THE SOUL OF KINDNESS

Elizabeth Taylor

THE SOUL
OF KINDNESS

With a new introduction by
Paul Bailey

The Dial Press
New York

To Elizabeth Cameron

Published by
The Dial Press
1 Dag Hammarskjöld Plaza
New York, New York 10017

First published by Chatto & Windus Limited,
London 1964.

Manufactured in the United States of America

9   8   7   6   5   4   3   2

Library of Congress Cataloging in Publication Data

Taylor, Elizabeth, 1912-1975.
The soul of kindness.

(A Virago modern classic)
I. Title.   II. Series.
PR6039.A928S6   1983   823'.914   83-2053
ISBN 0-385-27922-1 (pbk.)

Introduction

The Soul of Kindness: the title suggests a comfy, determinedly life-enchanting novel with Good Works as its theme. The book has a hero or a heroine, or both—a tireless missionary at some colonial outpost; a cheery district nurse, a plucky midwife, braving all weathers to ensure safe delivery. It's a title that promises warm feelings, the proverbial rosy glow.

Elizabeth Taylor's *The Soul of Kindness* fulfills no such promise, induces no such warmth. Its principal character, Flora Quartermaine, appears to be the very soul of kindness, but she isn't really. Flora is unaware that she is the victim of an appalling spiritual myopia, and of the damage it causes. She sees only what she chooses to, regardless of consequences.

"Les privilèges de la beauté sont immenses," Cocteau observes in *Les Enfants Terribles.* Flora has been granted all those privileges, all her life to date. Hers is a Botticelli-like beauty, fair and luminous, that enchants and captivates its beholders. With it goes a sweetness of temper, a beguiling gentleness. She cannot fail to be at the center of everyone's attention.

Slowly and deftly, Elizabeth Taylor reveals the true Flora. There is a sly hint in the opening chapter that the newlywed Mrs. Quartermaine is a rather awful kind of innocent. Flora's oldest and most devoted friend, Meg Driscoll, is watching her as she greets her husband:

> "Here I am!" Flora called to Richard as she went downstairs. For a second, Meg felt disloyalty. It occurred to her of a sudden that Flora was always saying that, and that it was in the tone of one giving a lovely present. She was bestowing herself.

In Chapter Two, we learn that Flora, who has now been married for four years, has given her father-in-law, Percy, a cat. He did not want the animal, but under gentle (always gentle) pressure from Flora, he had felt obliged to take it in. "Although as good as gold, she had inconvenient plans for other people's pleasure, and ideas different from her own she was not able to imagine." Thus Elizabeth Taylor goes about her cunning business of placing clues for the alert reader to pounce on.

Flora is in the habit of putting subordinates at their ease, as her mother's slightly dotty housekeeper, Miss Folley, is quick to notice:

> "Miss Folley, I can smell spice cakes," said Flora, shaking hands with her. It was just that touch of homely graciousness one connects with the Royal ladies, Miss Folley thought.

Miss Folley, in fact, is almost alone in not having disloyal thoughts about Flora. The two words—"disloyal" and "disloyally"—are employed several times in the narrative. Both Meg and Flora's husband, Richard, feel guilty when they think less than radiantly of the beautiful young woman:

> They had a quiet evening. After dinner, they looked at old photograph albums. Flora-worship, Richard thought disloyally. He kept nodding off.

On another occasion:

> "I so hoped that you'd come home to tea," she said. She spoke in a child's voice, as if she were only playing at being disappointed; and he thought she was far too tall for such a little-girl voice. Unlike her, he sometimes had disloyal thoughts.

But the most piercing insight into Flora's character

comes much later in the novel, when she invites the ever-attentive Meg to be the godmother of her daughter, Alice:

> Meg looked quite astonished. "I couldn't," she said. "I don't believe in God."
> "But of course you do, darling," Flora said comfortably.

Flora is comfortable for most of *The Soul of Kindness*. The men and women who are the objects of her affection and upon whom she sometimes bestows herself are nowhere near as fortunate. In the third chapter, Meg is looking for a small property in Towersey, in the Thames Valley. She spends the night in a dingy commercial hotel. Here she is, preparing to leave:

> When she had put the papers in order, she packed her overnight bag and took the Bible from the window and placed it on the bedside table, where it would be ready for the next desperate traveller. She had read some of it last night—the first time she had opened a Bible since her school days. It had a special index—for those in hospital wards, prison cells and hotel bed-rooms—to guide one to helpful passages, when Back-sliding, Leaving Home, Needing Peace or in the Failure of Friends. Nothing for her. Nothing for those needing a new home, in love with the wrong person, or sick of responsibility. Nothing in the index, rather. In the Bible itself everything can be found, she remembered having been told.

"The wrong person" Meg is in love with is Patrick Barlow, who is homosexual. Patrick writes unadventurous novels and dabbles in art criticism. (His choice of Gwen John as the subject of a monograph in, I presume, the early sixties indicates that Mrs. Taylor doesn't consider him a complete dabbler.) Patrick loves the wrong person, too. He has fallen for a dull youth named Frankie and sees in him qualities the boy patently doesn't possess. Patrick is grateful for whatever Frankie feels disposed to offer him, which isn't much. Frankie is on the make; he recognizes the precise nature of Patrick's besottedness, and knows that he can use it for his own purposes.

Frankie pays Patrick a surprise visit one Christmas Day, and the repressed and unhappy novelist is overjoyed:

> Frankie, wilting from being over-worshipped—nothing more tiring, he had found—finished his glass of wine, in several swallows. "I can't stay long," he said. Patrick was already on his feet, to fetch the bottle. Then having filled Frankie's glass, he became fussed about his driving home, and went to find some biscuits.
>
> "Of course. I know that; I understand that," he said, as he went. If the visit only lasted another ten minutes, he would still go happy to bed. For Frankie had come, against all hoping; and he must have wanted to come. It was right for him to go back to his mother on such an evening. Patrick was touched that he should think so much of her. He cherished those nice streaks in his character.

That last, masterly sentence is typical of Elizabeth Taylor's art. It is casually, effortlessly ironic, and it immediately solicits sympathy for the deluded—even hoodwinked—Patrick. The "nice streaks" he cherishes are almost non-existent.

Flora Quartermaine, in her happiness, wonders why Meg and Patrick—who see so much of each other, and are such good friends—don't marry:

> ...Flora said to Richard: "I can't think *why* Patrick doesn't ask Meg to marry him. They're so well suited. It would be such an ideal thing."
>
> "Darling, do use your intelligence."
>
> "Oh, I don't believe all that. I never have. I think people are just gossipy and fanciful."

"Then what in heaven's name is awful Frankie about?"
"I don't know Frankie: so I couldn't say."

Flora doesn't use her intelligence where Meg's brother, Christopher, is concerned, either. Christopher—or Kit, as everyone calls him—has vague ambitions to become a successful actor. Patrick, Meg and Richard—who have all witnessed him executing (in more senses than one) small parts in television plays—are convinced that poor Kit has no talent whatsoever, but the glowing Flora knows otherwise. She alone has *faith* in the struggling young man. Since Kit quite literally worships her, such misplaced faith has its dangers—dangers, of course, that Flora is blind to.

When Flora gives expression to her faith in Kit's genius, she puts on what Patrick calls her Early Christian look. It is he who makes the cattiest remark—one that far exceeds mere disloyalty—about the constantly, and irritatingly, radiant Flora, when Meg presents him with the perfect cue:

"She was under an anaesthetic."
"She always has been."

The sanest, and perhaps the most fulfilled, character in *The Soul of Kindness* is the painter, Liz Corbett. Liz is dumpy and running to fat and totally unconcerned about her appearance, or the effect it has on others. Hers, we are persuaded, is a genuine talent. She works in chaos, but achieves art of an exquisite delicacy. Elizabeth Taylor, with her customary quiet skill, keeps this beer-drinking woman on the periphery of the story, where her sanity functions, Chorus-fashion, as a counterpoint to the ultimately dismal glow that Flora causes to radiate about herself. Liz has a brief liaison—hardly an affair—with Kit, and after the last time they make love, she confronts him thus:

"I know all about her. I interpret what you tell me. And, my God, how you like to talk. Meg won't listen, so

I must. You love to say her name. It's an indulgence—
like playing with yourself. And then, when it's all said,
you jump into bed with me—having carefully put the
light out—very significant, that."

The alert and discerning Liz—who never manages to
look other than mucky—builds up a picture of Flora in her
mind's eye, and she does not like what it reveals. Nor, in
the chilling final chapter, does the reader.

The Soul of Kindness is a novel, then, that has at its heart a
creature without a soul, a phantom play-acting the kindly
virtues. Flora's mother, Mrs. Secretan, in a disloyal
moment, realizes that she could not depend on her daughter if she herself became ill. It is a shocking revelation—
quietly shocking, but no less real for that—in a book that
contains hundreds of similar insights. It is for such insights
that I remain loyal to the subtle and luminant artistry of
Elizabeth Taylor.

Paul Bailey
London, 1982

One

Towards the end of the bridegroom's speech, the bride turned aside and began to throw crumbs of wedding cake through an opening in the marquee to the doves outside. She did so with gentle absorption, and more doves came down from their wooden house above the stables. Although she had caused a little rustle of amusement among the guests, she did not know it: her husband was embarrassed by her behaviour and thought it early in their married life to be so; but she did not know that either.

It was a beautiful day. For the last week, friends had told Flora and her Mother that they were praying for fine weather for them, and Flora had smiled, easily, languidly, as if the idea of a shower of rain in September were absurd. The sun came in shafts through the open parts of the marquee and even quite brightly through the canvas. The purling of doves mingled with the sound of Richard's per-oration. He was a little reddened – from the nature of the day, the position he was occupying and his wife's inatten-tion. Then, just as he was coming to his last words, she stepped back again, close to him, and slipped her hand into his. She looked radiant. So everyone was saying a few moments later. 'Oh, I shall miss them,' she was thinking. 'My doves!'

'Such a lovely, tall, blonde bride,' her mother thought. 'A blonde bride is always best.' It was as if she had borne her – dear Flora – just for this wonderful occasion and, between her birth and now, all that had happened was forgotten; only the two triumphs counted for anything. So vividly, even to this day, she could hear Sister Willett saying, 'It's a lovely girl'. And 'Such a lovely girl!' all the

7

neighbours were saying this afternoon. Flora in white. She was born to be a bride. 'And no mother thinks any young man is good enough for her own girl,' Mrs Secretan consoled herself.

The bridesmaids bowed their heads smilingly over their champagne glasses as the best man praised their beauty, and the hubbub of conversation broke out again, given an airy quality by the height of the marquee and the thinness of its walls. Mrs Secretan circulated. 'Yes, *rather* a pretty frock, isn't it?' 'No, I don't feel tearful. Too, too *agitato* in church and too, too happy here.' She was widowed and had been for a long time and now faced loneliness. Her friends had expected tears, and still did. They watched her move on to Richard's father – a widower – and an idea occurred to some of them, for weddings beget weddings, it is always said. Most did not know that Mr Quartermaine's mistress was among them, a smart middle-aged woman called Barbara Goldman, talking at this moment to Richard – might well have been his godmother, some thought.

'They ought to be changing,' Mr Quartermaine said, reaching for a watch across his great stomach. The calyx of his carnation was showing, Mrs Secretan noted. She glanced quickly away from it, as if it were something embarrassing like undone fly-buttons. If anyone were to spoil the wedding, it would be he, she had thought over and over again in the last few weeks. With her zealous attention to detail, she had charged several of the ushers – cousins, for Flora was an only child – to see that he did not drink too much, and her own brother had been asked to keep him as much as possible apart from Barbara Goldman – whom she had not wanted to invite – lest he should call her 'Ba, old girl', and slap her bottom.

Mrs Secretan's enthusiasm for detail had foreseen all disasters. Lying awake in the middle of the night, she would suddenly envisage Flora stung on the nose by a wasp at the very last moment before leaving for the Church, and so the gardener was made to search for and dispose of windfalls, and Mrs Secretan herself made a dozen or more jam-pot traps and set them about outside the house. Precautions were taken against infections, fatigue and anxieties; but there were few precautions she could take against the bridegroom's father. What could be done, she did.

He was so large and Mrs Secretan herself so much shorter than her daughter, that it was a triumph when she managed to place herself between him and a waiter going round with champagne. One glass less, she thought. Every little helps, was advice she constantly gave.

'Where's Ba got to?' Percy asked. 'I'm sick of my relations. They make me feel old. That lad of mine went on too long with his speech. He should have sensed the people getting restless, wanting their glasses charged.' He twirled his own empty one. 'Even Flora got bored – feeding the pigeons.'

'Doves,' said Mrs Secretan.

'Well, she'll have to get used to listening to a lot more than that. We're all great talkers.' He had hoped to make a speech himself and, not having been asked to, he now told his hostess how old-fashioned the practice had become. 'Old-fashioned,' he repeated; 'and bourgeois. Ah, here's Flora, looking as fresh as a daisy.' A vague girl, he thought her. Not very bright, but biddable.

'Darling, there's something spilt all down your front,' said Mrs Secretan.

'But it doesn't matter. I'm just going to change.'

The best man had glanced at his watch and murmured to the chief bridesmaid. Mrs Secretan had arranged the schedule long beforehand.

'One last look,' she whispered and held her daughter at arm's length. When she turned round again, she saw Percy Quartermaine edging off, nudging his way among the flowered hats towards some more champagne: and then, to her dismay, she saw him slide something into a waiter's hand. She moved on, smiling gaily to right and left, to have a brief warning word with her brother.

Flora and her friend, Meg Driscoll, slipped out of the marquee as if they were up to some mischief, and hurried across the lawn to the house. With her train looped over her arm, Flora ran among the doves, calling to them and laughing.

'Oh, you and the doves!' a boy called. It was Meg's young brother, dashing after them with a camera. 'You and the doves, please!' Flora let go her train and turned and, putting out her hand, waited for a bird to settle on her finger-tips.

'It is a symbol, isn't it?' asked Meg, stepping aside out of the photograph.

'Before it flies away!' the boy, Kit, said with breathless anxiety as a bird perched. He put his eye to the view-finder.

'It won't,' said Flora.

'Bride and doves,' Meg said. 'It should be the best photograph of all. Except that there's no bridegroom.'

The photograph was taken and the dove cast lovingly into the air and Flora and Meg went into the house, Kit following.

'I didn't think boys were interested in brides and weddings,' Flora said, over her shoulder. Then, as she was stepping in through the drawing-room windows, she turned to smile goodbye to him. Coming too closely after her, he put his foot on her train and, as she turned, it was torn.

'Oh, Kit!' cried Meg. 'And why on earth are you following us?"

He kept his head down sullenly, choked with misery and embarrassment his freckled face reddened. But, quite wonderfully to him, Flora put her hand on his shoulder and began to laugh. 'In a minute I shall take this off for ever and ever. You can tear it to shreds and I shan't care.'

CHAPTER ONE

'Come, we must hurry,' Meg said and took Flora's arm. They were behind schedule in spite of Mrs Secretan, and Flora, fussing too long with her veil, had already been twenty minutes late at the church. The day now seemed to Meg to be dragging on.

'I shall send you the photograph,' Kit said, raising his head and looking up at Flora. The moment was too much for him, but he took what it gave, knowing that later he would need it. He bore with his embarrassment for the sake of having something to keep in the future, to be gone over on the dark Sundays of his last autumn term at school, those worst days – something better than the photograph, however that came out. As he walked away from her – for she had turned to follow Meg – the moment had already become a memory and he was at work on it, prolonging it, making her smile more personal, less vague. Richard, her husband, had often done the same.

'My dear, come! Flora, come!' Meg called down from the top of the stairs. She had gone running ahead to Flora's bedroom, to see if everything were ready. At school, she had been Flora's Nannie-friend, for it was clear from the day that Flora arrived there that what Mrs Secretan had done – the cherishing, the protecting – could not be lightly broken off. Someone must carry on. 'What do I do with this?' 'Where do I go from here?' were questions somebody must answer. Meg disapproved of Mrs Secretan's cossetting, but saw that it would be dangerous for it to be abruptly discontinued – like putting an orchid out into the frosty air, or suddenly depriving an alcoholic of drink. She had tried – so good she was – to introduce gradual reforms, but Flora peaceably ignored them, for she did not know that there was any necessity to stand on her own feet, or even that she was not doing so. The hard world was ahead, though, and Meg feared it for her. She sometimes tried to give glimpses of treachery and avarice, and Flora said, 'But no one would do a thing like that,'

and smiled forgivingly at her friend who had such unpleasant fancies. And now they – Meg and Mrs Secretan –
had handed their precious burden on to Richard, and
Meg, for one, was nervous.

'Here I am. I am here,' called Flora, in her high, floating voice, coming along the passage.

Guests – Flora could see from her window – were now
coming out of the marquee and wandering about the
garden, stopping to read the labels on the rose trees and
standing, as if hypnotised, by the beds of dahlias. At last
Flora was nearly dressed, and a maid tapped on the door,
to say that the bridegroom was waiting in the hall. To
placate him, Meg ran downstairs with optimistic assurances, to which his only reply was a glance at his watch.
'Once I can get her away,' he kept thinking. It had been
the devil of a day, and his thoughts were of escape and
driving off alone with Flora, stopping somewhere later for
a quiet drink. His head rang with chatter.

When Meg came back to the bedroom, she found Flora,
dressed but for her gloves, sitting at her desk writing a
letter. She was weeping. It was not the state of Flora's
emotions – for she wept easily – that filled Meg with
alarm, but the threat to her looks, of which she felt herself
to be in charge.

'What *are* you doing?' she asked, darting forward the
moment she had closed the door.

'I'm writing a little note to Mother. I'll leave it here and
then she'll find it when I'm gone. I'm so afraid she will
miss me.'

'Naturally she'll miss you. But she's a sensible
woman. . . .' Would that she were! Meg thought. Would
that she always had been! 'You can't go downstairs with
a tear-stained face, especially as you've been so long up
here. People will think you've had second thoughts.'

'Of course they won't,' Flora said, smiling and wiping her
eyes. 'How could I have second thoughts about Richard?'

'He's standing there, looking at his watch.'

'Well, he shan't have to wait any longer.' She sealed the envelope and stood up.

'Gloves,' said Meg, thrusting them at her.

'I shall miss everything,' Flora said, glancing round the room.

'Downstairs!' said Meg, and ran to open the door.

'Thank you, Meg. for everything. Not just today – everything, always.'

'Downstairs!' Meg said again. She had seen the tears brimming and sentimentality she knew to be contagious.

'Here I am!' Flora called to Richard as she went downstairs. For a second, Meg felt disloyalty. It occurred to her of a sudden that Flora was always saying that, and that it was in the tone of one giving a lovely present. She was bestowing herself.

'They are going away,' someone said in the garden and the word went round. Excitement grew – a rather feverish hilarity – as the goodbyes were said. Kit took more photographs. Mother and daughter were watched embracing. And then the pair drove off – no one else knew where – and the guests began to disperse.

When they had all gone, Mrs Secretan went up to Flora's room. Meg had tidied it, and the torn wedding dress was hanging in a cupboard and the ghost-like veil was spread upon the bed. Mrs Secretan took the letter and opened it. 'You have been the most wonderful mother,' she read. 'I had a beautiful childhood.' So it was to be regarded as finished? The words were the kind which might be spoken from a deathbed or to someone lying on one. If only, Mrs Secretan thought yearningly, if only Flora had written 'You *are* such a wonderful mother.' That would have made all the difference, she thought – would have made it seem that there was still a place for me. As it is. . . . She picked up the veil and popped it into a drawer, out of sight. It had looked so sad and wraithlike, lying there upon the bed.

But it had all gone off well and Percy had not got so very drunk. The surprisingly competent Ba had taken him in hand. Now the sun was setting and there were slanting shadows across the garden, in which the great marquee stood so vast and alien. She was tired, Mrs Secretan decided, as tired in every way as she had ever been. So much fuss, so much congregating together of people from far and wide, just so that Flora could start a new life, set up a home of her own. Mrs Secretan seldom thought of Richard, unless to hope he would prove worthy and to fear that he might not.

She opened the window and looked down at the lawn – it looked scuffed and trodden. Beyond the marquee and then beyond a row of poplars was the River Thames and the distant voices of people strolling along the towing-path. She imagined them seeing the marquee and wondering what it was for, or perhaps they had seen Flora leaving the church, had heard the bells making their commotion, and stopped to watch, feeling part of the excitement.

The summer was over and the dahlias, having served their purpose today, would have to be lifted. Mrs Secretan had not looked beyond this day and had hardly envisaged the evening ever coming. She wondered where they were – the glamorous two. Not to press Richard – for it was he who had been firm about secrecy – had been her resolution, as part of being a wonderful mother-in-law, which she now meant to be. 'Even I don't know,' she had said, when people enquired about the honeymoon; but she managed to make the words sound like her formula for keeping a secret.

The air smelt autumnal. In no time, there would be thick evening mists coming up from the water, a complete silence from the towing-path, and the river rising; perhaps floods. And Flora would be settled in London and never to come here again, except as a guest.

'I made all the plans,' Mrs Secretan thought; 'down to

the last detail. But I forgot this, I forgot myself and the future. I particularly overlooked this evening.' She read the letter through again, telling herself that Flora had meant well, meant very well, poor girl. In fact she had always meant well. That intention had been seen clearly, lying behind some of her biggest mistakes.

Mrs Secretan closed the window and stood for a moment with her eyes closed and a drooping expression on her creased but pretty face. She had a headache, but she must get ready to have dinner with her brother and two old aunts. They would go over and over the day's happenings and each would have noticed something different; but none of it would add up. It was too much like a dream.

Down below, some men were crossing the lawn. They had come already to begin dismantling the marquee.

Two

'A SEE-SAW, some men playing at tug-of-war, two sign-posts pointing in opposite directions, cross-roads, I think, and a funny little figure capering.' Flora tipped to and fro in the rocking-chair, musing over Ba's empty tea-cup. 'What signs of stress and strain,' she said, and smiled, leaning back placidly.

Since the first knowledge of her pregnancy, she had taken a great fancy to Ba's little sitting-room and especially to the rocking-chair. After four years of marriage she had begun to overlook the possibility of having children, and had been astonished by the doctor's diagnosis. 'A baby?' she had asked incredulously, her eyes so fixed on his in wonderment that he had to get up and take a turn about the room to hide his smile.

'At long last,' seemed to be other people's reaction – her mother's, Meg's, her father-in-law's. Only Richard was almost as bemused as she.

She put Ba's cup back on the table, turning away from her the side with the lipstick imprint, strokes ridged like the underneath of a mushroom. As she rocked to and fro, her stomach was a neat little mound under her silk jacket.

'Stress and storm. Thank you very much, honey,' Ba said briskly.

'Could all be obviated. Marry Percy.' Flora smiled complacently and clasped her hands over her stomach. 'Tell me,' she said lazily, 'what is in my cup, and I'll interpret it.'

'I'm not as clever as you,' said Ba, turning the empty cup and frowning into it. 'I can only see an owl.'

Flora leaned forward, gave her a sharp, stern look and

took the cup from her. 'That, dear Ba, means death.' She stared into the cup, said 'Owl, indeed!' and put it back on the table.

'So sorry, darling,' Ba murmured. Her hand, with the great diamond ring, hovered like a claw over a tortoise-shell cigarette-box. Percy-trophies, Flora thought. The ring, the box, the gold lighter which was now clicked smartly into flame. The room was full of trophies, yet was in itself so different – so cosy, sentimental, suburban. Flora had often noticed that women like Ba, austerely smart about their persons, inclined to prettiness in their sur-roundings, with a taste for pink lamp-shades, crinolined ladies on cushions and herbaceous borders full of del-phiniums – both embroidered on fire-screens and growing in the garden. Ba, in her elegant dress, looked out of place in the room she had created. She was tall and bony. Her once dark auburn hair was a dull colour now and drawn back in a bun. That she was Jewish was shown by her slanting, almond-shaped nostrils. Her dress was low cut, showing a lot of freckled skin, but her breasts went down and down, were only half-revealed. 'Such beautiful legs,' Flora thought, then glanced at her own, raising them a little from the floor, considered them, lowered them again, without coming to a conclusion. Ba's voice was a surprise to people. That she should be so bony, so race-horsy and have so soft, so husky a voice, lingering continually over endearments, was unexpected.

Ba had given up being puzzled by her friendship with Flora – so much, she knew, deplored by Flora's mother. She had not visualised Percy's family taking to her. It was agreeable when Flora seemed to, and after a while had fallen into this habit of coming at tea-time on early-closing days.

The little dress shop below the flat was Percy's most expensive present, the one Ba loved the most. Even now, in Flora's company, and in the evenings, too, when Percy came, she was aware of downstairs, was never not conscious of it – the silence and darkness, the blinds, with 'Barbara' in fancy letters on them, pulled down over the window and glass-panelled door, the muffling carpet and dust-sheets – a gentle stuffiness there, the scent of her ambitions.

'You're a lovely eater, darling,' she said, as Flora leaned towards the table and took a slice of cake. Ba put out food from habit, but never bothered to offer any of it. It was too improbable that anyone should want to eat at this time of the day.

'Why don't you have a cat?' Flora asked.

'I don't *want* a cat.'

'But it would be lovely for you. Percy likes cats.'

'Well, Percy's *got* a cat,'

Flora, in fact, had given it to him and he had been obliged to take it in. In four years, he had found that Flora was not biddable after all. Although as good as gold, she had inconvenient plans for other people's pleasure, and ideas differing from her own she was not able to imagine.

'He dotes on it,' she said happily. 'It keeps him company in that awful great flat.' She turned her head and looked accusingly at Ba, but then suddenly blinked as the child moved in her womb – this extraordinary thing happening to her. She felt like a birdcage with her furious prisoner. How shall we ever be friends when it *is* free? she wondered.

Ba threw her cigarette into the fire and took up some knitting. The angora wool made her sneeze and she sat with it held away from her for a moment, her eyebrows lifted, her eyes shut, waiting to sneeze again. 'Poor little baby,' she said, when the sneezing was over.

'Everyone but me is knitting. Mother is at it furiously,' Flora said. 'She has such heaps of it ready that I suspect she started years ago. Even Meg is making a thing. First, she knitted some leggings; but when she sewed them up, she found that both legs turned to the left. Poor Meg,' she added, as she always did nowadays when speaking of her. Her friend had all the troubles in the world, it seemed to her – her mother's death when her brother was still at school, her father's long before the responsibility of Kit's future, money worries, and a hopeless falling in love – hopeless and impossible to the verge of absurdity, Ba said.

'That reminds me,' Flora said, of an unspoken thought she had had. 'Patrick is coming for a drink.' She sat upright and stretched her back. Now it would be dark when she reached home, for the clocks had been set back. When she had put on her coat, she followed Ba down the stairs and through the shop. Ba went ahead, putting on lights and, when she opened the street door, Flora saw that it was evening already; a glowering blue, not quite darkness, hung over the parade of little shops opposite. People were hurrying away from the Underground station of this North London suburb. A moment before the road had been desolate, and would be desolate again until the next train came in. There were yellow leaves stuck to the greasy pavements. They must have been blown a long way, Flora thought, stepping over them cautiously to her car, afraid of slipping with her precious burden. There were no trees that she could see, but there was a definite thickening of the air, as if from drifting smoke, the autumn smell of smouldering bonfires.

It seemed so much more than six months ago when those leaves must all have been transparent on the trees and she was delighting in the spring, still a separate person then, without this other life joined to her own, entrapped by her.

Between trains, the suburb had a malignant air. The emptied streets and the haphazard lighting were ominous. The disgorged passengers who had hurried down the station slope, were now, or nearly by now, inside their bright hutches, shut up for the night in their wombs, their Englishmen's castles. Flora, driving on, thought first of a sunnier climate and then of her pretty house, her husband, her friend, Patrick, and hoped – but not enough to cause herself anxiety – to be there before them.

Ba – on this first evening which had had a hint of winter in it – locked the shop door and went upstairs and with no dissatisfied notions at all washed the tea-cups and put out the whisky in readiness for Percy.

*　　*　　*

Richard, waiting on the Underground platform, clutching briefcase, umbrella, evening newspaper and a bottle of gin wrapped in thin paper, tried not to read the poster advertisements over and over again, or count on the map for the hundredth time the number of stations between where he was and St John's Wood, where he wanted to be. Rush-hour tedium, hanging about in uncongenial places such as this one, threatened his reason, he thought – filling the vacuum of his mind with nonsensical names, printing banal pictures on his retina. He stared ahead of him at the dirty tiled wall opposite, his bowler hat tipped back on his head, his toe tapping the platform rhythmically. A little further down among the crowd, he had seen a neighbour from St John's Wood – Elinor Pringle – and was sure that she had seen him. They had recognised one another, but pretended otherwise; her eyes had dropped quickly to the parcels in her arms. Both wished to escape the effort of conversation during the walk at the other end, up the wide, quiet road to where they lived.

The wrong train came in. Richard's was always the second one, he told people, describing the hell he went through, full of rush-hour self-pity, and aggrieved that he must end his working day thus – obliged to visualise it coming towards him all the afternoon. With winter looming it must only get worse, the wet coats and the umbrellas, the appalling Christmas shoppers with their great parcels. He took a quick glance at Mrs Pringle who seemed to have started hers already. She was the sort to get ahead.

Now the right train came in and the doors in front of him slid open. No one got out and the passengers, packed in tightly, stared at him with hostility, not making room – in fairness, he doubted if they could; but, fussed, he hurried down the platform to the next car, pushed in, trod on someone's instep; hearing a hissing sound of breath drawn in quickly from sudden pain, he apologised and glanced round in time to see Elinor Pringle's look of fury change swiftly to a polite smile of recognition.

He apologised again, with more emphasis, swaying as the train clattered out of the station. He hooked his umbrella over one arm, gripped the bottle of gin between his ribs and his elbow and reached for a strap.

'It's perfectly all right,' his neighbour said. 'Herded like cattle . . . how can one help . . .?' She put her chin on the top parcel of the pile she held against her chest. Having no hand to steady herself, she would have staggered with every movement of the train, if there had been room for her to do so.

'Can I take some of your parcels?' Richard asked, putting out his free arm to steady her.

'No . . . very sweet . . . I shall drop the lot if I . . .'

He realised that he would have to walk up the hill with her now. There was no way out of what they had both hoped to avoid. 'If she had been Flora,' he thought, 'someone would have given up his seat to her long ago.' He had never known his wife have to stand in a bus or train – her gentle smile, her trusting look, always brought some man to his feet.

At Baker Street people got out, and Richard and Elinor Pringle sat down. She glanced sideways, reading someone else's newspaper. Richard unfolded and read his own.

It was quite dark in St John's Wood. Richard was allowed to take one or two of her parcels, and they set off along the leaf-strewn pavements, shivering after the stuffiness of the train. Elinor walked with small, brisk steps, although her foot still pained her.

'How is Flora?' she asked.

Here we go, thought Richard. 'Marvellously well. And Geoffrey?'

'*Very*. . . . Oh, well he has rather a heavy cold, as a matter of fact.'

'So many about.'

'Yes . . . one can't expect . . .' She was becoming breathless and he was already bored; but both knew that they must not walk in silence, being little more than neighbourly acquaintances.

'What a lot of parcels!' Richard continued, stalking along, trying to match his long stride to her tight-skirted trot.

'Yes. I'm so sorry.'

He hoped she had not thought he was complaining at having to carry one or two of them.

'Don't like it when the clocks go back,' he said. 'Don't care for it at all.'

'Nor *I*,' she said, with emphatic agreement, as if they had just discovered some fantastic, unimagined link between them. 'Dark so early.'

'A bit of help in the mornings, of course; though everything's so bad then anyway.'

'Oh, a great help then.' Her voice was flooded with relief, but most of it was at having arrived at her house. It stood, in darkness, behind two monkey-puzzle trees – a charming little stucco house. He and Flora had been there once for drinks on a Sunday morning. That was more than a year ago; although Flora had sometimes observed that they must ask them back, lately she seemed to have forgotten.

Elinor took her parcels from Richard and he held open the iron gate and said goodbye. As he continued up the hill, he thought how much he should hate to go home to a dark and empty house after the battle of the rush hour; but he could imagine her quickly putting the place to rights, against her husband's return with his heavy cold, going from one thing to another, methodically, so that rooms sprang into light, curtains were drawn, and flames began to grasp at kindling wood.

He turned off the hill into Beatrice Crescent. There were cracks of light coming between curtains at the downstairs window of his own house, Number Five, and he could see Mrs Lodge moving about in the basement kitchen. It looked cosy down there, with a red cloth on the table and some plants on the window-sill. She had not yet drawn the blind.

Flora's car was not in the garage, he saw. He climbed the two or three steps to the front door, between a pair of stone lions couchant, and stood in the porch, sorting out his front door key from the others. By the time he had opened the door, Mrs Lodge was in the hall. Hearing him, she had come running up the stairs.

'Mr Barlow's in the sitting-room,' she said in a low voice.'Madam expected him.'

'I see she's not back yet.' He took off his coat, but seemed reluctant to go into the sitting-room. The *end*, he thought angrily, the very end. He took some time to straighten his tie before the glass.

'I don't suppose she'll be a minute or two,' Mrs Lodge said. 'Perhaps the traffic's bad.'

At last, Richard pulled himself together, as if in the wings of a theatre, doubtful if he had it in him to give a great performance on this particular evening. He strode forward and, with an enthusiastic suddenness, flung open the door. 'Why, Patrick,' he said. 'I'm sorry you've been left on your own.'

*　　*　　*

Percy Quartermaine, still puffing from having climbed the stairs, flopped into his special chair, opposite the rocker in which Flora had been sitting earlier. He had hardly done so before Ba put a glass of whisky into his hand.

'Flora was here,' she said.

'Yes, I called at Richard's on the way here, and in she came. That chap was there, her writer friend, that creature. . . .'

'Patrick Barlow.'

'. . . lisping about art. "I like the old masters," I said. "Their sort of painting's good enough for me." Shut him up. No reply. I'll bet *he* hasn't got a Canaletto.'

'You haven't either, honey.'

'No, but I damn well know someone who *has* – hanging above what he cares to call the chimney-piece.' His expression became less peevish, then even tender, and he stared dreamily at his whisky, his thick fingers tipping the glass gently to and fro. 'I'd give a lot to have such a one – the Thames at London. You could well imagine you were there, looking at the real thing at a very magnificent moment for the light. When people talk about the river, I see *that*. Beautiful, like Venice. I don't see all those bloody new buildings. No, Ba, they really *hurt* me. Personally *hurt* me.' He was growing fierce again and had begun to pat his chest as if the pain and outrage constricted him there. Ba sat peacefully in the rocking-chair, smiling. Often, she wondered what his wife had been like, and once had asked him. 'Pretty little thing,' he had said vaguely. 'On the shy side.' Had she been timid of his explosiveness, cowering in the beam of his monstrous egotism, Ba wondered. She thought he must have been lord and master all the way.

'That fellow,' he said. 'What do these women see in him, for heaven's sake? Flora? Meg Driscoll?'

'He's kind, I think. He's sympathetic; yes, he's very sympathetic And quite a nice face.'

'But what *for*?'

'*I* like him too.'

'It's beyond me.' Too many things had been that in the last couple of hours – in the last twenty years, in fact – and he was barbed by what he considered to be pretentiousness or wilfulness. Things were done and said, he felt, simply for the sake of angering him. Even the high new buildings along the Embankments seemed designed to upset him, and he never looked at them without this sense of personal injury. 'You're fools to be so taken in,' he said.

'Why the hatred? Why the fear?' Ba asked, 'You begin to make me suspicious. It is out of normal proportion.'

'Normal proportion! Do you know, that girl Driscoll has actually fallen in love with him. How can that come about?'

'It's Meg's tragedy. Outside our domain. There is no one to be blamed and nothing to be done.'

'Well, *we* are all right,' he said, in a grudging tone.

'Yes. Perhaps it isn't a very noble attitude.'

'*Most* noble. And very grateful. I told you, I like gratitude.' He was sinking more deeply into his chair. 'I'd be very grateful for another dash of whisky, dear girl.'

Ba filled his glass and then went to get ready one of the snacky suppers they had on trays. He had a boyish fondness for baked beans on toast, and eggs and chips. 'Do you want the television?' she asked, before she went.

He shook his head; was preoccupied, and hardly heard what she said, ruffled and huffy because of some words of Flora's earlier. She had gone into the hall with him, as he was leaving and, while he was getting his coat, begged him for the second time to stay to dinner. 'I always go to Ba's.' he had explained. She knew it. 'And that worries me,' Flora said, her large, perplexed eyes fixed on him. 'It is difficult for a woman to live and work where she is gossiped about.' Or words to that effect, he recalled; leading up to the plea – her hands now tucked beseechingly under the lapels of his coat. 'I'm fond of Ba: so fond of both of you.

I dream of seeing you settled.' Ba had refused him a dozen times, but whenever he explained this to Flora, she smiled tenderly and gently shook her head; as if she knew better, knew something he couldn't grasp, perhaps that Ba wanted more persuading. To have been turned down was no matter for despair to him. He liked the arrangements that they had. Two homes are certainly more expensive than one; but there was enough money for the luxury. He enjoyed his do-as-he-pleased days, and looked forward to the cosy, domestic evenings.

It was such a long time since they had made love. He often forgot to kiss her goodnight, when he went home at ten o'clock; would sometimes remember this guiltily, driving back. His wife had minded about such things, would sigh and pout and let him know that she was hurt. Rather pretty, girlish ways, he had thought. Ba was not the sighing, pouting kind, and he was wondering now, as she fried chips in the little kitchen, whether he were not taking her for granted. He had just said that he liked gratitude, and now he thought that there was a lot due from him. Ba was giving him her life. She worked hard in the shop – buying, serving, doing accounts – and then she cooked all these chips for him in the evening. He felt uneasy about her wellbeing. If people gossiped – people in the neighbourhood where she earned her living . . . how could he find out if they did? He had heard stories before this of life in the suburbs.

'What did you do all day?' she asked, returning with his supper tray.

No one fries as well as a Jewish woman, he thought, looking at the crisp pieces of fish.

'I went to the factory this morning to have a look round.' Although he had retired, he still felt he should take an interest in the family business; and enjoyed causing an interruption, taking some of the older men off their work for a while, to have a chat about old times and to make family enquiries. Richard fumed, he knew. 'This afternoon I had my piano lesson.'

'How far have you got?' Ba asked.

'You only eating the fish? Silly girl.'

'Have you started a new piece of music?'

'Yes, *Fairy Footsteps*. It sounds childish, but it's really very pretty.'

'I must hear it when I come to measure for the curtains.'

'I'll practise a bit more first. Ba, this business about the curtains. . . . You do too much.'

'We'll go over one evening, or on Sunday, perhaps.'

'Can't I get some shop or other to do it? Ba, why don't we get some shop to do everything? You can have just what you want.'

'I?'

'Yes. Marry me. You might as well, Ba.'

As he reached for a bottle of tomato sauce, he glanced across at her.

She put aside her tray, her fish half-eaten. She had grown into a habit of eating very little. If they were married he could coax her more, he thought – would buy little treats to tempt her appetite.

'I think we are very well as we are, Percy. Quite all right. You said so yourself, just now. Baby, you can't drink whisky with fish and chips,' she said, as he held out his empty glass. She was thinking – as she got up to fetch the decanter – 'I suppose, one day, we shall. When he's very old, he'll need me.'

She filled his glass and sat down. 'I think we are best as we are,' she said again. 'And, Percy, make that drink last. You're driving.'

*   *   *

Richard and Flora were going to bed early. Flora, pink from one of the prolonged, hot baths she liked, put on her nightgown and her wrap, and began to brush her bright hair. She was thinking about her mother as she did when doing her bidding of long ago. Obedient still, she brushed her hair, counting. To be thinking of her mother meant that she was looking sad, because the idea of that lonely life by the autumn river, winter coming on, pained her and made her feel guilty.

'Can we go to see Mother soon?' she asked Richard who, drawing his shirt over his head, pretended not to hear. She sighed. The moment she put down her hairbrush, she brightened again. Once his head came out of the shirt, she saw that he wore a cross expression and decided to defer her question.

'Did you have a dreadful day, darling?' she asked instead.

'Fairly dreadful.'

'Poor you!' She opened a little jar of cream and began to pat round her eyes, leaning forward to the glass, watching him undress. 'What did you have for lunch?'

'Oh Lord, I can't . . . ah, yes, boiled beef and carrots.'

'But you *love* boiled beef and carrots. What on earth has changed you?'

'I haven't changed. I still adore boiled beef and carrots.'

'Darling, you're shouting at me,' she said, in a shocked murmur. 'I was only . . . I thought you said "boiled beef and carrots" in a tone of disgust. That was all.'

'I wasn't disgusted by *that*,' he said quietly, evenly. 'I was disgusted with my day. Father wasting my time this morning – everything gets behind. I was tired and irritated, and when I got home I didn't expect or want to find Patrick here, and to have him on my own all that time – to have to do all the listening and answering. He asks too many questions.'

'Did you have dumplings with it?'

'No, I refused dumplings.'

All the same, he had a stabbing, burning pain in his chest. He went into the bathroom and came back, mixing some white powder in a glass of water and Flora watched him anxiously, with another stirring of unease and guilt. The stomach disorders were a reproach to her. She, who was able to do so much to solve other people's problems, settle *their* disorders, had had no success with her husband's health. She blamed his work, his business life – for most businessmen had ulcers, she often heard, and said. On the other hand, for his work to have such ascendancy over his home, that it possessed the power to upset his life with her, was an affront. On this score, she felt her confidence weakening. His other world had escaped her influence. She had a vague understanding of what went on in the factory and warehouses, had been once or twice to that grim district and walked through one department after another, all smelling of glue and french polish; had sat – feeling a guest, with his secretary as her hostess – in his office, waiting to be taken out to lunch, while he, Richard, was constantly interrupted, telephoned. All had been bustle and commotion. She came to the conclusion that he should be made more inaccessible, blamed his secretary, saw herself in her place warding off callers, delegating.

Although he was supposed to be such a good businessman – his father always said so and had to all purposes handed over to his son – Flora thought, and was inclined to say, that there must be some flaw in the organisation for him to be so harassed.

She got into bed and sat looking at him, the skin round her eyes faintly glistening, her hair tucked primly behind her ears. 'Can't you *delegate* more!' she asked in a puzzled voice. He drank his medicine, swirled the mixture round in the glass, gulped down the sediment. Defensively, watching him, she stressed that word she often used, passing the buck.

He had no answer for her. He got into bed, switched off the light and lay there, waiting for the pain to shift away, smothering little belches.

She was glad that there was a way of coaxing him out of his black humour. She turned him to face her, her silky arms round his shoulders. An end to the sulks. Benignly, she made a present of herself.

Three

ON Saturday morning early, in a bedroom of a commercial hotel in Towersey, Meg Driscoll woke and heard the hooting of boats on the river below. She had sometimes during the night heard these haunting sounds as barges made their slow progress to London. It was possible, sitting bolt upright in bed, to see boats gliding past and some red-funnelled tugs moored near by.

She got up, put on her raincoat, and went along the dark passage to the lavatory. She tried, without much hope, the handle of the bathroom next door, but it was locked. Even over small things, she had bad luck.

When she had washed in her room and dressed, she went to the window, drawn, excitedly, to the scene of river traffic. This was where the estuary began, and the wide horizon to the east was littered with ships. Opposite, were cranes, funnels, masts. Pearly smoke was puffed up and changed shape and spread against the pale blue sky, and there was a glitter and business about the morning.

The hotel had a little private garden across the road, going down to the river bank. There were neat pieces of lawn, a path between sooty trees, and some seats.

She pushed up the sashed window from the bottom and was about to lean out when she suddenly imagined she could hear her mother's warning voice. There was some story from her childhood, of a young woman leaning from her window to whisper secretly to her love in the garden below when the sash had broken, the frame had come clattering down and the poor lady had been guillotined – or something like – before her lover's eyes. Warily, Meg straightened her back, and in fact, as she took her hands from the window, the pane began to slide down slowly. She thought of her dear mother, whose practical hints – how to clean hairbrushes and get earwigs out of lettuces and preserve oneself from the guillotine – would never be forgotten, though the look of her, the voice itself, were fading from memory.

The top half of the window was stuck and wouldn't move at all, so she propped open the bottom with a red-covered Bible she had found on the bedside table. Where she had a view of the river, she sat down to go through a bundle of papers from the estate agent. Some of the houses and flats she had been over the previous afternoon, and had gone to bed dispirited; but the fresh look and sound of Saturday morning gave her a different feeling.

It was Patrick Barlow who had had the bright idea of Towersey, when South Kensington became too expensive and Notting Hill Gate too depressing. He had sometimes visited a friend there – a painter, and had been charmed by the atmosphere of the little Thames-side town. He described to Meg the streets of small houses where customs officers and sailors and lightermen lived in their retirement, watching the river traffic from between parted lace curtains, or behind aspidistras in front parlours; sometimes, he had said, through telescopes. Such a small house would suit her very well, he thought; be within her shrinking capital. With a lick of paint inside and out, could have character, become an investment.

'Grass it over. Paint it white,' had been Meg's mother's advice, to friends in difficulties with awkward gardens or ugly pieces of furniture.

She would spend the morning sorting out possibilities and the afternoon, when Patrick Barlow was to join her, in coming – she hoped – to a decision. Kit, who was in Berkshire, working in a television film, his first job for months, was quite indifferent to whereabouts he lived, had left this decision to her; as he left them all.

When she had put the papers in order, she packed her overnight bag and took the Bible from the window and placed it on the bedside table, where it would be ready for the next desperate traveller. She had read some of it last night – the first time she had opened a Bible since her schooldays. It had a special index – for those in hospital wards, prison cells and hotel bedrooms – to guide one to helpful passages, when Backsliding, Leaving Home, Needing Peace or in the Failure of Friends. Nothing for her. Nothing for those needing a new home, in love with the wrong person, or sick of responsibility. Nothing in the index, rather. In the Bible itself everything can be found, she remembered having been told.

The morning light had hardened when she went out into the street. Clouds raced, smoke flew. Some swans took to the air for a second or two, adding to the commotion. Walking away from the river, towards the estate agent's, she could still hear the steady pulsing of the river traffic and gulls crying. The streets were busy already, Pakistani women, with coats over their saris, shivered as they went shopping; boys – some with turbans and incipient moustaches – played hop-scotch on the pavements or ran with home-made trucks over the cobble stones. Cats were everywhere.

It is exhilarating here, Meg thought. Perhaps despondency might be left behind in London. There would still – for her life – be those drab office afternoons with the sky minute by minute thickening with fog, dirty air pressing against dirty windows; but, with a different evening ahead – a home, with her mother's furniture about, instead of other people's tables, chairs, looming wardrobes and blackened gas stoves.

The exhilaration was to fade. Going round from house to house with the estate agent, her hopes fell. Front doors opened onto dark, narrow passages and rickety staircases. There were greasy wallpapers and stained baths and the same old blackened gas stoves. She looked at these things with her mother's eyes and sometimes, for no reason, with Patrick Barlow's.

*   *   *

'I suppose Mother would turn in her grave,' Meg said despondently. It was the best of a bad lot. Seven, Alpha Terrace.

She stood in the dusty bay window. Out of one side of it, she could just see a yellow funnel above some roofs, and a crane. 'There's the river,' she said.

'Look at the room differently,' said Patrick, kicking at some rotted linoleum which was stuck to the floorboards. 'Imagine it clean and painted. Tell me about your mother's furniture.'

There were two buttoned velvet spoon-back chairs and she described them to him. She pressed her fingers to her forehead, trying to remember; but the furniture had been stored for so long that she could not see it clearly in her mind.

'Well, the chairs are a good start. Let's go on from them,' Patrick said. He often had to jolly her out of sad humours and had a special voice for the purpose. 'I can see this as a little Victorian parlour. What colour are the chairs?'

'Yellow. A dark sort of yellow.'

'Charming. We can have curtains to match.'

'*We*,' she thought. She wished he would stop talking to her as an interior decorator.

They were alone in the house. She had the estate agent's key and must return it soon, before the office closed.

There was waist-high boarding all round the room, brown and varnished. He tapped it with his knuckles. 'This could be painted white,' he said. She did not even turn to look at him, but give a snorty little laugh. He wondered why.

Two girls had tied a piece of rope to the lamp-post out-side and one of them skipped in and out as the other turned it. The front path to the house was of unevenly set dark grey bricks. Against the wooden fence was a row of dead hollyhocks.

'I like the wooden fence,' Meg said. 'It might be in the country. It must be getting late. I shall have to take the key back.'

She was always much affected by changes of light, weather, the passing of the day, and by the day of the week. Her morning optimism had gone and she was pinned down by the sadness of Saturday afternoon – which could only be made tolerable, she was afraid, by being happily in love; in which case, a walk in the dreariest weather, or a twilight-darkening room might even have a delightful melancholy. As it was, *not* happily in love, she was nervous of herself; was afraid, in this bleak room, of making an appeal to him – with words, or not – of seeming to need cherishing, exposing her loneliness. She was in danger of herself here and wanted to get out into the streets with their busy shops, to tide herself over until the safe banality of Saturday evening would change her mood.

They locked the door and walked along the terrace, stared at by children and given a second glance by women coming home from shopping. The streets and alley-ways between the river and the High Street were poor, but had a neat, swept-clean appearance. Small corner shops were brightly lit. There was a smell of coal dust from a coal-yard behind some high gates and, farther on, of frying fish and chips.

The ornamental clock tower was the hub of the town and round about it were dull, plum-coloured municipal buildings, public lavatories, the post office and Wool-worth's. Meg left the key at the estate agent's near by and they walked on down the High Street until they found a baker's shop where they could have tea, although Patrick had promised, and had searched for, oak beams, copper pans and ladylike cakes.

'Every town has one, surely?' he complained, as they sat waiting for their tea at a tile-topped table under the bright fluorescent lighting. In this light, the butter on the tri-angles of bread – when it was brought – had a greenish tinge. And so had Patrick's hair, Meg thought, glancing at him as she gave him his tea. What there was of it. He wasn't forty, but it was receding fast. He had a pale face, and his eyes were different colours – one blue, one brown.

'These awful cakes,' he murmured. They were large, bright yellow, some covered with shaggy coconut. One had green marzipan leaves, shaped like a cauliflower; a rock cake was pitted with holes where burnt currants had fallen out.

'You pour out tea so prettily,' he said.

Sometimes, she wanted quite furiously to hurt him; now, for instance, to lean forward and snap at him: '*Why* do you dye your hair? I know you do. In this light it looks utterly horrible.'

She caught a glance from him as he lifted his cup. It was as if he might have guessed what was going on in her head. He's no fool, she thought, miserably ashamed. He had given up his afternoon, come out to Towersey on the train, had tried to be encouraging, was putting up with this tea, looking out of place. Instead, in his warm, elegant flat, he might have been writing his novel, cutting his goose quill pens, covering smooth paper with his beautiful handwrit-ing, pausing for reflection to take a pace or two about the room. Everyone's picture of an author. Sometimes he played records to accompany his inspiration. Incense fumes spiralled up. All day long, parchment-coloured silk cur-tains were drawn across the windows, and the lamps were lit. He wanted no one, least of all himself, to look out on the Congregational Church across the road.

'I am so grateful,' Meg told him. 'You have been very kind.'

'But I have quite a feeling of excitement over it. And something had to be done. You were living beyond your means.'

It was true. She had told him everything, gave him her bank statements to go over, showed him her few shares certificates. Kit was no good to her, understood nothing about money. There were three thousand pounds of her mother's money left and she should, Patrick had said, have something quickly from it, or it would continue to dwindle away in rent for furnished flats.

She had met him first at Flora's just after her mother died and found in him – briefed as he had been, of course, by Flora – a kind of sympathy, so light that even she could bear it; in the end had come to rely on it. From the beginning, she had known that *there* would be the end of anything she might expect from him, and had not worried, so wary was she of committing herself.

He was one of the various men Flora invited to the house whenever Meg was expected. She eagerly waited to hear Meg's reactions, when next they met alone – sometimes in Meg's lunch hour when Flora was shopping. If she could get Meg settled, Flora had decided, she herself would be quite happy, but her friend thought she went about it in strange ways and wondered what, if anything at all, Flora knew about people. Her mother had encouraged only the prettiest view of human nature and no later aspects she may have come across seemed to have made an impression.

'He is very nice,' Meg agreed, when Flora had sung Patrick's praises. 'Very nice, and kind.'

'I thought he was quite taken with you,' Flora said, with one of her smiles. 'He monopolised you all the evening.'

'You are talking like Isabella Thorpe,' Meg said. She felt her mouth stiffening with anger. 'And I don't like it,' she added.

But no one was cross with Flora, Flora thought, and her smile widened and she laughed. She hadn't the slightest idea of Meg's meaning.

Lately, though, she had rarely invited Patrick and Meg at the same time and hardly mentioned his name to her friend, who wondered if perhaps Richard had had something to say. She had bitter conjectures about what people *did* say. Her brave act probably deceived no one. It will go on all my life, she thought. And I shall be known for it.

Patrick was silent, glancing down sideways at the table. He often sat like this without speaking, and made other people feel uneasy, for it seemed that he had been just on the point of saying something, and then began to think better of it. He was not an impulsive person and was inclined to weigh his words; but to see him in the act of doing it was disturbing.

'Where does your friend, Liz Corbett, live?' Meg asked him. Liz Corbett was the painter.

'Down by the river, over an empty shop – very Dickensian. Next door to a pub called *The City of London*.'

'I saw that this morning.'

'Would you like us to go and call on her? Or are you tired? But then, you may not like her. She isn't everybody's cup of tea.'

Meg wondered just what sort of jealousy it was she suddenly felt – of an unknown part of his life, she supposed.

'Yes, I think I should like to go . . . if you would,' she said in an uncertain tone. At least this would be certain to make her evening with him last longer.

'Well, we can leave there the moment you want to.'

She opened her handbag and put away the packet of cigarettes she had left lying on the table, took up her gloves and smoothed the fingers; but Patrick for the moment did not stir and then he said, 'Meg . . .' in a hesitant way.

She realised that now he was going to say what had been

in his mind all this time. He stared down at the table. *She* stared at his signet ring. It had a dark green stone.

'Meg, about Kit. What's he up to?'

'I told you – the television film. He's a policeman in it; but I don't think he says anything.'

'I remember that. I meant, how long is he keeping it up? And how long are *you*? Keeping him, so that he can keep it up?'

'He's only young.'

'He wasted all that time and money at Drama School. Shouldn't we soon face the fact that he's not going to be any good?'

'*We?*' This time she repeated the word aloud, in a light, aloof way. She opened her handbag, looked into it for a moment, then quietly shut it and lifted her head.

'I dare say I presume too much. After all, you have Flora to confide in.'

'Flora?' Her voice was full of surprise. Then she said: 'Flora is the one in whom *Kit* confides. She encourages him very much, and always has done. There's no use in my saying anything down to earth, about money and the future, when Flora has been telling him for years what a great actor he is going to be one of these days.'

'It's strange that he pays such heed to her. He can hardly think that she's the kind of person who would know anything about it.'

'Since he was a boy at school, Flora has been a sort of goddess to him. He hasn't grown out of it. He still has a photograph of her which he took on her wedding day – clouds of veil, and surrounded by doves.'

'By doves?'

'One is perched on her hand.'

'How simply dreadful. I couldn't bear a bird to touch me. Has Richard got one, too?

'Richard isn't there.'

They glanced into one another's eyes; then Patrick stood

up hastily and took some money from his pocket and **Meg**, head bent, mouth tight, put on her gloves. In the street, they began to laugh and he took her arm. They walked briskly and when their laughter died down, he said: 'Those doves, Meg! The doves!' and fanned it alive again.

'One moment,' he said, stopping before a dim shop window. 'How about something from here for a Christmas present?' It was a tattooist's shop, and the window was full of photographs and designs. 'Look at this – the Cruci-fixion,' Patrick said. 'To cover whole back,' he read, 'in-cluding mourning figures.'

'The sailor's grave looks very sad,' Meg said. A dull blue ship was heeling over, and dark heads bobbed among peaked waves. ' "Love to Mum and Dad," ' she read. ·

'Here is Man's Ruin,' Patrick said, with his face close to the pane. 'Look at this one – naked girl sitting in a glass of champagne. The bubbles! What is this underneath? Dice?'

'Sailor's Ruin is only a bottle of rum and a bosom.'

'How could you *not* live here, where there are such lovely shops?'

They went down the hill towards the river. She walked rather awkwardly, with his hand tucked under her elbow. She was shy of her sexuality, shyness tinged with shame. When she stumbled on the uneven pavement, he steadied her.

'The river looks so beautiful,' he said, as they turned a corner and had a view of it at the bottom of the street. He took his hand from under her arm and stopped under a lamp-post, to look at his watch. 'Pubs are open,' he said. 'Let's call at *The City of London* and I'll get a bottle of whisky.'

He did not take her arm again, and she put her hands in her pockets.

'Oh, I can just imagine it,' he said, beginning to laugh again. 'Those awful doves!' And Meg walked beside him, smiling to herself, so glad to have made him laugh.

Facing the river, was a row of warehouses, the high brick wall of a brewery, one or two small shops and the pub – *The City of London*. Despite its name, inside it was like a country pub, with varnished settles and a darts board. There was only one other customer – an old man, staring into his beer mug, in the self-contained, ruminative gloom of solitary beer-drinkers.

'Your new local,' Patrick murmured to Meg, glancing about the bar. The landlord stood watching them drink, with his hands resting on the counter, in a patient yet suspicious attitude. A clock ticked with a solid, maddening sound: a fly-paper stuck over with the summer's flies hung from the dark ceiling.

As soon as they could finish their drinks, Patrick bought the bottle of whisky and they left.

'I loathe that stale cold smell of London pubs,' he said. 'Here it is.' He stopped by the empty shop. The window had been broken and inside were torn newspapers and broken cartons. He tried a door at right angles to the shop door, but it was locked. He rang the bell, and soon they heard someone coming down an uncarpeted staircase.

'Scheduled for demolition,' Patrick said. 'It has the smell of destruction already.'

Meg was feeling apprehensive, wondering what she was in for.

Liz Corbett – a fattish, short young woman with untidy hair – had a set face, a staring expression, which seemed incapable of showing a flicker of surprise or pleasure. She certainly showed neither now: her manner was as if she had been expecting them both, but without any en-thusiasm.

'I though you would have stopped work,' Patrick said, when he had introduced Meg. Liz did not answer, but reached past them to slam the door. 'Better go first,' she said and went ahead of them, up the narrow, musty stair-case, which had scurfy plaster walls Meg tried not to brush

against. Feeling antagonism, she followed the bare heels
up the stairs. With each step, they lifted out of the broken
sandals, yellow and bony.

The studio at the top was large, an old store room with
a big north-east facing window; and it was littered with a
tide of rubbish – the skeletons of dead flowers and cow
parsley, peacock's feathers, decaying set-pieces, dinner
plates on which paint had been mixed, a tangle of honesty,
some large shells, gourds, poppy heads and marrows.

Meg sat down on a chair with broken casters, and Liz
sat on the bed and took a large Persian cat onto her lap.
Both she and the cat sat still, staring at Meg. Patrick
poured out the whisky, and the glass he handed to Meg
looked smeared and breathed on. He was extremely particular about shining glasses in his own home. I hate it
here, Meg thought. How does she think that she can get
away with such behaviour? She kept her eyes away from
the canvas on the easel: to have looked at it would have
been, in her mind, like going to a writer's – Patrick's, for
instance – desk and reading a half-finished manuscript.

While Patrick was describing their afternoon, explaining their sudden visit, seeming perfectly at ease, Liz
turned to stare at him, and then again at Meg; as she
listened, twisting her coarse hair into spikes. Her blank
gaze went slowly from one to the other, and the cats' did
the same. He was an extension of her – as if there wasn't
enough, Meg thought – a second pair of eyes for her. After
a while, Liz got up, still holding her cat, fetched an electric
fire and set it down in front of her, chafing her mottling
legs.

When Patrick stopped speaking, she abruptly asked:
'Did you finish your novel?' as if this had been in her mind
all the time he had thought she was listening.

'No. No, I didn't. I haven't,' he said in a different voice,
and got up and began to walk about the room, with his
glass in his hand.

'Your name is becoming better known than your works,'
she said sternly. 'All this reviewing and broadcasting. But
you never do any *work*. You will soon be just a literary
gent.'

'Don't be quarrelsome, dear,' said Patrick. 'We all know
what a hard worker *you* are. Why don't you let us see what
you've been up to?'

Without any hesitation, and as if to imply that she, at
least, had something to show for herself, she put the cat
down carefully, detaching its claws from her sweater, and
went over to a stack of canvases.

The paintings she began to turn from the wall and set
up about the room, propped on chairs or against table
legs, astonished Meg. If, knowing nothing of Liz, she had
seen them first, she would straight away, she thought, have
formed the tenderest affection for the stranger who had
painted them. The rubbish on the floor and about the
room had been recreated, reassembled over and over
again, into delicate and intricate patterns, exposed under
a vibrating light. The same objects – the skeleton cow-
parsley, the chipped and cracked lustre jug which Patrick
had fetched water in for their drinks, the peacocks'
feathers – were in picture after picture, even the scattered
débris of the river scene from her window – flotsam,
smudged smoke and crane skeletons. There were also some
pale girl children, with staring eyes, holding the biggest of
the shells, or the cat, or the frayed straw hat, which was
now hanging by a red ribbon from the door handle.

'She's the most creatively orderly person I know,' Patrick said to Meg. 'Who would at first think it? Liz, you've
the patience of a bird, snatching up unlikely bits and
pieces from all over the place, to make a beautiful, tidy
nest.'

Liz, who had flopped back onto the bed, was picking a
scab on her ankle. 'Writers always talk embarrassingly
about painting,' she said scornfully.

43

Patrick read from the back of a canvas – '*Shells with Feathers* – I love the names of pictures. They seem so much more evocative than titles in literature. How one's heart would sink at the thought of a painting called *The Merchant of Venice*.'

'One's heart sinks anyway,' said Liz.

'I should like to read a book called *Mandolin and Fruit*.'

'I love the girls,' Meg said timidly, afraid of being slapped down.

'The pale, pale girls,' said Patrick, leaning to look at one, his hands clasped behind his back.

'Suffering from dysmenorrhoea my brother says,' said Liz. 'He's a medical student,' she explained to Meg. 'Not an art critic.'

Patrick straightened his back and walked away, took his glass to the sink and rinsed it, much occupied apparently with what he was doing. Liz watched him, with her head on one side.

'Don't you ever tidy up?' he asked crabbily, trying to find a space on the draining board.

'The whole place is going to be pulled down next year,' said Liz. 'So what's the point?'

'We had better go,' he said to Meg. 'You must be worn out.'

As far as conversation had gone, she had been a bewildered failure, she thought, and was glad to say goodbye.

'Come again,' Liz said surprisingly, following them downstairs. 'If you want to,' she added. 'But not in the daytime.'

'I have to work in the daytime, too,' Meg said primly.

'Only I lie on my day-bed and eat lotus fruit,' said Patrick.

As they walked towards the station, he said: 'Sometimes, in summer, I shall come down by river to see you. You know, you needn't bother any more with Liz, unless you want to.'

'Have you known her a long time?'

'I sought her out when I first saw her paintings.'

'And were you surprised with what you found?'

'I had one or two preconceived notions, I must confess. I find her rather a coarse character.'

'Her painting isn't coarse.'

'No. So one lives in hope of a revelation, an explanation.'

Now the pubs they passed – *The Pier*, *The Packet-Boat* – were noisy. Light streamed out from their doorways across pavements, and singing, laughter, and the sound of tinkling pianos.

'Let us have some supper at home,' he said. 'Mrs Clarke has left some cold game pie.'

Today would be the longest time she had ever spent with him, and her happiness brimmed over. It was bliss to have this lying ahead of her – the train journey, his company all the time, the Vivaldi records perhaps, and Mrs Clarke's cold game pie.

Four

'I DIDN'T tell her,' Mrs Secretan said to herself. 'I know I didn't tell her.' Her mauve lips moved tremblingly to the words in her head.

She stood at the window, looking down the wet gravel drive, waiting for Flora to arrive. Flora and Richard, in fact.

The garden was misty and threads of rain slanted across the window. The herbaceous borders edging the drive were full of stakes and withering Michaelmas daisies. A few greyish-brown sparrows hopped about on the wet lawn, and raked amongst the clutter of damp leaves underneath trees. The misty sky was of a glaring whiteness and against it, in the foreground, the pear trees still had a few tattered leaves – a dirty yellow – and their branches moved with silly, erratic gestures, like a puppet's limbs.

Mrs Secretan could hear the church bells ringing – the Misses Whitcher, the organist's daughter, and Colonel Young were practising. On and on, the four notes went through their boring sequence, sometimes stumbling in an unnerving way and rushing jangling together. The horror and sadness of the late afternoon were immeasurable, but it was part of living in the country, Mrs Secretan thought; she always had, but poor Flora no longer could. She had no wish to be in London where, no doubt, shops were already beginning to be Christmassy. Here, they would be well into December before Mrs Austen at the post-office hung a bit of tinsel in the window.

It was tea-time and they were late. Obviously, Richard had not been able to get away early, after all. But even now they might be driving through the village, past the war memorial with its two new poppy wreaths, past the church. Mrs Secretan imagined the bell-ringers coming through the lich gate (for the ringing had stopped), and seeing the car and waving. 'Mrs Secretan's got her daughter with her,' they would say when they got home. The whole village would soon know, if Miss Folley had not spread the news already.

Miss Folley came in now. She was Mrs Secretan's housekeeper, very much involved in Mrs Secretan's life, having had nothing much in her own. The visit of Flora and Richard was a great event to her.

The room had grown quite dark, Mrs Secretan discovered, turning from the window.

'Not here yet?' Miss Folley asked. She rearranged the cups on the tray, poked the fire, hummed and hawed annoyingly. 'Do you want the curtains drawn?' she asked. She wished to have the room looking cosy ready for the visitors. Mrs Secretan wanted to watch for them.

'No, I'll have the last of the light.'

'I am keeping the spice cakes warm.'

'Yes, I can smell them.'

It was mention of the spice cakes earlier in the week that had set up Mrs Secretan's uneasiness. A day or two before, Flora's letter had come and, as usual, she read it over several times and put in it her desk. She did not, for the present, mention it to Miss Folley, for she had a dread of something going wrong with the plans, of Richard finding himself after all unable to get away. It had happened before and Miss Folley's commiseration had been difficult to endure. What-might-have-been was the burden of her conversation all that weekend. If the young Quartermaines had been there, Mrs Secretan would not have gone to church alone, the sirloin would have been twice the size and Miss Folley herself would have been on the go all the time, making the young people's favourite dishes, especially the spice cakes Flora liked so much.

'Will you put some mace on the grocer's order?' she had asked Mrs Secretan earlier this week. 'I shall want it for the spice cakes.'

'What spice cakes?'

'For the weekend. They praised them to the skies last time.'

Unfairly to herself, Mrs Secretan blushed, as she always did when other people let themselves down. She hated it so much, was ashamed of her own thoughts, and embarrassed. She had been ashamed of her thoughts, ever since, and had tried to be especially considerate to Miss Folley to make up for them. She had insisted that she should bring in another cup and have tea with them, although Miss Folley had planned to have hers in the kitchen. She was pleased; but decided to drink her tea on the wing, as it were; not to settle down at all, or to eat anything – just one cup of tea, then a tactful withdrawal. This was the proper compromise, she had decided.

They will never come, Mrs Secretan thought. Watching from windows, one soon loses faith. A few cars had gone along the lane at the end of the drive, but she knew – from experience of watching and waiting – that they were going too fast to turn in at the gates.

'A watched pot never boils,' Miss Folley said – and what that had to do with anything, Mrs Secretan was wondering, when car lights approached, at the right speed; swung round at the right angle and soon flashed into the room.

Her eyes were full of tears, as she put her arms round her daughter, feeling the strangeness of her new shape inside the fur coat – so strange, this greatly enlarged Flora, that she felt almost shy. She took a handkerchief from her cuff and dabbed her eyes, then gave her cheek to Richard.

'Miss Folley, I can smell spice cakes,' said Flora, shaking hands with her. It was just that touch of homely graciousness one connects with the Royal ladies, Miss Folley thought.

Everyone was on their best behaviour. Richard told Mrs Secretan how well she was looking, and Mrs Secretan enquired after his father, while Flora, having thrown off her coat, went round the drawing-room admiring the flowers, and the bright fire. Mrs Secretan could not take her eyes off her, and Richard could not, who saw her every day. She looked far lovelier, he thought, even than on the day they were married. Her placid beauty was suited to pregnancy.

'She looks marvellous, don't you think?' he asked Mrs Secretan.

'*So* well. She was always healthy. D'you know, I hardly remember a day's illness?'

Miss Folley was thinking how nice it was to have a man in the house. Richard leaned back on the sofa, stretched his long legs, and ate one spice cake after another. It was a pleasure to cook for him, after Mrs Secretan, with her bird's appetite. Miss Folley had been begged to remain and, as another of her compromises, she perched sideways on the edge of a chair. It was very uncomfortable to her bony behind.

After tea, they went upstairs to Flora's old room, with its extra bed where, in other days, Meg had so often slept, the two of them lying awake talking half the night. Mrs Secretan, in the next room, would hear the continuous murmur and the muffled laughter, unable to sleep herself for fretting that Flora would have dark circles under her eyes next day: although she never did.

Mrs Secretan had spent some happy hours renovating Flora's old dolls' house for her future grandchild. She had made new curtains and bed-clothes and had cleaned the plaster food, which was set out on the table – a lobster, a pink ham, a dish of peas and a charlotte russe. A woolly cat lay in front of the painted fire. Dolls sat stiffly in chairs: those that could not bend at all had been put to bed in their clothes or were propped against furniture. The six rooms were greatly over-populated. Mrs Secretan switched on the lights, and Flora knelt down and gazed into them.

'It's so beautiful,' she said, 'that I should like to live in it. Won't she *love* it?'

'Suppose it's a boy,' said Richard, and Flora glanced up at her mother and made a little face.

They had a quiet evening. After dinner, they looked at old photograph albums. Flora-worship, Richard thought disloyally. He kept nodding off. The fire was warm and the women boring. Mrs Secretan kept handing him photographs and waking him up. He had seen them all before on other occasions, and in any case they could not recall happy times to him. But he felt quite peaceful and relaxed, and his stomach was better, had stood up to the spice-cakes and a rather rich dinner. 'I like to see young men eating trifle,' Mrs Secretan had said, as he took a second helping of it.

He thought his wife must have been – apart from Royalty – the most photographed child in the world. Willingly, tirelessly, she had smiled at cameras – Flora in a smocked dress with a fistful of flowers: Flora with her first pony: Flora feeding her doves; Flora at the seaside, and on skis, leaning against a ship's rail, and among ruins.

'This one of you, Mother,' Flora said. 'In Rome. It is one of my favourites.'

Mrs Secretan looked. 'A long time ago. People thought I had beautiful arms. I really regret them more than anything.'

'They are still lovely,' Flora insisted. But, nowadays, they were always covered.

'Here is Meg,' she said delightedly, as if she had never seen the photograph before. 'Those hats! Do you remember, Mother? The day we decorated the hats? Our old school panamas.'

Meg's rather Chinese face, with little dents beneath her eyes and a dark fringe almost touching her eyebrows, was

shadowed by a brim laden with lace and roses. Flora wore
a large bird's wing and had a veil tied under her chin.

'How is dear Meg?' asked Mrs Secretan.

'She has gone to live in an awful little house in Towersey. One of Patrick Barlow's bright ideas. He means very
well, but it seems such a sad thing for poor Meg. And
worse for Kit, of course, who will be there so much more.'

'Why should he be there so much more than Meg?' Mrs
Secretan asked.

A good question, Richard thought sleepily. He leaned
back and folded his arms across his chest. This very sofa,
he thought – the pre-marital embraces, Mrs Secretan having said goodnight and gone upstairs. Beautiful Flora, with
her hair untidy, so kind and sweet to him. Now he lolled
here beside her, and could hardly keep awake. '*Got* you,'
he had said grimly, holding her hand tight as they drove
off to their honeymoon. That was that.

'It's such a precarious profession,' Flora explained to
her mother, speaking of Kit. 'Especially at the beginning.
He is often out of work, and he minds so much, having to
rely on Meg.'

'Then can't he find some other job?' her mother asked.

Another good question, Richard thought.

'He means to be an actor,' Flora said quietly.

'Do you know, I believe those school plays have a lot to
answer for. They give grand aspirations to young people,
who would never otherwise have dreamed of going on the
stage. They hear the parents applauding for all they're
worth, and form the notion that they're Sir Henry Irving
or Ellen Terry. You know, this is just what happened to
Kit. Meg once took me to his school, to see him as Ophelia,
and very pretty he looked, apart from his hands and feet,
wearing a blonde wig. I was full of congratulations – had
no inkling of what harm was being done – Poor Meg! It is
such a worry for her, with no one to turn to.'

'She turns to me,' said Flora. 'But I can't agree with her

51

over this. She is too impatient. All the time, Kit does a little better, gets more work. This is only the beginning, and only very lucky actors don't go through it. But living out at Towersey, away from contacts, won't help him much.'

"Kit can't act," said Richard, suddenly sitting up. 'Even if he were to get the chance, he couldn't act.'

'I have faith in him,' said Flora, with what Patrick had once called her Early Christian look. She lifted her chin, and her eyes were steady. She glowed with confidence. She would easily carry Kit along with it, her mother thought – perhaps even agents and producers; there was so much.

Mrs Secretan felt tired from the excitements of the day – the preparations, the waiting and the arrival – and from the unease about Miss Folley that persisted all the time at the back of her mind. For how had she known? 'I know I didn't tell her,' she said to herself. Her lips moved, and Flora glanced at her. Putting her handkerchief over her mouth, Mrs Secretan pretended to be stifling a yawn. 'My bed-time,' she said.

It was strange nowadays, that when she went up to bed, Flora and Richard went, at the same time, to theirs. She had hardly spoken before they were on their feet. So different from the old days.

Five

AFTER the conversation at her mother's, Flora's sense of responsibility to Kit was deepened. She began to give little parties to which she invited anyone who might be likely to give him the chance of a lifetime and, at other people's parties, she kept her ears open for promising names. If there were any of the kind she was searching for, an introduction was good for an invitation. She would not have dreamed of behaving in this way for her own advantage.

Kit had become a tall, fair lank-haired young man. Even at Flora's parties, he did nothing to disguise his shabbiness – but there is nothing much that can be done about frayed cuffs and shiny seats. 'Scruffy,' Percy said to Ba. Richard thought the same. For his birthday, Flora gave Kit a dark suit. At first, he protested, refused to go for fittings: in the end, seeing her surprised and disappointed look, he gave in; but his thoughts kept swerving away from what he was doing – he was humiliated, and shrank from wearing the suit. Meg was angry. A sweater might have been one thing, she said: a suit – a smart dark suit, moreover – was gigolo stuff. Richard, when Flora mentioned her present, fumed; but by then it was too late. She was astounded by his cautions and predictions – how could anybody ever think such a thing of her and how – for that matter – would they know what she had done? And a boy of that age! She was simply, as an older person, trying to help him in his career. In other circumstances, she would have given him quite a different present. Whatever Richard might say, it could not possibly have anything to do with him, or Meg, or anyone else. A fuss had been made over nothing.

All the same, there was awkwardness all round when

Kit appeared for the first time in the new suit. His hatred of wearing it was mixed with pride at the change in his looks. He had hoped Flora would say something casual and be done with it, but to his extra embarrassment, she flushed and glanced away for a moment, came to talk to him only after she had regained her composure.

From meeting someone that very evening, Kit was later given a day or two's work, and Flora was quite delighted. 'His success is snow-balling, you see,' she had said to Richard. Before Kit telephoned to tell his news, they had been watching a film on the television in which he had a part. Richard, after his day's work and his dinner, liked above everything to slump down in his armchair and stare at the screen – at Westerns, quiz programmes, political harangues, Scottish dancing, ice-skating competitions. His retinas were kept busy; nothing else – except occasionally when he wagged his foot in time with a Highland reel or some catchy signature tune. Flora usually sat with her back to the set, trying to knit baby's vests. She would soon become fidgety and bring up deep sighs; yawn; get up and stretch, and go off early to bed. This evening, Richard pulled her chair round and they watched together. Flora could not make head or tail of the film – to do with a murder in a country inn. Kit's part in it was over in a flash. She was greatly disappointed, Richard swore he had not noticed him at all.

'But I saw him quite plainly,' Flora protested. 'He was one of the policemen standing behind the shot detective in the raincoat.'

'All I saw was that they'd come in out of that pelting rain, and their clothes were quite dry.'

'I thought he really looked the part,' Flora said. 'But to think he was down there for two whole days filming it. Perhaps they cut a lot.'

*　　*　　*

After signing the contract, Kit went straight back to Towersey and washed up the breakfast dishes.

There had not been enough time or money to carry out all of Patrick Barlow's ideas for redecorating, but some white paint and distemper had made a difference, and their mother's furniture was not all out of keeping. If he were not obliged to see so much of it, Towersey would have pleased Kit very much; but he had been so often alone there – guiltily reading for a whole day at a time, or doing housework, or walking along by the river. Sometimes – though he could not afford to – he went to the *City of London* for a drink, to meet Liz Corbett, whom he had first seen there with Meg.

He was sure that she would be there today. Always at about noon, she stopped work and went next door for a sandwich and a glass of beer. He decided to join her and went to take off his new suit and hang it away carefully and put on his old clothes.

It was a bright, cold noon-day, and lines of washing flapped strenuously on high-propped lines in gardens and back yards. Slate roofs and street cobbles were pigeon-coloured, drying after earlier rain. There was a smell of coal dust and of beer being brewed, and the streets were noisy with children coming out of school and the rattling of drays and coal-carts. Alongside the river, by the pier, there was a naval trimness – white-washed stones edged pieces of grass on which old anchors were displayed; there were newly-painted flag-poles, a row of seats overlooking the water and a huge figure-head, with curled lips and protruding eyeballs.

Liz, apparently temporarily affluent, was having what the landlord called 'the set luncheon' and his customers called 'a plate of dinner' – meat pie, tinned peas, mashed potato, all covered with thick gravy.

Kit fetched his beer and sat down at her table in a corner of the bar, trying to keep his eyes off her plate. At

55

home, there was some stew for him to warm up. Meg
always left stew. He told Liz about his new job and she
asked him about the money and showed that she was not
impressed. It did not seem to her that acting was his
obsession, as painting was her own, and she wondered how
in the first place he had drifted into the wilderness fringe
of it, in which he groped for his chances of work. If she had
thought there was any likelihood of a truthful answer, she
would have asked this question; but she could usually
sense when her words would be wasted. She knew that
there can be no rules for linking the characters of creative
workers to their work; but she discerned in him a pride –
worse, touchiness – which was too personal, went beyond
the work itself and landed him in evasions. She thought he
was trying hard to make the most of being in a false position and – again she did not ask – she would have liked to
know how he was encouraged in it. Not – by a long chalk –
by his sister, Liz had decided on the day of their first meeting. Meg's loyalty was staunch, rather than enthusiastic.
Patrick Barlow? she had wondered. Other thoughts had
then swarmed into her head, but – whether they were
wasting her words or not – those questions could not be
asked, even by her, though side-questions could be re-
vealing.

'Patrick Barlow,' she said, shaking a cascade of pepper
over what was left of her mashed potatoes. 'Why he so
religious?' She was often economical about verbs, as if
there were an extra tax on their use. 'Very rum – a grown
man like that going to church every Sunday.'

'He probably believes in God,' Kit said, with telling
vagueness, and relief flowed over her. He neither knows,
nor cares, she thought. 'He's got different coloured eyes.
Did you realise that?' Kit asked.

'What have they got to do with it?'

'Imagine him every night, praying for them to be the
same – down on his knees wrestling with the problem.

Everyone in the world wants to have them matching. It's the obvious thing. If you were to have a son, it's the first thing you'd hope for. Yet his prayer isn't answered. Of course, it may be that he can't make up his mind whether to ask for them both blue, or both brown. That's what it may be. There must be a damn good reason; otherwise definitely unfair. I'm not in the least religious – but the very first thing I prayed for, I got.'

'What was that?'

'Well, I can't say – it would be a breach of confidence, wouldn't it?'

'Why not keep on doing it?'

'It's a mistake to push one's luck.'

During this conversation, Liz had set free one of her suspicions; it had winged away into thin air and banished. For her part, she felt it a delightful sensation to have it leave her. She sat staring down at her plate, on which only mustard was left, until the barman came to take it, and added his thumb-print alongside.

'You're going the whole hog,' Kit said, trying to keep envy from his voice, as some suet pudding with custard was put on the table.

'Well, I couldn't have it every day,' she said.

'Why today?'

'I needed bolstering up, and that's what food does.'

'Why? I mean, why did you need it?'

She shrugged, getting on with the food. In her job, she had to keep her worries to herself – since she was the only one in the world who could solve them. 'Delegate' – Flora's word – did not exist.

She ate quickly, but without any sort of critical attention; when she was not saying anything, she stared about her expressionlessly. Her negligence, about most things – not her work – was disconcerting. Meg had found it so and, unjustly, Kit was sure, condemned it as a silly pose. He watched her take up her glass, groping towards it while she was glancing another way. As she drank, her eyes above the glass slid sideways to look at someone going past to the bar. When she had finished the beer, she ran her tongue over her lips, her teeth, and reached for the remains of her bread with her long, dirty fingers. 'Utterly unself-conscious,' Kit thought. 'What a bit of luck for her, if not for us!'

He liked her, in spite of himself; but he could not admire her, so that – such was his nature – she could have no real importance to him. She was easy to be with, set up no standards, regarded no conventions. She was comradely (they each paid for their own beer) and he found relaxation in this casual relationship. But, since boyhood, he had felt a need to admire and worship and be devoted to – words which Patrick Barlow would have used in a different connection. To be worshipped and not to worship, seemed to Kit the most wretched of fates. He was selfishly glad that it was not likely to be his; but it did not occur to him to have pity for gods and goddesses.

'I must go,' Liz said, sorting out on the table the money for the set luncheon, without a tip.

'You're bolstered up?' Kit asked.

'In every way.'

She was ready to go back to work now and would not let him delay her. When she had gone, he finished the glass of beer that he had made last so long, and went out into the street. He walked along by the river for a little way and sat down on one of the embankment seats. Here, he and Flora had sat, on a late autumn afternoon. It had been her first visit to Towersey and he had observed her trying to hide her dismay.

The little house had obviously depressed her. Meg and Kit had not yet moved in, and planks and buckets of whitewash stood about on the bare floor boards. Windows and sills were freckled with spots of paint. Kit, as Flora looked about wondering what to say, tried to scrape some

58

of them off with his thumb-nail. What can I do for them? Flora was thinking, in a panic. And what, for heaven's sake, had possessed Patrick Barlow to suggest such an awful place?

After the inspection of the house, she and Kit had an exploratory walk about the town. It was an early-closing day, and the dullness of the streets was deathly, with dark blinds drawn over shop windows, or unlit interiors glimpsed through glass doors or behind dummy figures or rolls of linoleum.

They had tea in the café where Meg and Patrick had once been, and passed the tattooist's shop without a glance at it, talking – as they so often did – of Kit's future, the golden glow of it, as Flora foresaw it. Kit had a superstitious reluctance to listen to her being so clear about it; but before long her confidence beguiled him, and he could remember now how they had come to some public gardens and he had walked with her along the asphalt paths, with a gentle sense of buoyancy, had enjoyed kicking his feet through drifts of dried leaves and sycamore wings, as if he were still a boy. The gardens had been deserted. Beds of shabby chrysanthemums had already been bitten by a frost. Where paths converged, there were notices pointing to the café (closed), the public conveniences, and the children's playground. There was a drinking-fountain of polished pink granite and a statue of a frock-coated town's benefactor – white and lumpy, like a thawing snowman, with green stains running out of his eye-sockets, and down his cheeks and dewlaps. A cold, but pretty day. He and Flora had sat on this seat at the river's edge, among pieces of driftwood, a scalloped fringe of grit, seaweed and old fruit-peelings. There had been a high tide, and a heavy wash, over the embankment.

'Well, it won't be long,' Flora had said, becoming – from her sunny nature – a little reconciled to Towersey, and fixing, in her imagination, a blue plaque to the wall between the bedroom windows – *Christopher Driscoll, Actor, Lived Here.*

Kit was, that afternoon, much more than reconciled to it. The town, under its early-closing spell, the dreary public gardens and the empty streets, had seemed a kind of paradise, into which the deity had temporarily, but in no way accusingly, dropped in. She had even given up her weekly visit to Ba, to visit him. As a schoolboy, when his devotion to her began, he had had his dreams about her; but such unambitious dreams that he had not thought of having her un-shared company for several hours together. He had allowed himself to save her life in countless situations, and sometimes she saved his – simply by sitting at his bedside while his fever dropped; or just by accepting his word, when the world did not. Her sense of fairness was the first thing about her that he had remembered. There was a broken cream-jug and spilt cream, and Meg and his mother cross with him; but Flora had seen his grand-mother's shawl fringe sweep it from the table, and would not let the senile child play out her crafty game, sheltering behind deafness and letting her grandson have the blame. The Christian martyr look was no new thing to Flora even then: she was pink with the injustice of their accusations – how beautiful she had looked, he had never forgotten. The apologies of his mother and sister, the fogged mumbling of his grandmother, were nothing; for justice had won and was beautiful. He was ten years old, and the long-lasting admiration had begun. He had not seen her often. Once or twice, she came with Meg and his mother to visit him at school and seemed like Persephone entering the under-world, and now was Demeter, with her swollen front and widened lap.

He had not desired her sexually – or had not given his imagination a chance, reining it in quickly when a hand's touch, a light kiss, disturbed him. He was rather more upset by the thought of her coming child, than he had ever

been by her husband. Once or twice he had made love to
girls of his own age, but could hardly remember them
afterwards, had always managed to slip out of entangle-
ments, even though, in his long-haired, untidy way, he
was attractive to women, and sometimes found them
tenacious.

The afternoon was going by, and he was so hungry that
he could almost face returning home to warm up the hated
stew. He could too easily imagine the thin, oniony smell of
it spreading about the house, and the golden sequins of
grease moving on its surface. Poor old Meg! It must be
eaten.

A girl who had sauntered by once, now sat down on the
other end of the seat, casually opened her handbag and
took out a cigarette. She rummaged about in the depths
of her bag and then glanced at him.

'I wonder if you . . .?' She waved her unlit cigarette.

'I'm sorry.' He thrust his hands into his pockets, knowing it was no use.

'Oh, well. It doesn't matter.' Sadly, she put the cigarette away, stuffing it back into its packet. 'Better for me
not to,' she said brightly. Her eyes had a full, glittery look
– from contact lenses, he thought; not tears. 'Could you
tell me the time?' she asked.

'It just struck three.'

'Oh, thank you.' She leaned back, crossed her legs, and
stared at her wagging foot, did exercises with it, flexing
and circling her neat ankle, humming softly. 'Not a bad
day,' she said. 'I quite like it here, watching the boats,
don't you?'

If she's going to *talk*, Kit thought. He got up and, as
politely as he could, said: 'I shall have to go home to
lunch.'

'To *lunch*?' she echoed, unbelievingly. 'At *this* hour.
You'll be in trouble.'

'No. There's no one to be cross.'

As he walked away, she stared after him dully, had let him slip through her fingers. When he was out of sight, she took out the packet of cigarettes again and a little lighter from the bottom of her handbag.

Moodily, Kit walked back along the embankment, wishing Flora were with him to restore his confidence. At times like this lonely afternoon, beside the melancholy-sounding traffic of the river, staring down at the thick brown tide washing the mossy stones, he began to see himself through Liz's eyes, not Flora's, and was afraid of doing so, more and more.

Six

RICHARD going sometimes into Mayfair for business-account lunches, several times, in a series of coincidences had glimpses of his neighbour, Elinor Pringle – once, sitting back in a taxi, yawning her head off; another time, in the window of a coffee bar, staring out at the street over a trough of plastic ferns. She wore such a sad expression that he did not like to catch her off-guard. He pretended not to have seen her and then, too late to do anything about it, was sure that she had noticed him going by, and seen through his pretence.

She was a tenacious shopper, he knew – indefatigably tracking down pieces of old furniture, jewellery, china; watching and waiting, perhaps for years, to get exactly what she wanted. She could always tell people the prices she paid, for they were so low as to start interesting conversations. One early evening, walking up the hill on his way home, he saw a dilapidated Victorian chaise-longue being carried in, and Elinor, flnging open the front door to it with an air of triumph.

Some time later, coming one afternoon into Marylebone Station after a trip to West Ruislip to soothe an irritable customer, he saw Elinor at the Left Luggage office, struggling to carry away a large picture, badly wrapped and tied up in thin brown paper. It was too wide to go under her arm and the frame too flat to grip. To make up for the occasion when he had passed the coffee bar without looking at her, he hurried now to her rescue.

'I must get it into a taxi,' she said. 'If you could help me. I have these awkward objects left all over the place.

This one is a really beautiful problem picture. I found it in a shop in the country.'

'Would you like some tea before we find the taxi?' he asked, handsomely atoning.

'I would,' she said, in her quick, emphatic voice.

It was before the rush-hour, and the station was almost empty; silent, too, except for a porter whistling. A slight fog from outside had drifted in and hung under the glass roof, where pigeons perched in the gloom.

The tea-room delighted Elinor, who had never seen it before. It was a great discovery, she said, gazing about her at the rich mahogany, the clean white tablecloths, the curly hatstands. It was so hushed that they spoke in whispers. There was only an old man, on his own, eating a poached egg, staring morosely ahead. Behind the scenes, a waitress was grumbling to another. ' "It's always been done that way," I told him, "and that's how it always will be done. By me." ' She emerged, straight-faced, took Richard's order without saying a word and then, out of sight again, resumed the harangue. 'It's the proper way. "It's not fair to the customers," I said, "leaving their butter exposed." ' There was a sudden hissing noise from a machine, which made Elinor start, and a sound of toast being scraped.

'I saw you the other day,' she told Richard.

'Yes, you were welcoming in a large green chaise-longue.'

'Oh, then! Really? did you? No, I meant when I was sitting in a coffee bar. You went past. In Davies Street.'

'Extraordinarily small place, London,' he said evasively. 'Once I saw you in a taxi going down Hay Hill.'

'Oh, I *don't* like people seeing me when I don't see *them*. They always tell me afterwards how strained I was looking.'

Not at all, you were yawning your head off, Richard thought.

The tea was brought and the strips of scraped toast,

criss-crossed on a thick blue plate. 'Exposed,' Elinor mouthed to Richard. The picture Richard had propped up on a vacant chair and the waitress skirted it disapprovingly. When she had poured out, Elinor leaned over and tore aside the thin brown paper, so that Richard could see. The painting was done in dark colours, and showed a woman in a cream lace blouse, boned at the neck, standing with her hand on a decanter and smiling to herself as she watched, in a sidelong gaze, a young man with his lips to a glass of wine.

'Is she a poisoner?' Richard asked.

'She looks as if she might be.'

'Or it might be a love potion. It's a nasty coloured drop of drink, whatever it is. What's the picture called?'

'*The Potation.* That's all. It's very lovely though, isn't it?' she asked, picking up one of the bendy strips of buttered toast.

'Dreadful,' he said. 'Simply dreadful.'

'You're not serious?'

'You're not, I should hope.'

The old man had finished his poached egg and as he waited for the bill, his eyes had wandered to the picture, but not with any expression of surprise or interest.

'It's awfully well painted,' Elinor said. 'You can see that's real Chantilly lace.'

'Is Geoffrey going to like it?'

'He won't give a damn. In so far as he sees anything, he seems to take against charm. He likes ideas, and for everything about him to be functional and make no demands on him. When he gets back from the House, he just shuts himself up with his history books – writing a play about the wickedness of the Crusades. I must say I agree with him about that, and I'm sure it will be a very good play when it's done.'

Richard thought of Flora and of how, at once, she would have been busy about furthering Kit's future, mentally decking him out in chain mail and helmet and setting him in the middle of the large stage. Then that went out of his mind, and he said: 'Aren't you lonely?' immediately wishing that he hadn't – definitely not a question to put to another man's wife.

'I have all sorts of interests, you know,' she said, looking round at the old-fashioned tea-room, as if it were one of them, and then at her picture. 'Sometimes I am,' she then admitted.

'You never do any of those things that other Members' wives seem to do – brightly opening bazaars, and looking absolutely stunned with delight at the sight of a bouquet of pink carnations.'

'As I'm on the other side, how could I?'

'That must lead to awkwardness.'

'Yes, it does; but there's nothing I can do about that.' She looked at him with bracing hostility, as she must have looked at other people – Geoffrey's agent? Geoffrey himself? They had forgotten to whisper and the waitress, flicking crumbs from a table, had her head on one side, listening. Richard thought how different Flora would be, were she in Elinor's place. He could clearly picture her loyal enthusiasm. No scruples she had ever had of her own would weigh against her constancy to him' 'Indefatigable,' 'unflagging', would be words his constituents would use of her. She would be affected by delighted wonder at every bouquet, and every sharp comment on him would wound her, rouse her indignation. Two years back, things had gone badly in his factory where they made fillings for upholstered furniture and Flora immediately saw herself as a poor man's wife. Her pathetic economies and sacrifices irritated him, for they were meaningless beyond the pleasure they gave to her. When trade returned, she suffered a spell of ennui, was not quite herself for a while – with fillet steaks back on the menu and having other people to wash her hair again.

'I don't know why you care so much,' Richard told Elinor. 'Politics mean too little to me to make an issue of them. The drab muddle it all is – the awful sameness, staleness. Who cares? About anything big, who of us will have any say? We shall be told afterwards. Anyone who is alive to be told.'

'There are lesser things that stick in one's gullet,' said Elinor. ('Worth fighting one's husband for? Richard wondered.) 'Honestly!' she said, leaning forward, her look, her voice full of quiet exasperation, as if she had read his thought. 'I can't be the sort of Socialist Geoffrey and most of his friends are. Being married to him doesn't suddenly make *that* possible. They all exasperate me. The high-minded talk that goes on in their nice houses; reading the *Times* in first-class compartments. If I had some serious illness, Geoffrey would send me to the London Clinic; if we had a son, he'd go to a public school. When I ask simple questions about such things, they prevaricate and rationalise. Call me naïve. Now *this* is typical, though not politics – Geoffrey's agent is a vegetarian who eats fish. "That's a nasty death a fish dies," I said to him once, as he was tucking into a couple of trout. But he had an answer, of course. Fish can't feel pain much – no brains, or nerves, or something of the kind; I forget. And I am told I must not over-simplify complicated matters. It is my besetting sin. I'm not valued for it.' She looked at the clock above the fireplace and decided that she ought to go home. 'If the fog gets worse, there won't be any taxis.'

The fog had been thickening while they were having tea and voices in the station were muffled and had lost their thin echo. Outside, lights were blurred and downy, and shapes of people and traffic made sudden appearances, weaving hesitantly forwards.

'I like it,' Elinor said. A cab crawled to the kerb and they got in. 'It's disorganising, like snow. It makes a different world.'

67

In the taxi, Richard had the picture propped against his knees. It seemed to him hours earlier that he had gone out to West Ruislip to pacify the customer. When they reached Elinor's house, he decided to get out and walk the rest of the way. He never took a taxi home. He carried the picture up the path for her and, when Elinor had opened the door, propped it against a chair in the hall. It was always a dark, empty house she returned to, he thought. He declined a drink and set off up the hill, keeping close to the railings. The fog thinned towards the top of the hill and Beatrice Crescent was almost clear.

*   *   *

Flora was in the kitchen with Mrs Lodge. She spent a lot of her time there, turning out cupboards and drawers, or cleaning silver, while Mrs Lodge was cooking. This was the easiest relationship she had ever known, and Mrs Lodge – because of the day-to-day intimacy – a closer friend to her even than Meg. There had never been a sharp word between them, and neither could imagine any; and it would often happen that one would make a remark which had been on the tip of the other's tongue, their thoughts havng run together.

Mrs Lodge had been a country girl and loved birds, luring them into this little London garden with strings of peanuts hanging from branches and crumbs of suet scattered on the grass. All through the hard winters, the starlings grew fat and glossy on her offerings, attacked crusts greedily, gagged and recovered, drove off thrushes and fought with one another. When the spring came, they tore the crocuses to shreds and snapped off polyanthus heads. But there were some triumphs for Mrs Lodge – tits nested in a box she put up, and a robin seemed to come for company, as well as nourishment.

It was Flora's bad dream that one day Mrs Lodge would decide to retire to the country, or (she was widowed) go to

live with her married son in the Green Belt which, although not what she considered country – so little was,
now – provided more varieties of birds, even reservoirs
where ducks came in.

'If you ever left me, I wouldn't, couldn't say goodbye to
you,' Flora said; for Mrs Lodge had been recalling how
different fog was in the country – just mist, really – an
outdoor thing: not this vile-smelling stuff creeping right
into people's houses. 'Obnoxious,' she said. The slightest
word of aversion to London, was enough to make Flora,
who understood the aversion, feel insecure.

'Don't think I'd dream of going with the baby on the
way,' Mrs Lodge said.

'But not ever. When it's born, I'll need you more and
more.' Mrs Lodge might have gone through the experi-
ences of birth and bringing up her child and being parted
from him, for the one purpose of learning how to advise
and comfort Flora when it was her turn for them. 'I just
want to take my good luck for granted,' Flora said. 'Not to
have to keep touching wood.' She blinked back tears, as
she polished a spoon, holding it up high, afraid that if she
bent her head the tears, instead of receding, might drop
info her lap. She wanted Mrs Lodge to say that she would
never leave her, but Mrs Lodge was too sensible. The unusual sensation of not getting her own way – even over a
meaningless pledge – ruffled Flora's spirits, and when she
looked at the clock – moving her eyes with care – she saw
that Richard was quite late. He had gone out to West
Ruislip on the two-twenty train, and she had expected
him home much earlier, had hoped that he might come in
in time for tea. Mrs Lodge, who had gone down the hill to
post a letter had said that the fog was quite bad. Perhaps
the trains were all late, which would make everything so
disagreeable. Flora hated chaos.

Mrs Lodge, with her head on one side, whisked up some
cream until it stood in peaks. Before she was married, she

had been in what she called 'good service', but as a par-
lourmaid. She still cooked with a sense of importance
which she could not have made other people understand.
Even when she was alone, she felt that she had an audience. It watched admiringly as she whipped the cream and
put her ear attentively to the oven door to hear the meat,
cooking beautifully, making little twittering sounds inside.

She liked cooking, and she loved Flora; but London
meant nothing to her. There was so little to look at. All her
visions, as she chopped herbs and stirred sauces, were of
the past. Her home, when she was a child, had been near
an estuary, remote, with wonderful wide skies, a beautiful
light. Terns used to gather on a sandbank at the edge of
the water, and looked as if they were dancing with their
frail, coral-red legs. They would spread out like a fan and
skim over the water, with their wings lifted – like a flock
of butterflies. So pretty. She could watch for hours. She
could still see them in her mind, and the herons standing
in shallow water; and hear the wonderful disturbance
when the wild geese flew over. At the great house where
she went to work, there were nightingales in a copse,
woods haunted by owls, elm trees clotted with rooks' nests,
swallows in the eaves. Richness. Here, in London, she had
some shabby sparrows, the fiendish starlings, and her heart
overflowed when the robin came onto the window-sill.
Two worlds, and the other the one she yearned for. To
herself, she used that word 'yearn'. She had discovered
that only this one described the pain and longing she felt,
softened by the tenderness and pleasure of her memories.

As Flora was wrapping the polished spoons in a chamois
leather, she heard Richard coming up the path, climbing
the steps, and she went upstairs to greet him. She always
left wherever she was and hurried to the hall when she
heard his key in the door. Her mother had told her that
she should, that it pleased husbands almost more than
anything.

He brought the smell of the fog in with him.

'I suppose all the trains are late,' she said.

He hung up his coat and said, 'Not too bad.'

'I so hoped that you'd come home to tea,' she said. She spoke in a child's voice, as if she were only playing at being disappointed; and he thought she was far too tall for such a little-girl voice. Unlike her, he sometimes had disloyal thoughts.

'There wasn't any question of it. I could have told you, if you'd asked.' He went into the drawing-room after her, and poured out some gin, tipped in some vermouth and took a long drink, still holding the bottle, as if he were dying of thirst. Then he began a boring rigmarole about the business at West Ruislip, his handling of the angry customer ... the personal touch ... pouring oil ... having his hand eaten from. Flora drifted across the room and straightened a picture on the wall. From her dreamy look, he knew that she was not listening to him and he couldn't blame her. The moment he stopped talking, to take another long drink, she flashed her beautiful smile on him. It seemed to sweep over him, like a stroke of brightness from a lighthouse. Then gone.

'How crafty you are!' she said admiringly. 'You twist these cross little men round your little finger.'

I am a bit crafty, I suppose, he thought. He had no idea why he had mentioned having tea with Elinor Pringle. So absurd not to – a chance meeting, such as that. To have kept quiet about it, had given it the significance of a secret arrangement. Now it was too late, and if Flora came to hear of it, as more than likely she might, a little puzzled frown would come between her brows – the expression she wore when she was bewildered by other standards of behaviour than her own. But we've preserved the face pretty well, between us, Richard thought; not fearing ageing lines, but the loss of innocence. So far, and by the skin of his teeth, he felt. The face was his responsibility now and

it would surely be his fault if it were altered. if the Botti-
celli calm were broken, or the appealing gaze veiled.

She sat down and clasped her hands upon her stomach.
'Well, you're here now,' she said contentedly. She still
looked like all those girlhood photographs her mother
cherished. Her glance might be enquiring, but it expected
a comfortable answer. The deceit of the world she would
hardly credit; the deceit of Richard would take her breath
away. By any other standards, he had never considered he
behaved very badly. Wanton and disloyal and ignoble
thoughts affected only him and, though frequent, were
fleeting. His irritability had gastric causes.

He stood by the fire, one foot on the brass fender. (Flora
glanced at it, but decided to say nothing, for it was better
to have a scratched fender than a nagged husband): his
elbow rested precariously in a little space between two
china shepherdesses with pink, smiling faces like his wife's.

She sat gazing in front of her. On a table at her side was
a piece of knitting which had not grown for days, and the
book by Henry Miller Patrick Barlow had lent her, which
she was reading with such mild surprise. ('What does *this*
word mean, Richard?' 'Truly? Well I suppose it had to be
called *something*.' How had she lived so long without knowing? he wondered.)

She seemed to be as busy as anything, just bearing her
child. Full-time job. He brushed a thought from his mind.
Just then he heard Mrs Lodge beginning to ascend the
stairs – his cue to move back briskly to the drinks table and
top up his glass as if he had no idea of the time. Every
evening, he managed to have a full one when dinner was
ready. He was a good way on to taking after his father,
some people thought. To be said to take after anyone is
usually derogatory to both parties; and it was so in this
case.

Seven

THE little house was as cold as a cave when Meg came home from work. Only the bathroom was faintly warm and still steamy. She picked up a wet towel from the floor and stood there with it in her hand, in a daze of tiredness, feeling sorry for herself. He took all the hot water, let the fire die, dropped her bath-towel on the floor, and then went out. It was in a fury with himself that he behaved like this, she knew. Once upon a time, he would not have done so, once he had been an affectionate brother and had tried to do things to please her. He didn't even remember my birthday, she thought, standing as if in a trance, frozen by self-pity. He went off to tea with Flora, and *she* reminded him. He had come back with a bunch of flowers tied up with string, not as a florist would have tied them, and Meg imagined Flora going round her drawing-room, taking them out of their vases, upsetting her arrangements, because the shops were shut. And Patrick Barlow had been there (Meg sometimes thought that she and Richard were the only ones who ever went to work) and he must have heard the whole discussion, probably taken part in it, seen Meg as an object of pity, whom everyone but Flora had forgotten. She was relieved that *he* had not tried to repair his omission by sending something late, with an apology. Meg had hated that bunch of chrysanthemums from Flora's, and as soon as the leaves had begun to wither, she had thrown them away.

She stirred and sighed, like someone on a sick-bed weary with pain. Coming out of her trance of misery, she hung up the towel. She fetched some kindling wood from the little yard at the back of the house and, still wearing her

73

coat, she knelt down and re-lit the fire in the parlour. *He has nothing to do all day, yet* . . . This phrase was always being churned over in her mind, although she knew that it was just *because* he had nothing to do all day that he left everything to her. It was the state of accidie into which he had fallen, Patrick Barlow said. A grievous waste and weakness, a sinful non-participation. It was something worse than being idle: it was self-destruction. He had said all this, and Meg thought that he exaggerated – whether from indignation on her account or from his religious convictions, she could not tell. She knew her brother better. It was simply pride that made him unco-operative. How easy it would have been for him to scuttle about tidying the house, making her bed for her, cooking their supper. He could have economised on the hot water, and gone without bacon for breakfast. And all that would have humiliated him and underlined his situation, as if he, himself, had seen the hopelessness of it. He would have been shamed by guessing Meg's thoughts ticking over – *he's a failure, he has no money: I have to keep him, but at least he does what he can.* She would have seen through his subterfuges – 'I like a cold bath occasionally.' 'I'm not hungry' – and insisted on the bath and bacon. He would rather be wholly a rogue. It was perhaps a less pathetic role.

She stood stirring the stew, still in her coat, wondering where he had gone. Liz Corbett? The pub? Both? Probably not far afield. Flora's was for daytime visits unless he were invited to one of her parties. Meg guessed that the arrival home of Richard, tired from the rush-hour and a day's work, made Kit uneasy.

She tried to spear a piece of carrot against the side of the saucepan to see if it were done but, although she had cooked the stew for hours before she went to bed last night, the carrots seemed quite raw. As this always happened, she was not surprised – only puzzled about why. The meat had disintegrated into coarse shreds and the potatoes had vanished.

74

What a useless wife I'd make, she thought. But she would never marry. Her life would turn out to be quite different from the one she had dreamed of as a child: it would be like that of Miss Williams at the office, who lived with her invalid mother and never went on a holiday or had an adventure. The books she read were sillier and sillier as the years went by – for reality had become upsetting, the truth disturbing. When, as a child, Meg had come across similar women – schoolmistresses, elderly spinsters in church – she had wondered how it came about that lives could dwindle so, and was convinced that hers never could, even though she had an odd sort of face and her mother could not afford to buy for her the beautiful clothes that Flora wore. She saw that things went wrong in some women's lives – things quite beyond their control – such as deformity or ungainliness or aged parents living on too long – but she believed that even in such circumstances, she would fight her way out of them. Yet, lately, she had felt dowdiness creeping over her. New fashions seemed absurd. She thought too much of her girlhood, went back to visit her old school on one occasion and was alarmed and depressed by what had already happened to some in the time since they had left. There were many Miss Williams in the making. I could have guessed it of them, Meg thought. But not of herself.

Miss Williams was such a warning to her that Meg was repelled by almost all she said and did. She averted her eyes from that sad, plain face as if it were some traitor's head, impaled and set up as an example to others, and especially to herself. Miss Williams was in her fifties, and when she retired, Meg would probably take her place, become the indispensable Miss Driscoll, for the rest of her working days – and there were so many to come – would sit there at her typewriter, high up in the office at the top of a building in Regent Street. From the windows she could look out onto roof-tops, dozens of different kinds of chimneys and cowls, sooty, rain-stained pediments and parapets which no one in the street could see. Her own view, though, for the rest of her life.

She was startled when, dreaming over the stew, she heard a bang on the front door. It could not be Kit. There was only one key and it hung on a piece of string inside the letter-box, so that they both could use it. When she opened the door, she found Patrick there, with a book in his hand. He was looking down the dark street to the lights on the river and, without turning to Meg, made a move-ment with his hand to draw her attention to the scene. She went out on to the step to look. A large ship was passing slowly along on its way out to sea; its funnels slid by above the rooftops.

'Yes, it is beautiful,' Meg agreed. For everything was suddenly beautiful. She felt as though the sun had broken through between clouds, yet had the sense of apprehension one knows on a summer's day in England, shivering and basking alternately, as the sun is covered and uncovered. Lest Patrick should suddenly turn and go or thrust the book he carried into her hands and at once drive off in the shabby car at the kerb-side, she stepped quickly back into the house and held the door open. Apologising for the smell of the stew, she went into the parlour, where the fire was burning nicely.

'I thought we might go out to find some dinner – per-haps that hotel farther down the river. I dare say we could get a nice frozen prawn cocktail, or some pâté maison out of a tin, and the ubiquitous fillet steak.'

All this sounded wonderful to Meg.

'I went to Liz Corbett's to collect a picture,' he said.

'Was Kit there?'

'No one was there. It was shut up and in darkness. I brought this for you.'

She took the book and handled it awkwardly, trying to put on an expression of great interest as she turned the pages. It was an essay on Gwen John that he had just had published, and she would not for the world have him know that she had hurried to buy it on the day that it came out and had already read it twice. 'Meg, with love from Patrick,' he had written. Then she turned the page hastily on which was printed 'For F'. She knew about 'F' and wondered what on earth *he* could make of such a book. She looked again at the beautiful illustrations – girls reading, nuns in church, the backs of chairs, cats. When he said, standing there by the fire, considering her, that he thought her rather a Gwen John person herself, she could not be certain what he meant, and wondered if he found some sadness in her, or loneliness.

'I sent Flora's copy by post,' he said. 'I know she won't read it. She never does. And she always has the same technique of getting out of it. It's amusing to observe. She manages for a while, by acknowledging the book the very moment she receives it; sits down and writes the letter before she could have had a chance to begin the first chapter. 'I shall enjoy reading it and, oh, the pleasure of having it at last, after the anticipation.' And so on. Then she keeps well out of my way, until some reviews have appeared, so that she had a phrase or two to tag onto it, or something unfavourable to be indignant at. "*How rude!*" she says. "How *terribly* rude!" Once, I met her by chance, before she was ready for me, and she said that she was taking the book in tiny sips, à petites doses, as Henry James wrote when he was up to the same trick – as if it were the most precious wine. That meant that she was bogged down in it.'

'Poor Flora,' Meg said vaguely.

'No one less so. Poor all of us, I say.'

'I used to imagine Persephone being like her. I could see her picking the flowers in a meadow in the sunshine. Because it was Flora I was imagining, the darkness, the underworld seemed so much worse. It was as if, by some

terrifying misunderstanding, Flora had found herself in
Holloway Gaol.'

'Well, Mrs Secretan makes a fine Demeter,' Patrick
said. 'Shall we go now, if you are ready? If Kit has gone
off with Liz, he can fend for himself. Leave a note. That's
Frankie's old car outside. He lent it to me.'

Frankie was 'F'. Although neither Meg nor Flora had
ever seen him, they had heard rumours. Percy had sat near
them in a restaurant – Patrick and Frankie lunching together – and brought back a description of him to which
Flora had listened uneasily. He – Frankie – was in his mid
twenties, Percy thought, had crinkly ginger hair and a
white, freckled face. He had sulked like a child, left food
scattered about his plate and boredly sat back, drinking
wine, had asked for strawberries out of season and kept
giving sharp looks about him, at everyone who came
or went and particularly, Percy said, at the tip Patrick
left on the plate. 'Did *you* enjoy *your* lunch?' Meg remembered Flora asking her father-in-law, quite without
mischief.

She went to turn off the gas under the stew and put on
her coat. When she locked the front door after them she
dropped the key back through the letter box. She walked
lightly down the path. Twenty minutes earlier, she had
been near despair.

Patrick was a bad driver, and the little car bucked
violently, kept starting and stopping. He was apologetic
about the driving – and more about the car, and probably
had to be so to Frankie as well, for Meg had no doubt but
that Patrick had bought it. She could imagine that young
man's face clouded with disappointment to find that such
a shabby thing was the best that Patrick could afford. We
are all vulnerable somewhere, she thought – and hoped
that feelings of pity were not going to ruin her evening.
Nearly all of us have blind, uncritical corners of our minds,
fiercely guarded and defended – and the awful-sounding

Frankie was in Patrick's who, though he did not bring him forward, could not resist saying his name. Frankie had put up some bookshelves for him. Frankie had driven him to Glyndebourne, although it was by no means Frankie's cup of tea, and when Patrick had flu, he had stayed with him in the flat and made him cups of tea – 'as black as night,' Patrick said indulgently.

That young man plays him up more than any girl would do, Meg thought. There was no peace for him – tantrums and suffering, insecurity, this utterly blind love in which he was exploited as a fond parent by a naughty child. All part of the self-deception were the pathetic attempts to cultivate Frankie's mind – Glyndebourne, the ballet, taking him to see the châteaux of the Loire. That had almost ended the affair. On his return, Patrick had frequently dropped in to see Meg, seemed to have time on his hands, could not work, or sleep, he had said. A fortnight on his own with Frankie had shown him many truths. Very early, Frankie had grown bored – not only with history and architecture, but with Patrick. He had refused to go into another great house or church, and had sat in the car all day long and sulked, would not get out of it except for lunch, and then had grumbled at the beautiful food. These charming foibles were described to Meg, as if they were the idiosyncracies of a genius, easily forgiven, even quite amusing in themselves. In those conversations with Meg, Patrick was rearranging the truth into a less painful pattern, comforting himself, concealing the darkness of mood he had really suffered. He might have deceived himself a little, but he did not deceive Meg. She had listened, and then put her thoughts in another direction. She did not want to know about Frankie, and she hoped that this might be an evening without any more mention of his name. She was tormented by his very existence.

*　　*　　*

Kit, on one of his riverside walks, recovering from a quarrel with Liz, saw his sister and Patrick, sitting in the bright window of the hotel restaurant. The embankment road ran between the hotel and its gardens, which sloped down to the river wall.

When Patrick had come puffing up the stairs, tapping on the door, Kit had been in bed with Liz, lying in the darkness, a short time after making love. From where they lay, they could watch the lights going by on the river, and Kit – in this darkness – could forget the squalor of the room. While Patrick was standing outside on the landing, they whispered to one another in the crumpled pillow, and Liz gripped Kit tightly with her short, fat legs. Their bodies, close together, shook with silent laughter. When they heard his footsteps go draggingly down the stairs, Liz jumped out of bed and went to peep out of a corner of the window. 'Yes it was,' she said. 'It's Patrick Barlow.' She watched him cross the pavement and get into his car, laughed at the hiccuping noises it made as he tried to start it. 'Sad old fairy,' she said.

Kit, as soon as she got out of bed, felt alienated from her, did not much like lying in the rumpled sheets alone, and thought what an extraordinary shape she was, crouching there by the window, chuckling to herself about nothing. The light from the street lamp, in which she watched Patrick's tussle with the car, fell over her breasts and shoulders, outlined against the window her tousled, spiky hair. She was oblong. This was how he had drawn people when he was a child – with arms and legs attached to the rectangle, hair scribbled on top of the head. Sometimes, he gave these figures a walking-stick, a hat with a feather; other times, secretly, daringly, what his mother always called a 'little tassle' hanging between the legs or – more from conjecture – a pair of round, high-up breasts exactly like Liz's.

'Gone,' she said, shivered and drew the curtain round her shoulders. 'It's beautiful out there.' She saw a large,

funnelled ship coming from the docks, passing slowly on
its way to sea. Tugs were hooting. Its passage set up a
commotion on the river.

It was while they were dressing that the quarrel about
Flora sprang up. Liz had never met her; but knew of the
soothing tea-parties, the tender influence. Slowly she had
formed a dislike of her – not from motives of jealousy, for
she was not in love with Kit. She would not dream of giving up even half an hour of work in the precious daylight
to go to bed with him. Her antagonism to Flora was simply
that the kind of woman she imagined her to be was the
kind that she had always scorned. She connected her with
romance, charm, fashion, elegance, fine feelings – all
spurious things, she considered. It was from curiosity – to
complete the picture – that she asked so many questions
about Flora and Kit's visits to St John's Wood. What was
she wearing? He could never remember; could only sometimes vaguely supply a colour. What did they talk about?
He did not like to say, realising that it was mainly about
himself. She even wanted to know what sort of dainty little
sandwiches they had for tea. With the crusts cut off? And
would snort with contempt.

This evening, her arms crooked like wings as she fastened her brassière at the back, she went too far. 'It's been
going on a good many years,' she pointed out. 'Haven't
you ever been to bed with her?'

Kit, with one leg in his trousers would, otherwise, have
rushed at her and shaken the breath from her lungs. They
stood, shouting at one another across the room, looking
absurd as they dragged on their clothes.

'Not even a kiss? Doesn't she clasp your head to her
bosom?' Liz asked. 'Too bad to have kept you at bay all
these years. Perhaps you think of *her* when you're in bed
with *me*. But that doesn't work, or so I've been led to
believe. There'a a damn good word for women like her.'
She said it.

'Do you think I'd ever come back to this filthy dump?'
Kit asked, getting into his clothes as fast as he could.

'I'll bet you do, all the same. The next time you come
back from seeing her.'

'You know nothing about her. You've never met her,
and I'll see to it you never will.'

'I know all about her. I interpret what you tell me. And,
my God, how you like to talk. Meg won't listen, so I must.
You love to say her name. It's an indulgence – like playing
with yourself. And then, when it's all said, you jump into
bed with me – having carefully put the light out – very
significant, that.'

He had slammed the door, run down the ricketty stairs,
tying his tie, and walked at a furious pace along the
embankment, too angry to go home.

'It's the truth that hurts the most,' Liz had told him.
'That's Flora's big attraction for you. You're safe there.
She won't hurt you.'

His mind was confused and his head ached. He had
quarrelled with Liz before – when she had splashed some
paint on his jacket, or been angry with him for trying to
interrupt her work, or told him – as she often did – to go
out and get a job. But he had not known her to be venom-
ous. He would never go back. She appalled him. She was
coarse and terrible, and she never washed her hair. As
soon as he had made the decision, he foresaw the awful
loneliness of his days, trying not to go too often to Flora,
lest she should think he claimed more of her time than she
could spare; loafing about the house; going for long walks
with his head quite dull and empty, no thoughts, nothing
to think; passing the time; playing his obsessive games –
counting the spikes on railings or the paces he could take
before a car passed by, touching every letter-box – even,
with shame, crossing roads to do so – and adding up the
score. 'I am going mad – mad.' Telling himself that with
another part of his mind. This evening, he forced himself,

with a great effort of will, not to count his footsteps and seal off his mind in doing so; but to think – to think hard – about his situation, to face all that he could. Was loving Flora, for instance, perhaps only loving himself? Because she was the only one who would tell him what he wanted to hear. She was his protection and disguise.

It was obvious that he needed her so badly because his ambitions were absurd. He would never make an actor. Bravely, he let the thought creep from the back of his mind, where it had lurked for a long time, like an animal in hiding. He could not look back and decide that what had fooled him was his desire for that particular life, or the hope of escaping some other kind – going to an office each day like Richard, for instance. As everyone but he and Flora had thought for long enough, he would have to find a job – there must be something even he could do – and he must find it without delay. He wanted no more solitary days, with only his own thoughts for company. He decided to go home quickly now to Meg and tell her of his intentions: then he would have to keep to them. The hibernation was over.

He had come to the gardens of the riverside hotel and he turned and began to walk briskly homewards. By the locked gate into the gardens was a pillar-box, and this time he crossed the road to avoid it. It was then that he was so surprised to see Meg sitting in the window of the hotel, smiling across the table at Patrick Barlow. She wore an air of gaiety and alertness he had not observed in her for a long time. So braced by his own new resolves was he, that he could spare a thought for her, as he too rarely did; could regret the turn her life had taken.

He walked past the window, unseen by them, and went on towards home. That ephemeral gaiety, that look of gentle radiance hurt him. Poor little sister! he kept thinking.

Eight

MRS SECRETAN had been finding the winter days trying, and was glad of the approach of Christmas, with the thought of Flora and Richard coming to stay. Next year, there would be the baby, too. She imagined holding her up to the lighted Christmas tree and on her little face the look of wonder that once she had seen on Flora's. If I am spared she always thought when she indulged in these dreams of the future. She had no desire to tempt Providence, and lately had been unhappy about her health. She had put off seeing her doctor, for fear of his giving some terrifying diagnosis which would completely ruin Christmas for her. She imagined the festive atmosphere charged with concealed horrors, a mockery, trying to hide the truth, arranging the decorations with a sense of doom, hardly daring to think about her granddaughter. I'm simply not brave enough to take the risk, she decided. So, from day to day, she just gently worried, could almost put the anxiety aside when she was busy; but in the darkness of night there were sudden, swerving moments of panic.

The behaviour of her companion-housekeeper added to the perplexities of her days. Since Miss Folley had announced that she had found a cache of old love-letters, Mrs Secretan's evenings had become really hurtfully embarrassing. The gentlemen who had written the letters to Miss Folley so long ago were eloquently described, and the letters themselves read aloud – often twice over – and dwelt on, a different one each evening. Mrs Secretan was embarrassed not only by their contents, but by the fact that she recognised the handwriting and the pale blue, mottled paper. At first she had listened from pity; but now she was repelled, sat tongue-tied, with her eyes cast down. She made attempts to escape her victimisation by many means – shut in her bedroom with a feigned headache (but a real pain in her chest), visiting her friends, or sitting at her desk, so deeply concentrating on her accounts, adding up on her fingers, her lips murmuring over columns, that Miss Folley would hover, with the letter ready in her hand, then sigh at last and go away.

To evade her was not easy. For instance, the places Mrs Secretan could visit were growing fewer. So many changes had taken place. She walked through the village, and saw the houses she had visited for years belonging to strangers now. They did not know who she was. They did not remember Flora as a child. And no one left cards any more. Mrs Secretan's always caused surprise, and certainly weren't returned. In what other way could one begin an acquaintance, she wondered. It was the worst part of growing old – one's friends died. Some of them died quite young. After middle-age, there were so many shocks: one hardly dared look at the deaths column; but somehow always did. And one made no new friends, so that there were not all those many people one could call upon. Each year there would be fewer.

Christmas, the arrival of Flora – and Richard – would be a break in the clouds, a great easement. They were to come on Christmas Eve – the same old story, Mrs Secretan thought: Richard could not get away earlier. With quite a good grace, knowing that respite was near, she resigned herself to Miss Folley's fancies on the evening before – she was obliged, in any case, to sit sewing, an occupation which made her most vulnerable – to finish embroidering a little purse for Flora's Christmas stocking. She tried to keep her thoughts on her stitches.

'I just found this by chance this afternoon,' Miss Folley said, sitting down across the room, from where she thought Mrs Secretan could not recognise the handwriting – although she might have known better by the ease with which Mrs Secretan threaded her needle with silk. 'There were some pressed violets between the pages, but they powdered to dust when I touched them. I'm sure I can't think why I kept the letter. For the poetry, I suppose. The man meant nothing to me. What he actually says is very over done. I think it may amuse you.'

Mrs Secretan thought, 'It's her reward, poor thing, for doing all that chestnut stuffing.' She was resolved this evening to be patient.

'He was a great one for exaggerating, Clive.' Miss Folley went on. 'We all have our foibles.'

We do, indeed, Mrs Secretan thought, watching her settling down to read the letter. She was as quick and nervous as a bird, even gave sharp, upward glances at the ceiling, as if she feared a hawk might be gliding there.

'*My enchantress*,' she began. Mrs Secretan, sewing steadily, was sure that it was going to be one of the worst of the letters. They were becoming increasingly bizarre. Each evening, unchecked by any word of distaste, any expression of incredulity on Mrs Secretan's blank face, stretched her imagination a little further. The situation would get more and more impossible, Mrs Secretan decided – 'Until she finally goes off her head. Or I off mine.' '*As you tread across the eternal spheres of my firmament*,' Miss Folley read. And it isn't even as if it makes sense, thought Mrs Secretan. She took up a pair of scissors shaped like a stork and cut off a piece of silk.

It was all very well this evening; she could bear it now, with Flora and Richard to look forward to tomorrow; but after – at that terrible time of the New Year, alone again, feeling ill, scared . . . but she set aside this picture with the firmness that came of long practice. She talked to her inner self, as if to a child. 'Not good for you to have such thoughts,' she said to herself, and her lips closed tightly together.

86

'*My Empress!*'' ('Empress!' Miss Folley! Oh, dear, how unspeakably droll, how utterly sad!) '*I cannot write more, for tears are falling from my eyes. Yet I am happy – knowing you, adoring you.*' Miss Folley at last folded the letter; but Mrs Secretan would not look up, lest she should see tears falling also from Miss Folley's eyes. 'I never saw him again. I sometimes have wondered what became of him.'

He hovered for a moment, like a ghost, between them, then vanished for ever. Clive. He had not even had a surname.

Mrs Secretan murmured 'Very nice,' in a polite but not encouragaing voice. At one time, at the beginning of the readings, Miss Folley had hoped that her employer would delve more into the matter, ask some questions about the writers of the letters. She had been ready with little facts and far-off memories. She no longer bothered; for Mrs Secretan did not seem to have grasped the rules of the game.

Silence fell. Miss Folley was tired, and leaned back and shut her eyes. They were both tired. The house was polished and fragrant, the larder 'groaning', as Miss Folley put it – the work of days, the work of love and excitement. Out in the garden, the rain whispered through the leaves. They were both listening to it with disappointment, having pictured snow, and the church bells clanging across the frosty air.

*   *   *

Richard awoke with indigestion in the very early hours of Christmas Day, his inside loud with acid gurglings. Across the room, moonlight fell on Flora, asleep in her old bed. Her eiderdown had slipped to the floor and he got out of bed and went over to hers. Her hands, with fingers laced together, lay between her cheek and the pillow, in the traditional pose of sleep, and gentle, puffing sounds came from between her slightly parted lips. Tied – but not conspicuously – to the bed-head was her Christmas stocking. Mrs Secretan had put it there before she and Flora went to the Midnight Service; and Flora, when she returned, had pretended not to see it. Although she must still have her stocking, she could not be expected to be asleep when it arrived. Richard had one, too – full of toilet things, which he had seen through the mesh. Everyone gave him dull presents like that. He was difficult, he knew, having no hobbies, or enthusiasms. So unlike Elinor Pringle. For the last few weeks, he had kept seeing presents to enchant her. There had been a Victorian Jubilee pin-cushion, for instance, with a printed picture of the Winter Gardens at Blackpool, studded with china-headed pins spelling *The One I Love*. It was giving out a little sawdust, but he would not have bought it anyhow.

Clouds went fast across the room as he stood by Flora's bed. Her face faded, then brightened again, with silver light on her brow and hair. It is impossible to cover up anyone who is asleep, without feeling deep tenderness. He stood for a moment, after he had put the eiderdown over Flora, filled with this fragile emotion: glad of it, to spite his stomach-ache, to spite all the irritations of the evening before – and then he got back into bed.

Lying there, the irritations took over again. Mrs Secretan had confided in him when Flora was upstairs getting ready for church. She told him of Miss Folley's increasing peculiarities, which Flora must not be worried about. The woman would have to go, Richard said. 'You can't live with a lunatic,' he added. At once, Mrs Secretan had half a dozen reasons why she should. Miss Folley was too good a cook; it might be impossible to replace her; she doted on Flora; she had nowhere else to go. The chief reason – that she could be relied on to look after Mrs Secretan if she were to have a long illness – was not brought forward. No conclusion was reached before Flora came downstairs, treading in the measured, balanced way of pregnant women, forging ahead, purposeful. This was something Richard found difficult to get used to. It changed her so.

He did not go to church with them, thinking it – funerals apart – a woman's job. Flora seemed to go only on pretty, gladsome occasions – Easter Sunday (no more to the gloomy Good Friday stint, which upset her), Harvest Thanksgivings, weddings, bells and carols she adored, she said: and Richard could imagine her picture of Christ – like the coloured illustrations in a book of Bible stories for children, an oval, insipid face, long blond hair curling gently on the shoulders, white robe, pretty lamb in arms. An English, un-Byzantine figure.

Flora and her mother had walked to the church. That was part of it, Flora said – part of the most magical night of the year. He had stayed behind and settled down, with his briefcase on his knees, to the work he had brought with him, and his hand straying out to the decanter of port which Mrs Secretan had placed beside him – perhaps the reason why he lay awake now, sucking a peppermint, wishing despondently that Christmas might be over.

*   *   *

The next day, there was more church in the morning. Social church, with hats. Richard was left with Miss Folley, whom he watched with a wary eye, tried to avoid. She kept offering him things – a mince pie, a glass of her sloe gin, a dish of marzipan strawberries.

He did not quite like to get out his briefcase and set to work again on Christmas morning, so he looked about for a book to read. No newspapers: no market prices. Mrs Secretan was reading *Elizabeth and Her German Garden* – 'for the umpteenth time', she said. 'Such a beautiful book. How much one would have liked to have known her.'

Richard thought that for his part he would have tried to run a mile in the other direction, if such a risk had risen. He had 'picked' at the book once, as he put it; and had been

vaguely repelled: but, because he could never justify his reactions to art and literature, he kept quiet. I'm a businessman, he thought. This bolstering-up reflection he also kept
to himself. At the same time, he straightened his back,
drew himself up, sure he had his own place in the world.

Ageing ladies' books filled the shelves – *My Life as This
or That* – he skipped the title – *The English Rock Garden,
Rosemary for Remembrance, Down the Garden Path, The Herbaceous Border Under Three Reigns.*

'If you're looking for a nice, pulling book,' Miss Folley
began, coming in to bully him with Elvas plums.

'No, no,' he said, straightening quickly, backing away
from the shelves, 'I never read.'

He would have his little joke, she thought; and laughed
accordingly.

'I-literally-never-read,' he insisted. She laughed so much
at this that she stood there with the dish of plums in one
hand, and held a handkerchief to her eyes with the other.
'Oh, dear! Oh, dear!' she laughingly gasped. 'I had a
gentleman friend once, who had a sense of humour like
yours. I was always in fits. Malcolm,' she added thoughtfully, her eyes suddenly clouded, as if with reminiscence or
invention. 'That was up in Warwickshire,' she went on,
with an air of explaining everything. She looked down at
the dish of plums, and advanced towards him. To fend her
off, he took one and put it whole into his mouth.

'Yes, Malcolm,' Miss Folley repeated, watching him
eating.

As soon as he could speak, he said that he must put his
coat on and go to meet the others from church.

'But the bells have only just stopped ringing,' she said.
'They'll be another hour.'

'Well, then, I'll have time for a stroll first.'

He made his getaway into the hall, and snatched up his
coat and opened the front door. A delicious smell of roasting turkey came from the kitchen. Miss Folley stood at the

door and waved him down the wet gravel drive, and then went back to the kitchen with a smile on her lips.

He detested walking about English villages on his own, and felt that he was stared at. This particular village, with its parade of shops, and hideous war memorial, and the late Victorian rose-red villas stained dark with rain, was extremely boring. In summer-time it was full of cars and bicycles, and people with rolled-up bathing things under their arms, licking ice-creams, waiting for buses. This morning, the place was almost deserted; blinds drawn over shop-windows; the pubs not open. Lighted trees in the little houses, holly wreaths on front doors already looked old stuff. Christmas was petering out. One or two fathers had their children out for walks – getting up an appetite, keeping out of Mother's way, displaying presents, such as fur gloves or mufflers. Little girls pushed shining new dolls'-prams.

The unfortunate thing was that the pubs opened at the same time as the church doors were thrown wide to let out the worshippers.

'Oh, he must have missed you,' Miss Folley said, when Flora and her mother returned. 'Wherever can you have missed one another?'

Mrs Secretan, in quelling silence, went upstairs, drawing off her gloves.

When Richard returned – only three-quarters of an hour late, after all, as he had kept telling himself, striding back, panting almost – they were in the drawing-room, waiting to have sherry. Waiting for him. Why did they have to? he wondered. Miss Folley had whipped off her floral pianfore and joined them. Mrs Secretan's tone was level. Flora's was anxious. It was a terrible thing to her if the two people she loved most in the world were to be at odds with one another. She did not know how much worse, should they combine to be at odds with her; this possibility had not occurred to her and was a most unlikely one.

They wished one another a merry Christmas, and drank their sherry. Richard, having been fortified by male company, put himself out at luncheon to be jolly and all that Miss Folley could wish a guest to be. Flora's anxiety disappeared; and Mrs Secretan, who was usually ready to give credit when it was due, saw how hard her son-in-law was trying, and relaxed. Miss Folley was in such a transport of pleasure that she appeared drunk. All the imagined Clives and Malcolms of the past were suddenly dispensed with, while she enjoyed the time-being.

Present-opening, in Mrs Secretan's house was after lunch. Then they sat round the drawing-room fire and made an occasion of it. Richard and his father had been casual about gifts, taking no trouble. In earlier years, Richard had been used to tearing off wrappings, alone, before dawn. He preferred that way. It was less gracious; but also less of a strain.

He unwrapped his parcels of soaps and shaving lotions, admired the beautiful cuff-links from Flora and the shooting-stick from Mrs Secretan, who seemed unable still to realise that she had a London son-in-law who never went to Point-to-Points, or gatherings of the kind. He watched the others undoing their parcels, as full of excitement as if they were children. But he could not manage to be a child himself, admiring the pretty wrappings, with such exclamations of surprise and delight. So much in this house made him feel old. Old and bored: two awful things to be. He had given out enough at lunch-time, it seemed to him.

He had been cut off from them both at the very beginning of the visit, when Flora and her mother – as soon as the suitcases were unpacked – had settled down to talk of other people. He hardly ever talked of other people, and he regretted Flora's constant preoccupation with the subject. He had heard it all before, and did not then and did not now care that Kit Driscoll was utterly miserable in the job he had at last found for himself; or that Patrick Barlow's little arty book had poor and few reviews. The real tit-bit of news this time – too good to wait until after unpacking – was Flora's personal triumph; that, through her tireless, but subtle machinations, she had persuaded Ba to be betrothed to Percy and Percy to imagine that he wanted this. 'About time, too,' was Mrs Secretan's reaction; but since Richard was there, she only said, 'How nice!'

Flora had more presents than anyone else, and continued to unwrap them while Mrs Secretan, looking well pleased, tidied up around her and Richard sat back and watched them both.

'So sweet of him!' Flora said, holding up a black chiffon nightgown – of the most appalling vulgarity, Mrs Secretan thought. 'From Percy,' Flora explained. Obviously chosen by that woman, her mother instantly thought. But Richard understood his father better than this, knew that he would be most happily at ease amongst the salesgirls in lingerie departments. He would have made quite an adventure of his shopping, for he had an exuberance Mrs Secretan did not appreciate, and could never pardon if she did in a man of his standing. It was a quality she could only forgive in what she termed 'people of birth'. And even then she would rather they did not have it.

'Charming,' Mrs Secretan said, nodding at the nightgown. Her good manners, thought Richard. He had to admit to himself that he had had his own embarrassing moments on account of his father, especially as an adolescent; and there were various old aunts and uncles he winced at the thought of Mrs Secretan's ever encountering. So far, he had seen to it that she did not; but it had been strenuous and tricky work – none more exhausting than being snobbish from an unadvantageous position. He envied those like his mother-in-law. They were so comfortable that it was hardly fair – wonderful to be so serene,

93

to have cupboards empty of skeletons, to take all privileges for granted – education, leisure (the Miss Folleys, Mrs Lodges who made it possible). The security of 'birth' seemed to him a chancy thing.

'*So* pretty!' Flora murmured over the nightgown, laying it back into its rustling paper.

Although Percy had made plenty of money early in his career – in time to send Richard to the public school Mrs Secretan took for granted, though in this case she would have preferred a better one – Richard could remember a childhood when they had lived in a semi-detached house without a garage. He could even remember his mother's nervousness when she engaged her first daily help. He was debarred from Flora's assurance. The next generation should do better, as he had done better than his father. If things went well, as they surely must. If he worked hard enough.

'There!' said Flora. She had opened her last present, made the last grateful exclamation. She sat back and twisted a ribbon round her finger, up to her ankles in screwed-up paper. 'I wonder how everyone else is getting on. Wouldn't it be nice if they were all having a lovely Christmas like ours? I hope poor Patrick isn't lonely. It must be so awful to be that on Christmas Day.'

'Patrick?' her mother said. 'Oh, yes. He's rather nil, isn't he, darling?'

*　　*　　*

Patrick was lonely. In the morning he went to church, and after that tried to forget the nature of the day. It should be possible, he decided, to ignore the dismal Christmas scene outside, groups of people homing fast, back to Mother and Father, until they were all cooped up in their families, leaving the streets deserted. The duties involved, the boredom and bondage of it – the idea of it was stifling to him. His gramophone records could surely cover the deadly silence of the day wearing on; the parchment-coloured silk curtains already covered the drabness of the sky and the slate roof of the Congregational Church opposite – the one to which he did not go. There was no reason why, just because everyone else was on holiday, he should not work, or go to bed and read all day.

At the thought of work, of the book he was writing, must finish, his stomach lurched, just as if he had come unexpectedly on something repellent. He was scared, too. Nowadays, he was so frightened of sitting down to work that he had to drive himself to grapple with it.

He had the most un-Christmassy lunch he could think of – two softly boiled eggs and thin bread-and-butter – and washed up everything before he sat down to work. He was very orderly, and the desk he sat down at had neat piles of paper, notes clipped together, and the cloth-bound books in which he made fair copies in his fine handwriting. The physical act of writing calmed and appeased him; but nowadays, to organise his imagination made him fretful. As if he were in the heart of a maze, he did not know which path to take.

He had been over-praised too early. *A Writer to Watch*, reviews had been headed. Those in the know, kept their eyes on him, as if he were a two-year-old colt which might later win the Derby; but he had not won the Derby. Critics, later on, always setting what he did against his first achievement, made an enemy of it to him. He winced when it was spoken of, loved only his poor failures, he said. He said it all the time – to anyone who asked; but chiefly to himself. On Christmas Eve, he had dreamt that, soldiering on with his new book, he began to find something familiar in it. Even the names of his characters he had heard before, and situations, then whole sentences were echoes of something that had gone before. At last, just before waking, he had realised with deep despair that it was all over again that first novel he had written, more than a likeness, more than he could expect to get away with.

Facing him on the desk was a photograph of his mother. She wore her hair in the flat, neat style of the 'twenties, had thin eyebrows and a rope of beads hanging against her chest – it could only be called that. Her large eyes were full of appeal, and her mouth had a sideways quirk, as if she were trying not to smile at something risqué which had amused her. She had been beautiful; and he had loved her deeply. When he tried to remember her as she had been before the war he found that, too, a difficult exercise of the imagination. Too often the later memories blotted out the happy ones. He could see so much more clearly the waxen face, the sunk eyes turning to him as he entered the bedroom; the head not moving on the pillows; the thin hand lifted an inch off the coverlet in greeting.

He turned his attention from the photograph and opened a notebook. He had all kinds of little tricks for helping him to start work – for instance, leaving off in mid-sentence the day before, or having some rough work to copy out, to carry him gradually into the atmosphere of the book.

It would have been nice if Frankie could have come, he thought. He had even risked devising a picture of them both – refugees from Christmas – shutting themselves in and making anchovy toast, as cosy as could be. He would have let Frankie play all the records he had bought for him, excruciating to him though they were. Tangled-up noises they seemed to him – Gerry Mulligan, Dave Brubeck. He had tried – but not very hard – to understand.

He put thoughts of Frankie out of his mind and took up the threads of his work. He wrote for a little, quite evenly, his elbow on the desk, his hand sheltering his weak eyes from the lamplight – bowed forward, like a nonconformist praying in chapel.

A sense of satisfaction began to creep over him – the satisfaction of getting ahead, and on Christmas Day, too. This was something extra, not really to be expected of him: a bonus of virtue.

It was quite understandable, he presently thought, that Frankie could not come. His mother would have been left alone, and she had sentimental ideas about Christmas. He admired Frankie for putting her first, for staying with her. It is what I should have done myself, he thought – to comfort himself. Then, No, I should not, he decided. He put down his pen and began to walk about the room. He wished the night would come.

It was his own fault, he told himself. There was no need for him to be lonely. He had friends who would have been pleased for him to join them. He could have asked Meg; or gone to Meg. He reasoned like this to himself, moving about the room, stopping to straighten a picture, or tilt a lampshade differently. The trouble was that he had hung on, hoping that Frankie would come after all. This happened a great deal lately. His life was beginning to have a waiting, rather negative quality. But sometimes miracles happened, and for that reason he stayed in the flat, refused invitations, glanced at the clock, peeped through the curtains into the street beneath, and listened for footsteps. He also wasted food – ordering special treats lest Frankie should drop in, and Frankie didn't.

At five o'clock, unexpectedly, there were steps on the landing. He sat absolutely still, bracing himself for disappointment, knowing he would have to bear with it as best he could, that it would last the whole evening; and knowing, too, how it would feel.

The unbelievable happened. The bell rang, and when, feeling rather weak-legged, he got up and went to open the door, Frankie stood there, with the horrible fluorescent landing light shining on his ginger hair, giving it a green tinge.

He was wearing the silk shirt Patrick had sent him for Christmas, and had brought for Patrick a tie his uncle had given him – a far too elderly, boring tie for him to be able to wear himself.

Patrick's pleasure in it was enormous. Frankie watched him with a smile as he admired it, got up at once and whipped off the one he was wearing and put on the new, standing before the glass, beaming.

We shall see a lot more of it, thought Frankie. Every time we meet one another; until it's threadbare.

Patrick would do it to please Frankie, who didn't care.

'But I wasn't expecting you,' Patrick said excitedly. 'I didn't want you to upset your mother.'

'My uncle arrived, so I thought I'd come over for a bit.'

He had come over from Clapham Common – quite a journey.

'I'm so glad to see you, my dear. It couldn't be nicer.'

He had rigid ideas about the times for having drinks and thought that just after five o'clock was far too early; but as it was Christmas, and Frankie was here – to celebrate the miracle, in fact – he fetched a bottle of wine. His hand – still trembling with excitement – trailed across Frankie's shoulder as he passed behind his chair.

'What have you been doing?' he called from the next room. Frankie was glad to hear the clink of bottles.

'Just eating,' he shouted back.

His mother had kept up the traditions. Although they were alone, she had cooked turkey and plum pudding and mince pies. It was rather touching, sad, he felt. He had pulled a cracker with her and put the paper cap on his head. It was their first Christmas on their own.

His father had quite simply removed himself from their lives. After one of the arguments with his wife about Frankie, he had walked out of the house and not returned. The arguments were caused – and had been caused for years – by Frankie's being cheeky, too big for his boots, as his father put it. He accused his wife of having spoiled him, and Frankie naturally did not take his side in this. It was always two against one and, unable to tolerate any more of it, Mr Parsons went to live in lodgings. 'He was dispensable all right,' Frankie told his mother; but nevertheless she had grown very subdued.

Frankie was a bright boy. He took up his cues quickly; could imitate anyone. He had tidied up his accent, expunged a London twang from his voice, and was ambitious. He was courageous, too. To his father's disgust, he had given up his job as a commercial traveller, and had gone to work with an advertising firm. He made less money there; but he was only at the beginning. His eyes were everywhere. He was in his mid-twenties, and learning fast.

It was a strange way for him to be beginning a Christmas evening, sitting by the fire in this swathed and insulated room. Just about this time on all the other Christmases he could remember, they would have been gathering round the dining-room table – his mother and father and relations on his father's side – including a girl cousin of his own age who worked in Selfridges. (None of these were this year invited.) A bright light would rain down on the white tablecloth, the red crackers, the jellies in their familiar shapes, a chocolate cake made like a log and, in the centre of it all the white cake with its paper frill, and the plaster Father Christmas, robin and eskimos, which were later washed and put away for another year.

Frankie had watched himself growing out of these Christmas tea-times, and for years now had endured them with distaste. It was a true sacrifice to the spirit his mother tried to foster, when he, year after year, offered his cracker to his cousin. Taking one end, she would turn her head away and screw up her eyes, ready to give a little cry of alarm at the bang. Playing her part, too, he guessed. Wearily, but wearing his fixed, Christmas grin, he would read out the motto, put the paper hat on his head. He did not feel at home.

He did not feel at home in Patrick's flat, either; but at least it was his ambition to do so. For instance, he had never read any of the books on the shelves; but he thought that listening to Patrick and other people discussing them should make it unnecessary. Even when they were alone together – as they usually were – Patrick talked a lot about literature, as if Frankie had really read any; but if, by an unavoidable chance, any of his friends were there, he would shield Frankie in conversation, deftly step in and answer questions for him, but not as if he were really doing so. Sometimes he managed to put opinions into his mouth. Cleverly done, Frankie always thought. I'm probably the only one who sees what he's up to. He shows me that he knows I know nothing. Also, that on those other times when we're alone, he's trying to teach me. Frankie liked tact. It was such a dangerous thing to practise. It has to be so very good, if it were not to be disastrous.

Patrick was not hurrying over fetching the wine and glasses. He rather lingered over it, pottering happily, humming to himself, thinking, in the next room is the one I love. The longer he took, the later Frankie would go.

He had bought a box of marrons glacés in case the miracle should happen, which had happened. Even standing in the shop, waiting for his change, he had not admitted to himself that the purchase had anything to do with Christmas.

'There are some cigars on the table,' he said, carefully carrying the tray. He did not smoke himself, and especially hated the smell of the kind of cigars which Frankie liked. In the mornings, afterwards, he was almost made sick by the staleness of the air and the smell which hung in the curtains. Then he was obliged to open all the windows, and let in the sound of traffic.

'You don't look very Christmassy,' Frankie said admiringly, glancing round the room. His mother, at home, had hung up paper chains and put sprigs of holly behind the pictures.

'I should hardly want to decorate a tree for myself; even if I'd wanted to be Christmassy, as you call it: and I didn't.'

'I'm sorry you were on your own.'

Patrick turned his back while he uncorked a bottle. He hated his pride to be hurt; yet knew of and disdained, this weakness in him. He feared his colour had risen, and made an extra fuss with the corkscrew to account for it.

'Oh, well, I needn't have been alone,' he said, handing Frankie a glass, hoping his hand wouldn't tremble. 'There was Meg Driscoll, you know, and her brother. I really ought to have done something about them. I have guilty feelings.'

'Ah, this is more like it,' said Frankie, settling back in his chair, sipping the Pouilly Fumé, which Patrick had put on ice before lunch, in hopes, and then taken off again, in despair.

Patrick sat opposite him, on the edge of a sofa. Between sips, he watched Frankie, with a most disclosing look in his eyes, then, his tongue following suit, he said: 'All lies, you know. I have no guilty feelings at all about Meg. If you couldn't come, I wanted to be alone; in case there was the slightest chance of your dropping in, after all. To think how vexed I should have been if I had gone to see Meg, and you had come. Or even if she had been here.'

Frankie, wilting from being over-worshipped – nothing more tiring, he had found – finished his glass of wine, in several swallows. 'I can't stay long,' he said.

Patrick was already on his feet, to fetch the bottle. Then, having filled Frankie's glass, he became fussed about his driving home, and went to find some biscuits.

'Of course. I know that; I understand that,' he said, as he went. If the visit only lasted another ten minutes, he would still go happy to bed. For Frankie had come, against all hoping; and he must have wanted to come. It was right for him to go back to his mother on such an evening. Patrick was touched that he should think so much of her. He cherished those nice streaks in his character.

Nine

PERCY and Ba went for a day or two to Brighton after the
wedding. They had often been there before, especially in
the early years of knowing one another. Flora had tried to
persuade them to be more venturesome, but her suggestions had set Percy off on one of his arraignments. 'I
can't stand people who go abroad,' he declared. 'They
come back and talk the hind legs off a donkey about
riding on a camel. That Geoffrey Pringle fellow the
other night at your place, Flora. Boasting about the cheap
hotels he stays in in Spain. The highlight of his holiday
is being taken into a filthy hovel to eat some bony old fish
with one of the locals. If you can't organise yourself
better than that abroad, I say you'll be better off staying
at home.'

So they went to Brighton as usual, and to the same
hotel. Ba even wore the same wedding-ring.

'This place begins to give me a sense of guilt,' she said,
looking round the bedroom before she unpacked: and for
the first time, she was embarrassed at being alone with
him. Their relationship had been set on a different basis –
more private. Yes, she thought, we are a part of society
now. Before, they had been secret (more or less), anonymous, selfish. She hoped he did not feel that just because
they were married she would expect him to make love to
her. About that, at least, she thought they should be
allowed to please themselves. There was no one, after all,
to know what they did, or did not do.

Percy grumbled a great deal to begin with. His sole, at
dinner, was not done in the way he had set his heart on –
a mistake arising from the menu's being in French. He

made his usual speech about that, and Ba seemed to find it as amusing as ever.

He was still muttering about the sole as he got ready for bed. 'If there's one thing I can't stand, it's cheese – cooked cheese. It lies on my gut all night.'

'It was what you asked for, honey.'

'You shouldn't have let me. You know I can't talk Frog language. How can I tell that Mornay stands for cheese? I like things to be plain. Very plain.'

'We may be on our honeymoon, but I think I know by now how you like your food.'

'No *sauces*. Just plain fish. The way you do it.'

'Thank you, my angel.'

She had creamed her face clean; was as sallow as·an icon.

'I'd rather have the bed nearest to the window,' he said.

'Yes, dear, I know.'

He tied the cord of his pyjamas, which were broad blue and white striped, like a schoolboy's. 'But you can have it, if you want,' he said, hesitating.

She shook her head, and at once he got into bed and pulled the bedclothes over his shoulder. Ba liked to read a little before she went to sleep, and she tilted the lamp nearer to her and opened her book. Her pale face glistened, and there were dark half-circles under her eyes. Her hair was plaited into a thin pigtail.

'Sorry about causing all that fuss, old girl,' Percy said drowsily into his pillow.

'What fuss?'

'About that bloody awful fish.'

'Oh, the fish! I shouldn't worry.'

'I'm afraid being meek and mild's not my strong suit.'

'No, honey.'

Peacefully, she turned a page. In a short time, he began to snore.

*　　*　　*

They gave a little party when they returned from Brighton. Things had improved there after the first day. A pale, wintry sun came out; there was a pretty sky, and the Regency houses looked their best. Percy discovered a tea-shop where they could have a four-and-sixpenny luncheon of tomato soup, cottage pie and jam sponge; and, for the evenings, a pub with a counter full of cold sirloin, Scotch eggs, York ham, and other British foodstuffs. Both menus written in English. He bought Ba an amber necklace in the Lanes and, as they were strolling along the Prom-enade, he was delighted to meet one of his old friends, a fellow Mason, a member of his Bowling Club. Ba did not feel herself at all slighted that he should so eagerly seek relief from her exclusive company. She was pleased to see him so revived. The days passed more pleasantly than she had expected. But she was glad to get back home.

Something – in fact, a very great deal – must be done about Percy's ugly old flat. She had a shop manageress living now in her own. She and Percy both missed their cosy evenings there.

Percy's flat was large and dark. The floors were covered with slate-grey linoleum, which always looked dusty; the walls were painted grey. It was stuffy, yet chilly; and it smelled of cigars. From their bedroom window, they had a view of dark red bricks, and a fire escape. For years, Ba had been making efforts to brighten it, with new curtains and different chair covers. Beyond this slight freshening-up, Percy was not inclined to go. He liked his black leather chairs and the Knole-style sofa in maroon brocade. Modern furniture, like foreign travel, he abhorred. ('Those little legs sticking out in all directions. They make the floor look like a thicket.') There were few ornaments, apart from some large, blood-coloured Chinese vases filled with bulrushes: no pictures, other than a sentimental version of Leda and the Swan, and a tinted photograph of Percy himself, younger, with a chain of office round his neck. His first wife had had it framed and hung.

Something must tactfully be done, decided Ba; but it was difficult to know where to begin, without causing an unheaval and unhappiness. Just for the party – she explained – she took out the bulrushes and put cream chrysanthemums in the Chinese jars. At a touch, the bulrushes almost exploded; they disintegrated, and their seeds filled the room. Percy nearly exploded, too. He was practising at the time, sitting at the piano playing one of *Four More Advanced Studies for Two Hands*. The downy seeds flew about him, made him cough, got into the opened top of the piano. And he had liked the bulrushes. They could not often be seen in London, he said. He had brought them all they way from Dorset, at great pains. And Ba might laugh! He thought it childish of her to laugh.

'Childish!' she cried, wiping her eyes, blowing fluff from her bosom.

'And not very kind,' he said.

His fingers were stiff. At his age, he couldn't afford to give up practising, even for those two or three days at Brighton; so, if he stumbled, it was her fault really. And he liked to have an audience for the perfected thing; not while he rehearsed. He was not used to that. He kept making mistakes and muttering 'Sorry!' 'Blast!' and a shorter, less polite word – one of his favourites (to Ba's and to Richard's dismay).

The party was both for Ba's birthday, and to celebrate their wedding – neither of them good reasons, thought Percy, who was determined to get into a corner and drink whisky with those he called his cronies. Their wives could stand by the fire and talk about their grandchildren. They always did.

In the dining-room, Ba laid out the table – a large stuffed and decorated fish, a jellied leg of lamb, salt beef, spare ribs of pork, savarins, tortes and babas. The cronies'

wives exclaimed in admiration. Flora, plate in hand, went
to find her father-in-law.

'Don't you feel lucky?' she asked him. 'To have such a
cook as Ba for your wife?'

'Well, she's always cooked me nice suppers,' Percy said
rather peevishly. He had no intention of showing gratitude
to Flora or to anybody else., 'And we didn't entertain
then,' he added. 'I hate entertaining.'

'Very naughty,' said Flora, smiling and shaking her
head. Raillery he did appreciate, and smiled back at her.
'That's a very pretty rig, if I may say so,' he told her,
looking at her pleated maternity frock, which was rather
like a lampshade.

'Thank you.'

'Oh, I always say the right thing, my dear.'

He forgave her for having telephoned to ask if she might
bring Patrick with them. He had dropped in for a drink,
and seemed at a loose end, she thought. 'But of course!' Ba
had said, truly delighted. Percy, listening, had raised his
eyes to the ceiling and clicked his tongue, and she glanced
towards him and put a warning finger to her lips, though
still nodding and beaming at the telephone.

The rooms of the flat were high, and there was not too
much babble. The grandmothers chattered, drank champagne, and peeped at Ba's birthday-cards on the chimney-
piece. They were seemly cards, with pictures of bluebell
glades and kittens. There were no sick barbs, for she was
no longer of the age when there could be rallying jokes
about birthdays, and the number of them. She was to be
comforted now, with pretty scenes and kind little verses
set out in curly print.

She was an energetic hostess, making up for Percy.
Chiding and exhorting, she bent to refill glasses, giving
the long view of her bosom, and called across the room,
'Don't smoke your *own*, for heaven's sake, honey.'

Patrick was rather uneasy amongst so many strangers,

all from such an alien world. 'This is Patrick Barlow, the writer,' Ba had introduced him to the women; above all, meaning well. The husbands, as usual, had gone to another part of the room.

'Oh, tell me! What sort of things do you write?' Patrick was asked. No one there had heard of him.

'Novels, books about painting,' he began miserably.

'Romances?'

'No. No, not romances.'

'True-to-life stories?'

'I don't know if they . . . perhaps . . . I hope . . .'

'How simply marvellous! To be able to express yourself!'

'Really, it's only a job like any . . .'

'Do tell me, the titles of some of your books.'

Oh, *my God*! he thought, horrified at the idea of going into such a recitation. Besides that, he hated saying aloud the titles of any of his books. It was almost a superstitious dread he had of hearing himself saying the words.

'Patrick,' said Flora, coming to him and handing a tray, 'Will you take this round for Ba?'

When he had gratefully gone, she told the guests all about his books – which she herself had never properly read – and praised them lavishly.

'We shall look for them in the library,' her audience promised.

'Thank you, Flora,' Patrick said later. 'And what a lovely party!' he went on, to repay her kindness. He was really rather fatigued by the evening.

'Doesn't Ba look happy?' Flora said. 'Don't they *both* look happy? I was always sure that they ought to get married, but neither of them seemed to know what was best for them.'

'I can't imagine how anyone can know that marriage will be *that*. The very idea of wanting to be with the same person, day in, day out, the same bed even, shut up together for a lifetime; well, even for *half* a lifetime. Just imagine, as a child, being told that some day one will have to belong to some other person, so finally that only death could put an end to it. You couldn't blame the child for bursting into tears at the idea. To be under the same roof till kingdom come.'

He was a little surprised at his own vehemence, and he had an echo at the back of his mind – *under one roof, under one roof*. He was pained and excited by his own words. He wondered if he had drunk too much champagne.

Flora said simply, 'But I love Richard, and that's all I want. Just to be under the same roof as him.'

She sat down on the arm of one of Percy's black leather chairs. She was rather ungainly now, very large. 'I should like to have a child, though,' Patrick thought. He imagined it being very wonderful to have someone young, who would look to one, love one.

'And I love Mrs Lodge, too,' Flora went on. 'And I wish that *she* could be under the same roof, for ever and ever. I should like to be sure of that.'

After supper, Ba put on some gramophone records. She and Richard sorted them out. They were all very old.

'I'M *looking* OVER *a four-leafed* CLOVER,' Ba sang, doing a few nineteen-thirtyish steps.

'Weren't they lovely, the old tunes?' one grandmother said wistfully to another.

'If anyone wants to dance,' Ba said, kicking back the hearthrug. But no one did, and after a while she put it straight again.

'Have you seen Meg?' Flora asked Patrick, who could tell how her thoughts had been running.

'We went to the Ballet together.'

'Ah, yes. she told me. I'm so glad. She doesn't go out a great deal, darling Meg. Isn't she the most wonderful person?'

'A very nice girl.'

'Oh, far more than just that. If I don't know her, who *should*? A nice girl indeed!'

'I like her very much. I enjoy being with her. I admire her. What else, dear Flora, can I say?'

'What *else*!' Flora thought indignantly.

'You mean a great deal to her, you know,' she said.

'And *she* means a great deal to me,' Patrick said lightly. In a way it was true. He looked down sternly at Flora, thinking, 'You saved me once this evening. Only to submit me to something worse.'

'It's my greatest desire,' Flora said, 'to see Meg happily settled. My very greatest desire. Oh, and Kit as well. That awful job he's doing.'

'Meg says he doesn't seem to mind it.'

'But the waste of it! Richard darling,' she said, putting her hand into her husband's as he came to stand by her. 'I was just saying what a waste of Kit that ridiculous job is. If only there were something one could do to help.'

'I should leave well alone,' said Patrick. 'And if you ask me, I think Meg would say the same.'

On the way home, after they had dropped Patrick at his flat, Flora said to Richard: 'I can't think *why* Patrick doesn't ask Meg to marry him. They're so well suited. It would be such an ideal thing.'

'Darling, do use your intelligence.'

'Oh, I don't believe all that. I never have. I think people are just gossipy and fanciful.'

'Then what in heaven's name is awful Frankie about?'

'I don't know Frankie: so I couldn't say.'

*   *   *

'Seems funny, Ba – not going to your place in the evenings,' Percy said later, lying in bed.

Ten

FLORA's daughter was born under the sign of Aquarius – a little earlier than was expected. Richard had to take Flora to the nursing-home suddenly. That evening, there was a dinner party for Geoffrey and Elinor Pringle, Meg and Kit. After dinner Flora went upstairs with Meg and Elinor and stayed there. Meg came hastening down to speak to Richard.

Flora had quite thought she had time to fit in this little party and had almost done so. Pouring out the coffee had defeated her, and Elinor did so while Meg was packing a small suitcase.

Flora came downstairs, wearing her fur coat, trying to look unconcerned. 'Please stay,' she said. 'Richard will be back in a moment. I'm very sorry about it. Kit darling, will you see to the brandy?'

He went to the sofa table where the tray was, not able to look at her, filled with jealous agitation. She was on her way to this alien experience; nothing would be the same afterward; separation was in the air. He wished that she would go, before he had to begin pouring out drinks with his shaking hands.

The childless Elinor, having seen to the coffee, leaned back, as if this interruption were of no interest to her. Her husband stood up straight, his hands spread on his chest, his deep eyes very alert. He always looked as if he had spent boyhood and adult life out-of-doors, climbing mountains, tramping moors. His clothes were tweed and baggy, proper camouflage in the country, but not at all in St John's Wood, or the House of Commons. He was the kind of Englishman one notices so much abroad.

'If there is anything we can do,' he said. 'Have you plenty to read?'

Flora hadn't thought of that, and picked up *Vogue*.

'Goodbye,' she began, her face suddenly whitening, then growing rosy again. 'Please forgive me.'

'Fare thee well,' Geoffrey said, giving her a smiling look of encouragement.

'Thank you for the delicious dinner,' said Elinor, lest they should lose sight of why they were there.

In the hall, Mrs Lodge embraced Flora, but could not speak. She watched them drive away, then quietly closed the front door.

'Well, well,' said Elinor, glancing round the room. Her voice was both amused and disapproving.

'Cutting it a bit fine,' said Geoffrey.

It was for my sake, Kit thought, trying to carry a glass of brandy to Elinor without slopping it.

*   *   *

It was only a few days earlier that Flora had come to Richard in a state of great excitement. 'Darling, the most wonderful thing! I saw Elinor Pringle in the coffee shop, and she says Geoffrey's written a play and it's going on in London.'

'Yes, I know.'

'You know?'

'I saw Elinor, too.'

'You didn't say.'

'I often see her, going up and down the hill.'

'*Why* didn't you tell me? There's so little time left. We must ask them to dinner straight away, the first evening they can manage. There might very well be something in the play for Kit. I'm sure Geoffrey would put in a word for him.'

On her way to the nursing-home, some waves of pain and her sense of apprehension did not prevent her from wondering if anything had after all been accomplished by the dinner party. Kit (for the promising young actor she had described him to Geoffrey) had seemed gauche and tongue-tied. Worse than that, Elinor had remarked casually, when they were discussing Geoffrey's play, that once he had written it, it was done with as far as he was concerned; then, other people took over. It appeared that, by now, it was out of his hands.

*   *   *

In spite of all the rush to get to the nursing-home, the baby was not born until late on the following day – the most terrible day for Mrs Secretan, who sat near to the telephone and could not eat her meals. 'It is much, much worse than having one onself,' she told Miss Folley. By the time Richard rang up with the news, she was worn out; but she rallied quickly, and spent the rest of the evening telephoning her neighbours. It turned out to be one of the nicest evenings she had ever spent.

*   *   *

The baby's birth caused a great activity of telephoning. Elinor rang up to ask Richard to dinner on any night he chose. 'You just come whenever you wish,' she said. 'I am always here, even if Geoffrey isn't.'

*   *   *

Meg telephoned Patrick to tell him the news.
'Splendid,' he said. 'And what sort of time did Flora have?'
'She was under an anaesthetic.'
'She always has been.'

*   *   *

'Alice. Yes, after me,' Mrs Secretan kept saying happily into the telephone.

*   *   *

It was the happiest day of her life, Flora kept marvelling. This particular day, out of ten thousand or so others, mostly happy ones, she had already had. Trying to do the multiplication sum in her head, she grew confused.

It seemed a little strange to her that she should be having this happiest day lying in bed, mostly alone. Nurses came and went; the Matron paid a visit; the baby was taken from the cradle at intervals and put into Flora's arms. She was so unbelievably light – the shawl round her seemed to weigh more. Suckling the baby, Flora examined what she could see of her with great attention – the fragile, veined skull covered with dark down, a narrow, mottled hand which detached itself from the wrappings and wavered uncertainly in the air, spread delicate fingers, caught a flaking gauze-thin nail in the shawl.

Flora loved nursing her; but there was something unexpectedly beautiful about lying in the quiet room with the baby in her cot near by – sleeping mostly but, from time to time, stirring, making the faintest puppy noises, or suddenly sucking furiously against her fist.

For most of her happiest day, Flora was in pain. Her womb contracted with cramping spasms; she seemed full of wind and discomforts and her breasts ached – vexations she had not foreseen, the pangs of anti-climax; but they counted for nothing with her. She felt stranded, deserted, at peace; as if she were a battered boat washed up after a storm.

Richard had very little part in her day. She thought of him occasionally, wondered what he was doing, imagined him feeling important, telephoning a great deal, buying chaps drinks. She could not suppress the idea that she had been more clever than likely, and that he would be proud of her.

Bliss! she thought. The delightful word was continually on the tip of her tongue.

She lay propped on pillows, gazing placidly at her

flowers, for hour after hour. All day, they kept arriving. 'Just like a fillum actress,' the Irish nurse told her. She always said that. Her head was full of automatic phrases to address to both mothers and babies. She also thought she was a dab-hand at arranging flowers and was always appreciative of plenty of gypsophila and fern.

Outside, above Richard's yellow roses in a place of honour in the window, the sky thickened, began to take on its bronze, over-London kind of darkness. Richard came. It was his second visit. That one of the evening before Flora hardly remembered – just tiredly, she recalled, taking his hand and then becoming bored with holding it, but having no strength to let go.

This evening, the Irish nurse smartened her up – just as if she were a doll. She tied the bow of her bed-jacket and held up the looking-glass while Flora combed her hair. 'There's two pretty girls for Daddy,' she said, putting Alice's hand back under the blanket.

She was even more lively when Richard arrived, called him 'Daddy' to his face and kept popping in on little duties which he thought could have waited until later. 'Now we can't have Daddies sitting on the beds,' she said, shooing him off.

'My God, doesn't she drive you dotty?' Richard asked.

'Oh, no; she's awfully sweet,' said Flora.

He seemed uneasy, sitting on a hard chair amongst all the flowers, yawning and yawning. He had had rather a distracted day, and too much to drink at lunch-time. He had felt talkative and quite disinclined to work. His father – to make matters worse – had come down to the factory to commiserate with him for not having been granted a son. 'Next time,' he had kept saying. 'You're bound to be lucky next time.' But Richard's thoughts were on *this* time; on now; on having a daughter. He imagined her grown to be eighteen, tall and fair like Flora, walking with her arm through his. Where were they going? he wondered. Up the aisle of a church? Lord, no, not that. Somewhere out of doors, with her hair blowing back in the wind. She was laughing. Or he might take her out to dinner. He scattered several of his friends about the restaurant, for an audience. And Alice preferred to be with her father than with any of those young scoundrels who hung about her. They were always out together, people noticed. Flora wasn't there in any of these pictures. Perhaps she was at home with their sons. He hadn't day-dreamed since before he was married, and the pleasures of it came as a sweet surprise.

Flora looked at him and smiled. He looked different, she thought; not his usual neat self; had the slightly *farouche*, untidy appearance some widowers take on. Just two days parted from me, she placidly thought.

'What are you thinking, darling?' she asked. This was one of her favourite questions, for she did not like his thoughts to separate them.

'About –', he nodded at the cot. He had been going to say 'Alice', but it seemed early days to be referring to the baby by her name. It was only in his mind that she was eighteen years old. 'The baby,' he said. 'I hope she grows up to be as beautiful as you.'

For the first time he had known, Flora made a deprecating murmur at being complimented. Her usual gracious composure, her pleased acceptance, deserted her. She saw herself suddenly as certainly not beautiful enough, with nothing like the sort of looks which would be proper for her daughter, who would need to have a straighter nose, for one thing; and smaller hands.

She considered the question for a while, going over her faults, hoping for the best. Then she said, 'You know, in just one day I suddenly understand all sorts of things about Mother that never entered my head before.' (Things that must have secretly pleased her, she reflected; and other things that may have worried her, Flora not at the time conscious of the possibility.)

She pulled off a few grapes from the bunch on the bedside table and threw him one. 'Death-bed grapes, Meg and I call them. This black kind. Oh, well done, darling.' He had caught the next grape in his mouth.

Larking about, Nurse Murphy thought, hearing their laughter; but for the moment she could think of no very good excuse for going in.

Richard, charmed by Flora's good spirits, remembered the evening before, with her drowsy murmuring, as she turned her head on the pillow, tangling her hair. Her pale face was glistening; she smelled of anaesthetic. But still she had her touching, troubling beauty.

'Did Mrs Lodge do something with the rest of the chicken?' Flora asked. The dinner party seemed a year ago – a most disordered, botched-up occasion. She turned her thoughts from it.

'Yes. Very nice. I can't quite remember what,' said Richard.

'What about this evening?'

'I was thinking of going to the Pringles.'

'Oh, yes,' said Flora. 'She sent those gentians. So unusual.'

*   *   *

The next day, her mother came. Mrs Secretan felt quite shy and self-conscious as Nurse Murphy showed her in. She brought a little parcel of spice cakes from Miss Folley, and Flora began eating them at once. She offered one to Nurse Muprhy, who put it into the starched bib of her apron.

Mrs Secretan, when she had kissed her daughter, approached the cot. She leaned over it, making gentle clicking sounds with her tongue, her eyebrows raised as if she expected a reply. Cautiously, she drew down the blanket and stroked one of the little mauve hands with her finger. Disappointment, dismay even, overcame her. She smiled in spite of it, for Flora's sake, and whispered, as if happily, to her granddaughter. 'And *is* it then? And *is* it? Aren't you a pretty girl?'

The baby was not in the least like newly-born Flora. The faint eyebrows, the shape of the head were completely different. The dark, downy hair would remain dark, Mrs Secretan was sure. The child was going to take after her father – Richard's long upper lip and pointed ears. Heavens above!

Mrs Secretan moved away and sat down on a hard chair. Here's a pretty kettle of fish, she thought. A possibility of this kind had not entered her head. But one should be *thankful*, *thankful*, she told herself firmly. The child might have been born deformed.

'Isn't she sweet?' asked Flora.

'Adorable. Oh, how I wish your grandmother hadn't died. She lost this lovely experience of having a grandchild. I missed her so much when you were born. I wanted to show you to her. "She didn't see Flora," I used to say to your father. "She didn't see our darling Flora." And wouldn't *he* have loved to see little Alice?'

Tears of sympathy came into Flora's eyes. When Nurse Murphy came back from eating her cake in the bathroom, they both seemed on the verge of weeping. She had to make quite an effort to cheer them up.

'Now isn't that a smashing baby?' she asked Mrs Secretan. 'And isn't she just the spitting image of her Daddy?' she went on, not knowing what she did.

The baby began to make peaceful sucking sounds. She turned her lashless eyes towards the window to contemplate the unaccustomed light outside.

*   *   *

Other visitors called in the days following. Ba came one afternoon, without Percy, who did not want to enter a nursing-home. A friend of his had just died in one – of cirrhosis of the liver. This had greatly disturbed Percy. He was trying to cut down his drinking, and to think of other things than mortality. He was utterly depressed; his thoughts grew so out of hand, so monstrous, so alarming that he had to have another glass of whisky to steady himself.

'Are those *diamonds*, honey?' Ba asked Flora, bending over to admire the bracelet Richard had given her.

'I don't know, Ba.'

'You don't *know*?'

'Well, Richard gave it to me as a present. I could hardly ask. I hadn't thought about it. I don't know much about jewellery.'

'They're diamonds all right,' Ba said, leaning back.

'You will be one of Alice's god-mothers, won't you, darling?' Flora asked.

'It's very kind of you, but may I remind you that I'm Jewish?'

'Oh, that doesn't matter. Of course it doesn't matter,' Flora said.

* * *

When Meg came, Flora asked her the same question. Meg looked quite astonished. 'I couldn't,' she said. 'I don't believe in God.'

'But of course you do, darling,' Flora said comfortably.

To Richard, that evening, she said: 'It's so miserable of everybody. I thought it would please them to be asked. It would please *me*. And if I were in their place, I'd do anything rather than spoil my happiness.'

For the first time since Alice's birth, she felt a little depressed and suffered from a sense of anti-climax. Richard left her, to go to dinner with the Pringles. They were being so very kind, she thought.

He had brought an *Evening Standard* for her, and she glanced through it, but it was full of either boring or horrifying things. She would rather not have had it.

She was glad when her supper came.

'Now tuck in,' said Nurse Murphy, excitedly whipping the cover off the dish, as if it were the last garment in a strip-tease. The smell of cauliflower cheese escaped.

Flora encouraged her to stay and Nurse Murphy, before she took the flowers outside for the night, lingered to pull off a few dead petals, and stood with them in her cupped hand, talking of love.

'There's a fish bone in my cauliflower,' Flora said, more surprised than reproachful.

'Well, you wouldn't credit it, would you?' Nurse Murphy said, not paying attention.

The next course was some cold custard and red jelly. Flora ate it slowly. She always finished everything.

'And well, so this young fellow and me, we joined up with Sister Blackie and her young man from the Rugger Club, and we went to the Police dance. It was like a ball more, and evening-dress and all, for the ladies.'

Flora put her spoon quietly on her empty plate and sat listening, like a little girl. As the story grew more interesting, Nurse Murphy sat down – on the side of the bed, Flora noted.

Eleven

'I know it would be easier for everyone if I gave in,'
Elinor said. 'It would save Geoffrey a great deal of
embarrassment; save me . . .' she slowly shrugged, and
then went on. 'It would mean I could travel with him
sometimes, and meet people. I suppose I could have gone
with him now, to Prague. I should rather like that. I need
not have an idle moment, you see.'

Richard had found her with a map of England and a
railway timetable. She did not mope over her loneliness:
she made plans.

'But it would be such a meaningless capitulation,' she
said. 'I don't think I could bring myself to it. I'm too self-
conscious for false attitudes. Or I haven't the humility.
Now, where shall I go?'

She shut her eyes, circled her hand over the map and
stabbed down her finger. 'Nearly in the sea,' she said,
peering rather short-sightedly, 'I make that Cromer.'

'My dear Elinor, you'd be frozen there at this time of
year.'

'I oughtn't to cheat. And I must go somewhere for a
change. I'm rather tired of Cathedral cities, though
they're good in winter. They have bookshops and antique
shops and cosy tea-shops and rather nice pubs as a rule.'

She feared to mope, left in an empty house. He could
understand that. So she made excursions, was a tireless
sightseer – still alone, hardly speaking a word from day to
day; but occupied. She even went to race meetings on
her own.

'How was Flora this evening?' she asked, realising suddenly that so far they had only talked of herself.

'Glad to be coming home tomorrow. She was feeling a bit peevish, I believe; wept when I left her. The baby had been sick.'

'I don't suppose that's anything,' Elinor said vaguely. 'I expect she just feels low.'

'Yes.'

It was the last evening, Elinor kept reminding herself. Tomorrow, she would be back on her own again. She got up and went to the kitchen to turn the roast potatoes. Richard had suggested going out to dinner, but she would not. She could not explain her personal rule that she would have lunch out with men; but not dinner. 'Dinner' caused talk. She had brought about too much embarrassment to Geoffrey – simply by being absent: she did not want to bring about gossip and conjecture, too.

Almost every night, during Flora's fortnight at the nursing-home, Richard had looked in, had an air of making an escape to Elinor, for the cosy atmosphere at the nursing-home was oppressing, and Nurse Murphy enraged him. All her dreadful sayings he recounted to Elinor, who laughed.

'Yes or No?' That's what she asks poor Flora every single day.

'Yes or no what?'

'Bowels,' said Richard. 'So it seems. And do you know, Flora cottoned on at once to what she meant. Isn't she marvellously intelligent? But I don't know how she stands it there.'

He carved the loin of lamb and she sat opposite, beyond the candles, and watched. It was a far more intimate setting, she realised, than one in any restaurant; but at least it could do no harm to Geoffrey, or his cause.

'Flora had boiled cod and parsley sauce,' Richard said. He popped a little piece of outside meat into his mouth, just as if he were at home. 'They brought it as I was leaving. It smelled horrible. Perhaps that's what made her cry.

Poor old Flora. Mrs Lodge has pheasants for tomorrow. That should cheer her up.'

He adores her, Elinor thought. All the time he wonders what he can do to please her, and just as the thought of Geoffrey came into her mind, Richard startled her by saying his name. 'Have you heard from Geoffrey?' he was asking.

'No. He's not a very picture postcard sort of person and there would never be time to write a letter. Well, quite frankly, he's so occupied, I doubt if the thought of me ever enters his head.'

Richard was going to make come conventional protest, or sound of protest, as soon as his mouth was empty, but before he could, looking at him steadily across the candles, she said, 'We're not like you and Flora, you know.'

He kept his eyes down. It was quite unlike his idea of her, that she should talk as personally as this. The peacefulness of his companionship with her was ruffled. On other evenings, her conversation was all of things, not people – of porcelian marks, and figures lying on tombs, whose lives, however turbulent while they lasted, could not be boringly involved in his own. He had liked this about her – safe talk, but interesting.

'We quarrel,' she said in a defiant voice. 'There's some undiagnosed bitterness between us. Perhaps because I haven't been clever like Flora, and had a child.'

She knew she was making a mistake, could tell this from his downcast look. He will never come to see me again, she thought, trying to warn herself. But he wasn't coming again, anyway, she thought.

'There are such a lot of booby traps,' she said. 'And quarrelling must be the easiest to fall into, because one rather enjoys it at the time; at least one feels that something is going on.' His glum silence forced her into a spate of words. 'There's so much to learn, and things one hardly wants to know. For instance, how not to go on bickering too long. Until it's suddenly fatal and final. I know it all in cold blood. How to be particular in one's recriminations, not general. So that they can be dismissed in good time, and not remembered for ever. I always mean to be fair. I'm fair in rehearsal. I practise when I'm alone, and waiting. "I thought you were rather unjust to me this evening, darling." I might have it all ready to say in a reasonable sort of voice, and then, instead, I suddenly find myself saying, "Oh, trust you to be unfair about everything," and my voice cracks hideously with scorn and self pity. So ugly.'

'Now, I can't imagine *that*,' Richard said firmly. 'May I carve you another piece?'

'Have *you* never quarrelled with anyone?'

'I've had some tiffs with my father.'

She paused. 'Well, I expect I've exaggerated,' she said. 'But no doubt it's a good job that Geoffrey's away so much. It's when we are alone together for too long that the trouble starts . . . holidays, oh, my God, the holidays we've had. He won't go on them any more, hasn't for three years, and I don't blame him.'

'He told me before he went to Prague that he wished you were going too,' Richard invented. 'He said how much he misses you, when he's away. Are you sure you won't have some more meat?'

'Do help yourself,' she said, shaking her head. 'No, he never thinks of me. I know it. He could leave me in the morning lying stretched dead on the floor. And if anyone later in the day asked him how I was, he'd say, "Fine. Fine. Thank you"; and then he might suddenly remember and say, "Well, no, as a matter of fact, she's dead." '

Richard, carving off another chop for himself, laughed loudly. He was deeply relieved that the conversation had taken a lighter tone.

*   *   *

Mrs Secretan was full of aches and pains: one day it was one thing, the next day another. She had not found the courage to see her doctor, and tried to avoid meeting him socially, turned her back on him at village cocktail parties and hurried away through the churchyard after morning service, if he were there. Once, at a wedding, he had cornered her, barred her way with a dish of canapés, asked her (with a penetrating look, she thought) how she was. He could tell at a glance, she thought. *Riddled with cancer.* His diagnosing eye slid over her as she took a canapé; he stopped to pick up the wisp of smoked salmon she had dropped on the floor. 'Very well,' Mrs Secretan replied firmly. 'And you and Gertrude?'

It had been only a social enquiry, she told herself afterwards. He had expected a cheerful or a non-committal answer, similar to the one he had given her, although Gertrude – as Mrs Secretan very well knew – was miserable with rheumatism. After all, they had been at a wedding, where no one was expected to launch into a catalogue of ailments.

Lately, to those ailments had been added a dragging pain in the small of her back. This was very impairing and depressing, but she did not mention her discomforts to Miss Folley, for fear of in this way making them even more real to herself. Her favourite dream was that her pains would all prove to have been psycho-somatic; but it was only on her better days that she could indulge in this charming fancy.

Nowadays, everything she did fatigued and disheartened her – even walking to the nearest pillar box, or cutting a bunch of forsythia; sewing, she soon grew cramped. And the weather did not help: nearly all day, and every day, the pale rain fell steadily against the dark fir trees in the garden.

It was all the wrong way round in life, she felt. It tailed off. It was like a party that began all right and then began to drag and bore interminably. No; far worse than any party, fatigues greater than anyone could suffer in one night, accumulations of anxiety, sometimes panic.

Only in her bath was she in the least comforted. She gave up bathing in the morning, to save this soothing thing for later in the day, when she was tired and fidgety and at a lower ebb. At first, six o'clock; then earlier, earlier. Lulled and relaxed, safe from Miss Folley, she would lie there, doze a little, aches and pains smoothed out, feeling light, leached, enervated, and would at last dry herself and dress and go downstairs hoping, against all hope, that it would not be one of Miss Folley's inventive evenings. The store of love-letters did not run out. They must weigh many pounds by now.

I really must not go up before five o'clock, Mrs Secretan resolved, just as she could not dream of taking a glass of sherry before seven. The bathroom was beginning to be associated with guilt. But the afternoons were so very long and dark. The best of all the week was the one when she sat down at the davenport by her bedroom window and wrote to Flora. With her pen in her hand, she gazed out from time to time at the sludge-coloured river beyond the trees, at the wet green garden and Flora's doves walking on the gravel, with frozen-looking pink legs and feet. A starling pecked at some crocuses, and she opened the window and clapped her hands at it. After all my kindness, she thought – feeding them with suet through the bitter winter.

'Such ingratitude,' she said to Miss Folley, who had tapped at the door and put her head round it. She came across the room with a letter in her hand.

'It's an invitation to Doctor Wilson's,' she said. 'A large party, the postman was saying.'

Mrs Secretan by now feared the sound of Doctor Wilson's name, almost as much as she feared to hear the names of diseases.

Miss Folley hovered, pretending to be looking out of the window and Mrs Secretan, opening the invitation, neatly dropped the envelope on to the page she had been writing. She knew that Miss Folley's eyes wandered, that she identified herself so closely with her employer that she felt she should share her correspondence.

I shan't go, Mrs Secretan decided. I shouldn't dream of going. I shall find some excuse. I shall say I'm ill. No, I can't say that. Something else.

She put the card back in the envelope and sat with her hands clasped on the letter to Flora, waiting for Miss Folley to go away.

'The rain!' said Miss Folley, and sighed.

The weather seemed to have been very bad since Flora went away.

'Appalling,' Mrs Secretan agreed. 'And the river begins to look very high.' She could see its rain-pitted surface and patches of twig-collecting scum floating by. 'It was so clear when I was a girl – a beautiful clear olive green, and smelled so good.'

Everything around her was changing for the worst, not only the polluted Thames, but the ugly cement lamp-standards that had replaced the Victorian ones in the village street, the new, brash supermarket, the council houses beyond the church, and the block of flats where once her old friend, Lady Brotherhood, had her villa. It was a village no longer: it was an overcrowded, noisy suburb. People had to live somewhere. Whenever she grumbled about the state of affairs, she always added that, grudgingly. But why here? Why did they not go up to Scotland, where she understood cottages were empty and derelict. The Orkneys, for instance, were becoming seriously depopulated. And people had far too many children. The world was teeming dangerously. There should be a law to limit progeny: one person allowed to reproduce himself, herself, once only. Childless parents or the unmarried might transfer their quota to the family-greedy. Might sell it, perhaps. There were difficulties, she mused, staring out of the window; but none – she was sure – that could not be resolved.

Miss Folley did not go. She had now turned her attention to a little picture above the chest-of-drawers, was peering at it as if she had not seen it before.

'I always admire this,' she said, 'although it *is* modern, futuristic.'

It was a *pointilliste* landscape painted before the turn of the century. Mr Secretan had bought it many years ago – as an investment, he had said at the time.

'That red earth reminds me of Devon,' said Miss Folley, standing with clasped hands, head thrown back, eyes narrowed. (the picture was called *The Poppy Field*.) 'One of my favourite counties. Although the Thames Valley runs it close, of course.' (Oh, go *away*, Mrs Secretan thought, shutting her eyes for a moment; but keeping her hands where they were.)

'What's it done in?'

'*Done* in?' Mrs Secretan repeated, mystified.

'Yes . . .' Miss Folley waved her hand vaguely at the picture, at a loss for a word.

'Oils,' said Mrs Secretan. 'It's an oil painting.' She took advantage of Miss Folley's back being turned to press both fists to the small of her own.

'It's so good, I've always thought it was needlework.'

Mrs Secretan sat out a long silence, as if her thoughts were far, far away and at last Miss Folley, with another look at the clasped hands resting on the desk, went away.

At once, Mrs Secretan took up her pen again. She wrote, smiling as she did so: 'I know it is wrong to make fun of simple people, but I really sometimes wonder what Miss F is going to say next.' She was quite grateful to her at the moment, for it was not always easy to find things to tell Flora.

She finished the letter and then, on an impulse, added a postscript: 'I shall be in London on the 27th for the dentist. (Alas!!) May I pop in in the late afternoon, early evening?'

She sealed the envelope and went to the bedside telephone to ring up her dentist. The 27th was the day of Doctor Wilson's party.

When she went downstairs, Miss Folley was hanging about in the hall, pretending to water a plant.

'I have to go to the post myself,' she said. 'As soon as it eases up.' She put out her free hand to take the letter.

'There isn't any hurry,' Mrs Secretan said. 'And I haven't a stamp.'

'I have some.'

There was nothing for it but to hand over the letter and go to fetch threepence from her purse.

'You shouldn't have bothered,' Miss Folley protested, when she returned.

The rain didn't ease up until some time after tea. Mrs Secretan went up to take her bath and, when she came downstairs, Miss Folley had gone. There was only a light drizzle and the gusts of raindrops shaken from the trees.

In the kitchen, the windows were quite steamed-up. There was a kettle of very hot water on the stove.

I begin to have suspicions, Mrs Secretan thought. She opened a window and sat down on a chair, feeling quite ruffled and put out. A disconcerting sense of shame grew in her, even though she kept telling herself that it should really belong to Miss Folley – if, indeed, any shame there were.

But, my *God*! she thought, and kept remembering words, phrases. *Wrong to make fun of simple people.* Hadn't she written that? Well, it *was* wrong, and she had done it. I, who have all the advantages as they are called, she told herself sternly.

She closed the kitchen window and went to the drawing-room, not knowing how she could face Miss Folley when she returned. They could not surely, she felt, go on living in the same house with this embarrassing and unmentionable thing between them, or – at best – Mrs Secretan having to give Miss Folley the benefit of the doubt, not finding it easy, always wondering. . . .

It was twenty minutes to seven and Mrs Secretan, breaking one of her personal rules, poured herself out a soothing glass of Bristol Milk.

Miss Folley was a very long time returning. Perhaps she was walking off her rage, Mrs Secretan thought; or trying to arrange an innocent or nonchalant air.

Well, listeners never hear good of themselves, and it is the same thing, Mrs Secretan said to herself, nearly aloud – her lips moved. Half a glass of sherry had made her feel defiant. She raised her chin, looked down her nose. Two pink patches spread on her soft cheeks.

The defiance left her when she saw Miss Folley come slowly up the drive, her head bent, a scarf looped round her head against the drizzle.

If she's been crying, I can't bear it, Mrs Secretan thought. She asked herself, what have I done? But what she had done, she tried to reason, was what everyone had done at some time. Miss Folley it was who had done what no one does – or had better not do.

*   *   *

Elinor was solitary in East Anglia. By now, she had been solitary all over England. Here, the towering clouds and their dark reflections in water, the spare landscape and sombre knots of trees were so much like all those painted by John Sell Cotman and Crome that she had begun to love them for themselves.

To be here, whatever the weather, was a change, was more positive than just staying at home. She kept telling herself this, on the short excursions she took in the wind and rain, as she tried to peer through steamy, spattered bus windows, driving along the inland roads.

On most days, towards late afternoon, the skies cleared and a pale sun shone for a while. Then she liked to walk on the esplanade and look down at the lower sands – brown and grey and beige shore colours, wet and shining, ridged like the wing of a skate – and the pewter darkness of the North Sea. The hotels, on higher ground, were of red brick, standing in shadow.

'Now, what next?' She would wonder, turning into one of these hotels as soon as the sun had gone down.

In the lounge, elderly women, all wearing spectacles, were draped with stoles. They read *The Illustrated London News*, or knitted. A place at the writing-desk was coveted, watched for.

In the dining-room, they had their own packets of cereals and health foods on their tables – Bemax, All-Bran and Energen rolls. With little fusses, they filled their days, yet seemed quite devoid of the despair that kept welling up in Elinor, taking her walks about the place, going alone into pubs, sitting in her bedroom, asking herself from hour to hour, What next?

She thought she had much better go home. Richard had been right. It was a wrong time of year for going away in England. What she had expected, she did not know. Days went by when she spoke only to waitresses or bus conductors. To the elderly women in the hotel, she was a matter of conjecture: they looked thoughtfully at her over their spectacles when she left the dining-room. She was always one of the first to leave, having hastily eaten, with a book open on the table, from which she scarcely ever raised her head.

After a few days she could bear it no longer; but, before she went home, she sent off a picture postcard. 'You were right; absolutely right. It is too grim,' she wrote on it; but addressed it to both Richard *and* Flora.

*　　*　　*

131

When Ba was shown the postcard by Flora, who seemed pleased to have had it, she thought gravely, as she had done before of Richard's visits to Elinor. Only once, during the time Flora was in the nursing-home, had he spared an evening to visit his father. Was going to the Pringles, he always said when invited – 'The Pringles' was not a deliberate lie, Ba thought. By this, he could perhaps have meant the Pringles' *house*, although, as Ba knew, Geoffrey was abroad.

Ba handed back the postcard, thinking that there is nothing so threatening of danger as a neglected wife. She was nursing the baby. Flora was the kindest hostess. She always brought Alice from her pram or cradle when Ba and Meg called, behaving, with self-conscious generosity, like a nice child with a special toy to share.

*　　*　　*

Miss Folley had betrayed herself by sulking. She was helpless to behave in any other way. Recollected words bit into her pride like acid. Phrases kept springing to mind. *Folly by nature as well as name.* For Mrs Secretan had a tartness of tongue and pen, which occasionally bewildered her daughter, who would usually resolve the matter by blaming herself for having misinterpreted her mother's words.

Deep shame and a state of wariness developed between Mrs Secretan and Miss Folley. They did not care to catch one another's eyes, played an evasive game and were always glad of a third person. No word could ever be spoken of what occupied their minds. Mrs Secretan racked her brain to remember everything she had written in the letter, and kept recalling, in increasing confusion, one thing after another. Miss Folley could not bring herself to pretend amiability. She was shocked and preoccupied, and showed it. She had to reorganise all her old ideas about her employer and their relationship. In no way did she blame herself.

Sometimes, optimism briefly unsettled Mrs Secretan. 'She *could* not have read it and *stay* here,' she would tell herself. But then how account for the sudden glumness, the grim silences, the averted glance? And the letter-reading in the evenings had ceased. Awkward as they had been, those days seemed better than the present. Now Miss Folley found jobs to keep her in the kitchen. With a martyred air, she made chutney and lemon curd and more marmalade than they would ever eat for all the rest of the breakfasts of their life, thought Mrs Secretan.

She was counting the days to her appointment with the dentist. It would make such a nice little break: tea with Flora afterwards was something to look forward to. She got on busily with her sewing. The lawn dress she was making for her granddaughter was edged with real lace – she did not like the other kind, and everything for Alice must be the best. If she were to be so ill-favoured with looks, such a quaint, un-Flora-like little thing, they would have to be especially careful about her clothes.

'I'm afraid I've used up the saffron,' Miss Folley said one lunch-time, in the tone of one no longer afraid of anything. She set down the dish of rice in front of Mrs Secretan and stepped quickly back. 'Perhaps when you're in London for the dentist you could get some more. They never have it in the village.'

Mrs Secretan, serving herself, blushed. *That* was in the letter, too, she thought. She had not breathed a word about going to London. That clinches it, she thought; that's final. She wished with all her heart that it was not.

She was all Miss Folley had, and she had destroyed, with trivial indiscretions, her own image. Nothing she could think of would ever repair it.

'I shall leave her something very handsome in my will,' she had decided. 'A nice sum of money, and that fob watch she admires. Then she'll know that though I laughed, I was grateful.'

Nowadays, all her possessions she saw as having some different life after her death. In her mind, she tried pieces of jewellery on her friends and relations – the diamonds were for Flora, of course – but there were lesser things of seed pearls and garnets that would bring unexpected pleasure to other people, poor Meg Driscoll, for instance.

Meekly, she promised to get the saffron, and Miss Folley, who had given up her old habit of lingering, went out, shutting the door very, very quietly. Not knowing about the fob watch, she remained huffy.

Twelve

Flora saw very little of Kit. The afternoon tea-parties were over. He had long hours now, working as a publisher's traveller. He did his job with a mixture of both boredom and relief, and seldom any more thought about acting, even when Geoffrey Pringle's play – without himself being involved – was put on and, shortly after, as it happened, was taken off.

The spring came, and Flora all the time was happy. The baby grew, her dark, puckish face delighting her parents, although most other people thought it a pity. 'With those *other* looks in the family,' they said.

As usual, Flora's worries were other people's worries; with these, she tirelessly concerned herself. More than she could ever be indignant with most of these other people, she was with Patrick Barlow; for Meg, growing older, was developing some old-maidish traits; she looked sad, and often dowdy. Much of her old charm had been slain by Patrick's not having seemed to succumb to it. Some selfishness, Flora thought, had made him obstinate. He took Meg to the Ballet, or to some foreign film, on Friday evenings, and had done so since Christmas, without ever altering the night or adding to the number of occasions. If for some reason it could not be Friday – if Meg were unlucky enough to have a cold on that day – no other evening was ever suggested.

He sometimes called on Flora after tea. Having sat at his desk for most of the day, his back and shoulders ached with tension: he just wanted to walk about a room with a glass in his hand, but not alone.

Flora always seemed pleased to see him. 'Don't bother

to telephone first,' she begged. ' I am always lonely then – Alice gone to bed, and Richard never home.'

'I shall still do so,' Patrick said. 'Do you mind my walking about like this? I feel a bit stiff.'

'But of course not.' Flora moved a small chair, to give him more room.

'I loathe it myself when people drop in,' he said sourly. ' "Drop" is the word. And it's sometimes a job to stop one's face doing the same. What's the telephone for, if not to allow one a chance of saying "yes" or "no"? And, after all, the only people one could bear to see unexpectedly are the very ones who would never dream of letting it happen. In one of Robert Liddell's novels someone says that he can't imagine Bernard Shaw or Virginia Woolf ever ringing the bell and going empty away. I simply no longer answer the bell.' (Frankie's scampering up the stairs, prolonged ringing, he could recognise by now – but sometimes, trying to make sure, he also made a mistake.)

'I'm always pleased to see anyone,' Flora said. 'But surely Bernard Shaw is dead?'

Patrick agreed.

'Did you enjoy the Ballet on Friday?' she asked.

'Yes. Yes, it was quite nice and prancey.'

'And did Meg?'

'Meg more than I, I suspect. She knows what they're supposed to be doing – you know, those names of what they're up to.'

'We both went to ballet class at school,' Flora explained. 'I'm afraid I was rather slow and heavy at it, but mother thought it was better than too much horse-riding – though I really liked that more. I had a fat pony called Silver . . . and guinea-pigs . . . oh, and my *beautiful* doves. To get back to them all in the holidays – the summer holidays. Meg used to come and we had picnics on the river. The most heavenly weather in those days. I suppose one purposely forgets the gnats and midges.'

A toile de jouy world of innocent country pleasures, he said to himself, almost moving his lips as he paced about the room, and could imagine the girls dressed as shepherdesses, one pushing a swing, the other flying upwards, ribbons fluttering. A quite different world from any nowadays, with different weather.

'Poor Meg,' Flora said, sighing.

Patrick did not answer her.

'Her world was altered when her mother died. So little money, and Kit having to take jobs not worthy of him.'

'Kit is being sensible at last,' Patrick said sharply.

'But such a dreadful waste of talent; and what he's doing won't lead anywhere.'

'If he sticks to it, he might; and he wasn't going anywhere before, unless slightly potty from loneliness and having nothing to do.'

'There was no need for him to be lonely. He knew he could always come here.'

'One can't make much of a career out of having tea with married women.'

Flora looked perplexed and hurt. 'Whether I'm married or not has nothing to do with it,' she said mildly.

'No,' Patrick agreed, and then more definitely repeated 'No' again. 'Well, it's a relief to Meg, at any rate, that he's come to his senses.'

'She doesn't look any happier for it,' Flora said. She gave him a rather timid and reproachful glance, then looked away.

'Flora,' Patrick began: then he put down his empty glass and in a different voice said, 'I shall have to go.'

He never stayed long and Richard, for one, was glad of that. He did not like to find people cluttering up the place, as he put it, when he got home tired.

'Don't come out,' said Patrick. He stopped and kissed her cheek, looked down at her for a moment, and then said, 'Compassion's all right: reason's better, you know.'

Its small voice, he thought, going down the outside steps.

*   *   *

As Percy would not deign to go abroad, Ba went on her own to France for a week to visit relations. Percy did not like other people's relations, either. He drove her to the airport in his large dark car, which looked, Richard said, as if it ought to have a Flanders poppy on the bonnet all the year round.

It was too affecting, saying goodbye. He made up his mind never to do it again. And Ba, waiting to go through to her departure channel, felt suddenly tearful and guilty. Percy was so much on his dignity that she could not bear it. She dabbed her eyes with her handkerchief, then shut it in her handbag with a brisk, expensive-sounding click.

'Don't hang about, honey,' she said. 'Off you go. Look after yourself, and remember the casserole is in the fridge. But if Flora should ask you there, it will do for another day.'

'I shan't be going to Flora's. I prefer my own home, thank you. I've been alone in it before now,' he said crossly. 'And I don't like other people's cooking.' He was quite flabbergasted that she should leave him in this way. 'I'll go back home and do some practising. It's a long time since I had the place to myself.'

'Yes, you do that,' she said soothingly, not in the least hurt.

'You're sure you've got enough money?'

To be abroad was bad, he thought; but to be abroad counting every outlandish coin was a horror he would wish on no one, not even on Ba as a punishment.

The airport building gave him the feeling that the whole world was on the move, the words *departure* and *arrival* echoed threateningly about him. There was a suggestion implied that to stay in one's own country was an eccentricity. He did not like it. He went off to buy some magazines for Ba, was making an effort to forgive her, lest he should never see her again. As he did not want their last minutes to be bitter ones to look back on, he decided to leave. He kissed her and gruffly murmured a warning against taking foreign lavatories for granted, and walked sadly away, conveying by his slow tread, he hoped, both courage and a sense of injury.

Ba watched him, wondering how soon he would recover. Her optimism was of the self-induced kind of parents leaving their children for the first time at boarding school. (*They settle down in no time. Everyone says so.*)

Driving back to London, filling the closed-up car with the smoke of his cigar, Percy's spirits slowly rose. He decided to go and pester Richard at the works. He got in his son's way for as long as he could, giving his criticism freely, and then wondered what next to do. On other occasions, he took his complaints and forebodings back to Ba. This afternoon, there was nowhere but Flora's to go for this purpose. He drove off in that direction, thinking it was more than likely that she would ask him to stay for dinner.

Mrs Lodge opened the door to him. Although it was only half-past five a faint but appetising smell of roasting meat came up the stairs. It must be a very large joint to have been put on so early, he decided. There would be plenty for him, but he hoped there wasn't going to be a dinner party. Of course, they lived well, he thought vaguely, taking off his overcoat and handing it to Mrs Lodge, who almost staggered under its weight.

Patrick Barlow stood up as the drawing-room door was opened. Always here, thought Percy. He wondered why Richard did not put his foot down. Flora sat on the sofa. Alice was on her lap, having her napkins changed.

Good God, thought Percy.

Flora clasped the little feet together in one hand and

lifted the bright red bottom from the steaming napkins, saying 'How nice to see you, Grandpapa. Do sit down, Percy dear. Wherever you'll be most comfortable.'

'I've just called in on Richard,' Percy said, taking a chair by the fire and keeping his eyes away from the baby. *In the drawing-room*, he thought. *In company.*

Flora gave a little sigh in her mind; the only place where she *could* give it. Those visits to the factory of his she dreaded, or dreaded, rather, the repercussions of them. She began to dredge Alice with powder. Then she pinned her into clean napkins and handed her to her grandfather. She went out with the wet napkins and left Percy with Patrick. A long string of dribble swayed from Alice's mouth and attached itself to his shoulder. Her head bobbed uncertainly on its frail neck. He was afraid that she might nod it right off. Some talcum powder came off her legs on to his sleeve. With both hands needed to hold her, he could not protect himself. He kept his head back, rigid, as far from her as he could, but her face came nearer and nearer and with a sudden lurch she fell forward, her wet, open mouth pressed slobbering against his chin.

'Shall I take her, sir?' Patrick asked.

In spite of his relief, Percy resented the 'Sir'. A dozen years younger than me at most, he thought sourly, and wildly inaccurately, as he brushed and mopped himself. Far less hair than me already. Be quite bald at my age. That's too much headwork. You can't grow grass on a busy road, they say. Men of action usually have good heads of hair.

Patrick was walking about the room with the baby held against his chest. He kept putting his lips against her soft cheek, breathing her faint, sour and powdery smell. Her mouth explored his face and neck in vain. She was hungry and began to cry.

'The days are drawing out,' said Percy.

'Yes, they are; at last,' Patrick agreed in a cautious

voice, wondering if the old man's remark was a sarcastic comment on his own silence, his preoccupation with the baby.

'And how was Richard?' he enquired.

'Richard's a worry-guts.' He left it at that. Further comments on his son could wait for Flora's return.

'How is your wife?' Patrick plodded on.

'Fair. Very fair. Gone to France.' That, too, could wait for Flora's return. She was a long time away. Must have been having a word with Mrs Lodge he decided, when at last she came back and at once invited him to dinner. 'Just chops,' she said apologetically.

Even Patrick, who had smelt the roasting meat when he arrived, was surprised. He wasn't as disappointed as Percy, for he was not staying to dinner. He rarely went out in the evenings except on Fridays, when Frankie took his mother to the cinema. Were they having the roast cold tomorrow? he wondered. Percy was dumbfounded for a moment or two, and even then could only speak in a voice of gloom.

'Thank you, my dear, I'd be glad to. I saw poor old Ba off. My wife's gone and left me,' he said, turning his stout body round to address Patrick, who was still pacing up and down with the baby cradled against him.

'Only for a week,' said Flora.

'Just because we're married,' he said accusingly. 'She never left me before. In those days we always went on holiday *together*. She was quite content with Brighton or Torquay, where at any rate you could get a tot of whisky at a reasonable price. If she was ever fretting to go abroad, she never said so.'

'She'll soon be back,' Flora said comfortingly.

'What happened to that old photograph of me standing outside the factory? I see it's gone from Richard's office.'

'I don't remember it.'

'Me standing outside the factory,' he repeated. 'About the time we first moved there.'

'I don't think I've ever seen it.'

'Of course you've seen it. It was hanging up above the filing cabinets.'

'I'm sorry, I can't help you, darling. Ask Richard.'

He had been too proud to do so, and only his increasing irritability had made him mention the matter now. He was wounded, too. Probably his son was a snob and didn't care for his staff to know what a very small factory it once had been, or for them to see his father standing there so proudly in the photograph, under the sign with his own name, and wearing a cloth cap.

'I don't think I shall stay for dinner after all,' he said. 'I always get very restless in the evenings.'

'Oh, dear; but whatever you want to do, of course,' Flora said in the soothing voice which Patrick admired. 'I know Richard will be disappointed, but I quite understand.'

'I always used to enjoy my evenings in the old days,' Percy said. 'I can't seem to settle down the way things are now.'

He hauled himself out of his chair.

'I must go, too,' Patrick said, putting Alice carefully into Flora's arms.

If he had known *he* wasn't staying to dinner, Percy thought, he might have stayed himself. Too late now to change his mind. He put his hand with a vague gesture on the baby's head, and she began to cry again. Her mouth squared, her face darkened, and she let out a loud and angry wail.

'Quite a little person, isn't she?' said Percy.

'I must feed her and put her to bed,' Flora said.

She went into the hall to see them off and then carried Alice up to her nursery, where Mrs Lodge had already lit the gas fire. Flora sat down in the old rocking-chair – her mother's – and began to unbutton her blouse. Alice pushed her tear-wet face against her and her crying ceased; but, even with her mouth fastened furiously to her mother's breast, she still made little hiccuping noises, the echoes of sobs, as if resentment lingered.

The room, at the top of the house, was quiet; there were the gentle sounds of the child sucking and the bubbling murmur of the gas fire. Flora leant back in her chair, thinking of Percy, with a smile of amusement on her lips.

* * *

Percy's flat, when he returned to it, had a vacant look, as if he had been away for a long time, not just half a day. There was the melancholy sound of a tap dripping in the kitchen, and when he opened the drawing-room door the sudden movement of air caused one of Ba's big shaggy chrysanthemums to collapse; its mass of petals slipped softly on to the floor.

'Make untold work – flowers,' Percy said aloud, walking round the petals on his way to the television set. He sat down opposite it, waiting for it to warm up, his hands clasped across his stomach, his face wearing a patient expression. That nuisance-cat Flora had given him came to rub against his legs but he pushed it aside. He was all ready to pass judgment. The picture suddenly swam out of nothing, following the sound. A quiz programme. Two rows of people facing one another. A pompous, school-masterly man asking the questions. Those answers that Percy knew he spoke out loudly and promptly; when he was at a loss, he pretended (as if he were not alone) that he had not quite caught the question, or was too busy blowing his nose to make his reply, or had to go to help himself to whisky.

He also contradicted and made rude remarks to the quiz-master who, like so many other things today, irritated him. 'Speak up, you bloody fool. You didn't say anything of the kind. Any idiot knows that. And goodbye to *you* until next week, only I shan't be there, thanks.'

He got up and refilled his glass and lit a cigar. Now began some hideous music – horrid cacophony, he fumed, as if to someone else in the room – and three young men in tight trousers gathered round a microphone, posturing about, singing a load of rubbish simply to annoy Percy, who had to get up and switch to the other channel, on that to find teenagers talking to a clergyman about sex. He switched the set off altogether. That was that, then. That was what he paid his licence for. Sacred youth drummed into him day and night. What was so marvellous about being young? It happened to everyone. It was growing old that did not.

'Juvenile delinquents. Louts,' he said. With the bomb for their excuse. It unsettled them, it was said. They talked about it all the time. They feared it. But what about us, me? Percy asked himself. The bomb won't just drop on the teenagers. He was sick and tired of the word. Not worth an ounce of dripping, none of them.

He lifted the lid of the piano, propped it open and sat down on the stool. Not that he actually knew any young people, he reflected. Who was there? That Driscoll lad, Meg's brother. A case in point, he decided grimly, turning the pages of his book of studies. *For Smoothness* he settled for. It was smoothing he wanted himself. He began to play, peering at the music-book through cigar-smoke, his thick, nicotine-stained fingers plodding up and down the arpeggios – the cigar burning away in an ash-tray at the end of the treble notes – and an occasional oath springing from his lips.

*   *   *

'What happened to that old photograph of your father outside the factory?' Flora asked, suddenly remembering, as she lay in bed with Richard that night.

'I chucked it into a drawer, I believe.'

'I think he was hurt that you'd moved it.'

His voice, when he answered, had some of the irritable tone of his father's. 'Look, darling, *I* run the factory now. *He* wanted to retire, and he can't have it both ways. He's enough of a nuisance as it is, coming down there and taking up everyone's time, gassing to the old chaps about the old days. He nearly drives me mad. And the thought of those stuffy old times stifles me. Backward glances are no good.'

'Yes, I suppose . . .' Flora murmured meekly. 'Poor old boy,' she said presently. 'He was such a cross-patch today.'

But Richard did not want to talk about his father. Instead, he turned over to take her in his arms. 'We're the lucky ones,' he said. She was lying on her side and he curved his body round her, as close as a carapace.

Thirteen

GEOFFREY PRINGLE often said that the more time one
had, the less one did. His own life was organised quite
differently from that. He did not have to add this rider,
knowing that it was perfectly plain for everyone to see.

He had taken the failure of his play good-humouredly –
even amusedly, it appeared, or seemed to appear, from his
continual light allusions to it; although his face would
often cloud a little and his tone change to one of serious
concern, mentioning the actors and all those others involved, with their livings to earn.

In spite of this concern, he began straight away to risk
their livings once more, writing another play, this time
about the present day, and Parliamentary issues. There were
to be no women in it, so Elinor thought it must be very dull.

'Apart from everything else, men look so very mono-
tonous, unrelieved,' she warned her husband. She was not
in a very good humour, and his placid smile, as he went on
making notes, irritated her.

'Anyone would think there *weren't* any women M.P.s,'
she said.

'Everybody knows there are.'

'Well then.'

'The moment a woman walks onto a stage, the audience
thinks of love – who is she in love with? and who will fall
in love with her? – I can't risk even a women M.P. doing
that to my play. I wouldn't even take the risk of Edith, or
Bessie, passing briefly by upstage.'

'But a committee room,' she said, contemptuously stress-
ing the last two words. 'What a boring set to have to look
at, for one thing.'

She liked a stage full of atmosphere – *things* to look at: love seats and painted screens; heavy drapings, oil lamps, someone carrying in a samovar; or cobwebs and a broken window.

'People sitting round a table,' she went on. 'It simply won't work.'

'They will get up from it now and then,' he said, as if he were talking to a child who would understand things better later on.

'But the struggle for power,' Elinor protested, in a disgusted voice. 'Darling, we *know* it all. We've watched it all time and time again, the same intrigues, the same conclusions drawn from them. It's such old stuff, Geoffrey.'

'And so is love old stuff, and death, and all the other themes we've also seen time and time again.' He did not look up this time, and had stopped smiling. He wrote quickly, paused, then looked about him frowning, as if the thread of what had occupied him was lost.

She left him alone as he had wanted her to, and went upstairs.

Their argument had not been about the subject of his play, but about something quite different. She realised that, and thought he had too. It was not *what* he should write his play about, but whether he should write it at all. It was a Sunday afternoon and she was lonely. He knew well that she reached her lowest level on Sundays, or did, rather, as soon as lunch was eaten and she had washed up. Then the day heeled over into a frightening sea of boredom. She floundered in it, letting herself, as the hours went by, sink dully under, with the sound of church bells in her ears.

Religious people were a vexation with their selfishness. They took one whole day out of seven – out of every *seven* – and put a curse on it for other people. Even abroad, even in non-Christian countries, Elinor had always known when that day came round. It carried its staleness with her wherever she went. Only love, being blindly in love, made it endurable – as *that* made so much else.

She washed her hands, and they trembled with impatience as she dried them. She put on a jacket, took a book from beside the bed, tied a scarf over her hair and went downstairs.

'I'm going out,' she said, opening the study door.

'O.K.', said Geoffrey, cheerfully.

'I don't know when I'll be back. I may go to the cinema.'

'All right. Don't worry about me.'

'Don't worry about me,' she muttered through her teeth, slamming the front door.

The streets were almost empty. There were hardly any cars going up or down the hill. A few people were exercising their dogs. Her footsteps rang like a chant upon the pavement, as her thoughts rang in her head. 'I could say "don't" to him. I could plead. I could try to explain what I feel. I could even have taken a different turning myself long ago. Now it's too late.'

She hadn't made up her mind where she was going. Cinemas weren't open for another hour. She wondered if it were warm enough to sit in Regent's Park and read her book. It was a windy afternoon. In the St John's Wood gardens, lilac trees tossed and lowered their branches, heavy with battered blossom. It was surprising what they could endure – or had to endure – of strain and stress. 'Oh, yes! *God*,' she thought bitterly. ('I'll spend my Sunday tormenting those lilac trees I made.') They haven't even got free will, she thought dolefully. So that no one can make that an excuse for their misery.

To pass the time, she went into the Park and sat down on a seat by the lake and opened her book. *The Princess Casamassima*. There were plenty of *things* in Henry James.

But she could not read. It wasn't really reading out-of-doors weather, and she felt self-conscious. 'There's poor

Mrs Geoffrey Pringle,' she imagined the sauntering pass-ers-by whispering to one another. 'How very odd to come and sit on a park bench on a Sunday afternoon, alone, when everyone else in the world has company.'

For they had – all had – company. Here, this afternoon, no one walked alone. Lovers, entwined like woodbine, and giggling, bored her – as they are bound to bore those for whom love is over; has been, but is over. Family parties irritated her – they looked so sedate, so Sundayish that she felt she hadn't missed much. Mum and Dad strolled ponderously, silently by, all said, all gone. Is that what I want from Geoffrey? she asked herself – such companion-ship – her mind chock-full of derision and sarcasm.

Whether aloud or silently, she could not help talking to herself, she found, when she was bitter and disturbed; and staring with fixed, angry eyes at the path or the lake water, she carried on a conversation which she knew she would never have with Geoffrey. For it isn't even as if he were a great dramatist, would be a loss to the world, she reasoned. It was for something almost worthless that he was letting their marriage fall to pieces.

She looked at her watch, as she looked at it a great deal nowadays. She might walk on slowly; no need to sit here any longer. The diversion of queueing outside a cinema was a little thing to look forward to. If the film were bad, she would be bored; if it were good, she would feel the worse pain of wishing to have shared her pleasure.

She walked some way down Baker Street, looking into shop windows or, instead, meeting her reflection in drawn blinds; then she got on to a bus. Crowds of foreign people were milling about Piccadilly Circus, or sitting wearily on the steps below Eros.

Elinor joined a queue outside a cinema, and stood there, reading her book; then, just as they all began to shuffle forwards, she suddenly felt that she could not endure to go inside, to have those two or more solitary hours facing the screen. She hesitated, wondering, where else, what else, then? and while she hesitated was pushed on into the foyer.

Waiting for the film to begin, she could not read her book, for the print was too small, the ceiling lights too dim. Colours changed on the ruched, draped curtains and an engulfing noise from an electric organ gorged the theatre.

So she wasn't the only solitary person in London! As the cinema filled, she could see one or two people sitting alone. There was a young man, twisted sideways in his seat, trying to get a little light on to his Sunday paper. *Vice Racket*, in big black letters, Elinor could read. A girl sat alone, smoking, her legs crossed and her head bowed; perhaps trying to find an inner refuge from the noise of the organ. She was rather beautiful, looked intelligent and wore interesting clothes; must be alone from preference, Elinor thought; but she could not really imagine people being that, and wondered how much she was ever a subject of guesswork, herself.

When the organ music occasionally briefly stopped, a hum of desultory conversation could be heard about her, the voices of people dully passing time. At last the curtains silkily parted, and a cartoon film began. Ill-drawn animals with squawky voices spitefully pursued one another, were catapulted through space, ricocheted, eyes wide with surprise, tongues flapping crudely to the sound of folksy, mawkish prattle. As far as Elinor could see, there were no children in the cinema, and she wondered for whom this nonsense was put on. She closed her eyes until it should be over, and wished that she might close her ears as well.

Cocooned, isolated by darkness and by vicarious emotions, she felt all the more vulnerable when it was time to emerge; but that chrysalis state had had no development – no change had taken place, and it was just the same Elinor who pushed her way through the shuffling crowds outside the cinema, having passed time; nothing else.

This part of London always depressed her – and did so

especially on a Sunday and under a rain-laden sky. Dirty pigeons walked in the litter round the fruit barrows; a smell of hot dogs hung about the streets, and canned, echoing music, the rattle of slot-machines and a waft of stale air came from an amusement arcade.

Pubs were just opening and beginning to fill rapidly. She went into one on a corner of a side street, fetched her drink from the bar and carried it to a table. She took her cigarettes and lighter from her bag, settled down, sipped her gin-and-tonic, then opened her book.

'Poor Mrs Geoffrey Pringle,' the stranger in her imagination said. 'I saw her sitting in a pub all on her own the other Sunday evening, pretending to read a book.'

She lit a cigarette and glanced round her defiantly. But she did not see anyone who was likely to be the stranger, the faceless person in her mind, whom she imagined saying those things.

At the next table, a more than middle-aged man, jauntily dressed, in a navy-blue blazer heavily badged, and shoes with pointed toes, was also sitting alone. He covered his mouth with one hand, and with the other worked with a pick among his gold or rotting teeth, eyeing every woman who came in.

'Nasty sort of evening,' he said, catching Elinor's glance as she looked round the bar.

She agreed rather coldly, was about to return to her book, but took up her glass instead.

He put the tooth-pick in his pocket, folded his arms casually across his breast, leaned back, and said, 'I wonder what sort of summer we're in for this year.'

Elinor disdained to say that she wondered, too; and she could think of no other reply. She was quiet, looking down meditatively as she flicked ash off her cigarette.

'It seems pretty general,' he said. 'This filthy weather, I mean. One of my china's just got back from the French Riviera. Very disappointing, he said. The Costa Brava's been the same, I hear. If you can't be sure of some weather there, where can you be?'

Nothing he had said so far seemed to her to lead in any way towards a conversation. His half-questions hung in the air, and she ignored them. Realising this, he became more direct. 'You made any holiday plans yet?' he asked.

She raised her eyes and looked coldly at him. What a wretched sort of creature, she thought. 'No, none,' she said. She could not take up her book again now. She had left it too late. Instead, she lifted her glass and drank from it, a long drink. She wore a reflective air, as if she might be sitting there quite alone, with little problems to ponder.

'May I be allowed . . .? What is your pleasure, drink-wise?' He had got up quickly and was standing in front of her. 'The same again? Gin and ton, I gather.'

During the moment of sheer surprise before she could answer, he had turned away, had disappeared across the crowded bar. Again she was too late. She was annoyed at this awkward development. Now she would be obliged to talk to him. At the bar she heard him calling authoritat-ively for large drinks. He returned with them. He put the glasses on separate tables, but twirled his chair round in one hand to bring it closer to hers, at a better angle for conversation.

Oh, the boredom of it! she thought crossly. The bore-dom and embarrassment. 'I should have stopped you, but you were too quick,' she said. 'I was just going home.'

'No damage done. And where is "home", may I ask?'

'North London,' she said in a vague voice. 'Well . . . thank you,' she added. She hesitated, and then took up her glass.

'Cheers!' He made a gesture with his glass towards hers. 'Here's to us.'

Whoever we are, Elinor thought.

'And is this one of your regular haunts?' he asked. He had a heavily arch way of speaking – of asking his questions – as if he were really quoting something they both knew to be amusing and full of meaning.

'No, I've never been in here before.' The one and only time, she added to herself.

'Nor me. Our paths were brought together.'

'I just dropped in after the cinema,' she said prosaically, afraid that the conversation was taking a romantic turn.

'On your lonesome? What a shameful waste!'

'Waste?'

Her manner impressed rather than subdued him. Because of it, she was unlike other women whose casual acquaintance he had made, and the situation titillated him simply by not progressing as it should, as he expected.

'Waste of you – your company,' he said.

'Do you always talk like this to women you don't know?'

He flushed, she was pleased to see, and looked downcast; but then disconcerted her by saying, 'No. I hope you'll forgive me. Since the wife died, I've been lonely. Like to share a social glass, you know. It's no fun drinking on your own. No harm meant.'

Whether she believed him or not, she was bound to murmur something in an apologetic voice. Having to do this prolonged the circumstances; for she had been just about to go. When she had finished her drink, she opened her handbag and put away her cigarettes and lighter. There was something so deliberately final in this, that he began to make hasty suggestions for a visit to another pub, or a bite of something to eat – as he put it – or for accompanying her home, even a small part of the way home.

She was in too great a hurry, was late already, she explained, and despised herself for mentioning her husband.

'I'm sorry,' she said, realising that she had wasted a valuable part of his evening. It was a misunderstanding for which she saw she was partly to blame. Now he would have to begin all over again with someone else, a different kind of woman, probably, one who from practice would slip easily into the routine.

'Thank you for the drink,' she said, standing up. Time *and* money she had wasted.

He stood up, too. 'Then we shan't meet again.'

'It seems rather unlikely. I'm afraid I am poor company. I hope you find someone more interesting to talk to.'

'I'm afraid I don't know what you're driving at. I don't go round London picking up any strange women I happen to see.'

'I'm sorry,' she said again, more gently. Then she said goodbye, and pushed her way through the bar to the door.

Her face burned as she walked towards the bus-stop. 'Mrs Geoffrey Pringle,' the voice in her head began, 'I saw her being picked up in a pub by the most disreputable-looking bounder.'

All the way, sitting in the bus, staring out of the window at the drifting, eddying Sunday-evening crowds, she was wondering if in time, some terrible deterioration caused by loneliness would take place in her – so that a man would not be mistaken in – as this one had been this evening – expecting some response from her, and for it to be far from impossible that she should spend an evening in his company. From reading and her knowledge of life, she knew that lonely women are prone to such forms of degeneracy – the rich old widows making themselves figures of fun on long sea-cruises, the garrulous divorced women sitting in pubs, mistaken sometimes for prostitutes, but having quite a different attitude to men, more than willing to receive nothing, give everything.

She got off the bus and went the long way round, along Beatrice Crescent, a walk she sometimes took and, doing so, passing their house, pictured Richard and Flora inside it, pursuing their happy married life: sometimes she could hear the baby crying, and once saw Mrs Lodge going out with a shopping-basket.

Richard was one of her given-up hopes. She had not
wanted much of him – his company and conversation. So
often, women irritated her, her attempts at wives' prattle
did not ring true, and she felt that others knew it. Uneasily
she had sat in coffee shops in the middle of shopping mornings, trying to join in, to talk of children's illnesses and
cooking and the charitable works in which they all seemed
so severely involved. Her part in it was false, and lately
she had made very little effort.

She drew near to the house. A laburnum tree hung over
the railings, not yet in bloom. They would most probably
be in the dining-room, having supper; Mrs Lodge's afternoon and evening off, so Flora would have brought up the
cold joint and Richard would be carving it.

But she had imagined it all wrong. Richard had been
putting his car away and, as he turned from the garage, he
saw her and waved and called to her.

He had scarcely seen her since Alice was born. She
couldn't be blamed, he felt, for thinking he had just made
use of her – for company (at a time when he was at a loose
end), or for his evening meals.

'Come in for a drink,' he said, opening the gate, trying
to make up for his neglect by the warmth of his smile.

'But won't you be having supper any moment?'

He opened the gate.

'I had a sandwich at a pub on the way back from
Berkshire. I took Flora and the baby to stay with her mother
for a day or two.'

Gladly, she went up the steps with him and he unlocked
the door; but the silence, darkness of the house made her
feel nervous. He's really my only friend, she thought. How
dreadful if I did something to lose him. It was all she
wanted – and had happened with miraculous luck – to
talk, to sit and have a drink with him, for him to be at ease
with her, to take her for granted. She had not fallen in love
with him, and desired nothing that belonged to Flora: but

he must have something left over from that, which he could spare her; everybody has *something* left over.

Marital complications she abhorred – husbands and wives in a changing pattern. Complications; embarrassments. If, for instance, as he crossed the room now with her drink – if, instead of handing it to her, he should put it down on the little table beside her and take her into his arms . . . even imagining this she was overcome by confusion and dismay.

She took the glass in steady fingers and wandered across the room to look at a photograph of Alice – as far away from him as possible.

'She's like you,' she said, but not in an interested tone.

'What have you been up to?' he asked – very exuberant, very genial.

'I went to the cinema on my own, and then into a pub near Piccadilly where some perfectly frightful man chatted me up and bought me a drink.'

The bright, slangy account was not in her character, and he wondered what it was disguising or concealing. He picked up her book. '*The Princess Casamassima*,' he read out. 'Is that how you pronounce it?'

'Have you read it?'

'My dear, Flora would tell you that I have never read anything. She's not much better herself. She *opens* a lot of books, but that's about all. She drops off without turning a page. Do you always read in the cinema? I should have thought it would be too dark.'

'No, I took my book to the Park first, but it wasn't really warm enough to sit about.'

'Is Geoffrey away again?'

'No. He's at home.'

'My dear, do sit down. Shall I put on the electric fire?'

'Don't for *me*.'

'Now tell me about the man in the pub,' he said, settling back to listen.

She described the nameless one in a haughty, mocking way, and again he felt a stirring of unease at her manner. 'Will you have another drink,' he asked, when he had listened, and shown himself properly amused.

'No, thank you.'

'So Geoffrey doesn't care for going to the cinema?' he asked, getting up to help himself.

'Geoffrey is writing another play. He is awfully persistent about it.'

'It must be lonely for you.'

She faced this warily. She wanted his sympathy; she wanted to indulge herself, angle for it, luxuriate in it; but she guessed that it might be a mistake, and perhaps a deadly one. Cautiously she said, 'I am rather used to it, you know.' He made no reply, and she felt compelled to go on. 'My own fault, really. I ought to know more people. I seem to have lost the knack of making friends – though "knack" suggests something more clever than anything I ever had.' Stop! Leave it there! she told herself, but added, 'If I had children, it wouldn't matter.' The self-pity she had never intended at the beginning of the sentence, had crept into it before the end. She had meant to be very brisk.

She stood up. She had talked about herself in a way that must alienate him, could bear no more of it and must go. Ali day she had been in a self-destructive humour, and it was, after all, a cruel chance that had brought her to his house in such a mood.

'You must come round and see Flora more often,' he said.

He was always easy with her, always kind and equable; but behind his urbane manner might conceivably be bored, or irritated, or embarrassed. As she walked down the hill, she wondered if he were indeed any of these things; but could only imagine him shrugging his shoulders, forgetting her, sitting down at his desk – for she knew he brought work home.

'You must come round and see Flora more often,' he had said. Kind, neighbourly words. All he had to offer. We all talk like it most of the time, to make the wheels go round.

It was dark, and late. As she opened her front door, she hoped that Geoffrey had missed her, even if only because he had been hungry.

But he had not. He had made himself a beef sandwich, and was eating it contentedly as he wrote. He raised it in his hand in greeting, and went on writing and munching.

Fourteen

'I COULDN'T take it, Madam,' Mrs Lodge told Flora.

(Geoffrey Pringle detested the form of address she used. 'In this day and age,' he would say – a phrase often on his lips. To Mrs Lodge, 'Madam' was a part of her professionalism.)

Flora was trying to give her her old fur coat. 'It will keep you warm when you go shopping in the winter.'

Shopping in a fur coat! thought Mrs Lodge. 'It wouldn't be suitable in my position,' she said. 'Fur coats cause talk – about anyone like me, I mean – if you'll excuse me saying so.'

This was not her real reason for refusing, which would have to be brought out now, she could see. She had put it off for too long; her head was weary with rehearsing speeches. As it was, she didn't make a speech at all. She simply said, 'No, Madam, I'm ever so sorry, but I've made up my mind to go.'

Flora, with the fur coat still in her arms, sank down on the side of the bed, her eyes suddenly widened in a startled expression.

'Go where?' she asked.

'I don't know. I haven't made any plans yet. I wouldn't leave you in the lurch, you may rest assured. It's just that I couldn't stand another London summer. I don't know why I ever thought I could.'

Flora pushed aside the fur coat and stared at Mrs Lodge, who, not able to face her, continued to clean the window.

'But why?' A tear or two began to run down Flora's cheeks, but she was too stunned to notice, or brush them away.

'Baby's older now. I wouldn't have gone till she was

settled. You know that. And I won't go now until you've got someone in my place.'

'But I don't want someone in your place. I only want you.'

'I get that fussed and restless, Madam.' Mrs Lodge turned, with the chamois leather in her hand, and looked pathetically at Flora. 'You were brought up as a country child, too. You must know what it's like.'

'Being with those I love means more.'

'That isn't really fair, Madam. You know I love you, and little Alice. But I'm just hungry for the country, and I really can't bear it any longer. It feels like being in prison. I miss so many things. I haven't heard a cuckoo this year. I wake up and wish I could just hear it once – but you never would in London, and if you did it wouldn't be the same.'

She was silent and stood there so quietly by the window. In her imagination she could hear the sudden, erupting cry, bursting through the early-morning mist, echoing from one tree to another.

'You get a better class of bird in the country,' she presently explained. All those young summer birds she had missed – the pale slim thrushes especially!

Birds more than I do, Flora thought, shocked. After all, I left my doves when I got married.

'It wasn't easy to say, Madam, I haven't been happy about it.'

Someone under her roof unhappy, without her knowing – this upset Flora and she got off the bed and went over to Mrs Lodge and put her arms rounds her. 'Forgive me,' she said, 'I won't make it harder, I promise. I'll try to be grateful for having had you at all. I'll try to think in that way.'

Then she went quickly from the room, so that they might both cry a little, separately.

*   *   *

Ba came to tea that afternoon and was told the dreadful news.

'Just birds, birds,' Flora said in a plaintive, mystified voice.

'Babbling of green fields,' said Ba.

'No, just birds,' Flora said again.

'Richard will be surprised.'

'He is – I rang him up at the works to tell him, and he couldn't believe it. I can hardly believe it either. It's so awful. And she'll go the minute I find someone else. And, of course, I'll have to try, *properly* try – though it's like signing my own death warrant. And after that I suppose I'll never see her again. Or at best she'll call on me when she comes to London; if she ever does come, which I doubt. She'll wear her best clothes and sit down in here and drink tea, and I'll be racking my brains for something interesting to tell her. And it won't be at all the same as just chatting about the house while we work. And Alice will have forgotten her.'

'Don't cry, honey. She might come in.'

'I just can't stop.'

'You're worrying Alice.'

Flora wiped her eyes and blew her nose. 'Of course, it might be worse,' she said. 'She might have died. You see, I *do* try to look on the bright side. I must, for *her* sake. It would be a sort of blackmail if I upset myself. I'm sorry, Ba, to have been such a misery. How's Percy?'

'I begin to think Percy retired too soon. He's restless. He doesn't know what to do with his evenings. He mopes about the house, and in the end goes out. In the old days he used to visit *me* – but nowadays I'm *there*; so the evening brings no diversion. It's all bowls and billiards now; drop in at the Club, and so on. Ah, well, this is married life, I suppose. . . . It's not the same; but I expect there are compensations. We're not getting younger.'

Flora looked rather shocked and said, 'But surely, if you explain to him how boring it is, being left alone . . .'

'I tried it. He said, "What about that time you went off to France, and left *me* all alone?" '

Then Mrs Lodge came in with the tea-tray, and was given a dazzlingly cheerful, but watery smile by Flora.

* * *

Patrick had learnt to call on Flora after Alice's bed-time. Although he dearly loved to see the child, he realised that, at that hour, he was less welcome than he used to be. Setting out later meant that much longer at home after finishing work, nearly another hour of pacing about the room, yawning and stretching; tired, so tired, his shoulders as stiff as a coat-hanger. Anyone watching him must have thought him a madman; for he shrugged, and swung his arms, blew out his cheeks, scratched his armpit – poor, apeish, worn-out novelist: then his bath, which could not restore what was drained out of him; and then a drink, but not alone. So, frequently, he went off to Flora's, every so often taking with him a bottle of gin about which she gently protested.

This evening, when he arrived, Mrs Lodge opened the door to him and he noticed that she had been crying. Flora's eyes were also red. She was sitting in the drawing-room with Ba. Patrick wondered what on earth could have happened. He fairly soon established that the baby was not dead; or Richard declared bankrupt, or gone to prison or both; but, whenever he mentioned any trivial thing that might happen in the future, Flora twisted her hands together, Ba gave him a warning glance.

'Whatever's up?' he asked her, when Flora, thinking she had heard Alice cry, had gone flying upstairs.

'Mrs Lodge is leaving,' Ba whispered.

'Good Lord, why?"

'She wants to go and live in the country.'

'I must say I feel relieved – I thought something was badly wrong.'

'It is. Someone always has to look after Flora, and let her think she's looking after them. And love is also involved – comfortable daily love, a very nice kind. It must seem trivial to you, though – just losing a housekeeper – especially as you were expecting the worst.'

'It doesn't seem trivial to me,' he managed to say before Flora came back.

She was all watery brightness. Mrs Lodge's weeping had left her blotchy; but Flora had the aqueous beauty of Venus risen from the sea – her eyes swam, her cheeks had pearly tracks upon them. She had not blown and scrubbed her nose into a red smudge like Mrs Lodge's. She had more or less let her grief be.

'I am very sorry to hear,' Patrick began, while Ba shook her head slowly at him and frowned, and Flora's eyes began to glitter more than before.

She smiled as best she could, and said they would all have a drink.

But when she went to the drinks tray there was no gin there. Mrs Lodge, bringing in a bowl of ice, was full of apologies. 'Oh, Madam, my head's gone all to pieces. I meant to remind you, when I put the last empty bottle out. They finished it up the other night when Mrs Pringle was here, and I couldn't find another one in the cupboard.'

'Mrs Pringle?'

'Yes; Sunday night, that was.'

Flora still with a puzzled air, said, 'Oh, yes, Sunday.'

'Lord!' Patrick said to himself, his eyes on the carpet. 'Yes, I'd like some whisky,' he said aloud. Well, *I'm* often here with *Flora*, he reasoned with himself. But no one cared about that. No one would keep secrets about him.

As they drank, little gusts of chatter came from Flora; but he could see she was preoccupied.

'Are you writing anything at the moment?' asked Ba. His was another world to her, but she felt bound by

163

courtesy to enquire about it. 'Anything on the stocks?' she added – inevitably.

'I've just finished one – so I suppose that's quite *off* the stocks now.'

'How thrilling! And have you begun another?' she persisted.

To him it was almost the worst kind of conversation. 'Barely,' he said.

He thought Flora looked relieved at that. He wrote too much for her comfort. His books were a burden to her, as H. G. Wells's were to Henry James – they arrived too frequently.

'Do you think it all out beforehand?' Ba went on.

He sheltered timidly behind another writer. 'No, I'm like Lewis Carroll, who said he had sent his heroine down a rabbit-hole without any idea of what was to happen to her afterwards.'

In his case, this was utterly untrue; but his anxieties, his fussings, were his own, he felt.

'But *your* books aren't at all chaotic.'

During this, Flora sat silent, her thoughts elsewhere, he could tell.

'Thank you,' he said vaguely to Ba, hoping the conversation was over. There had been the strain of trying to speak in another language of which one knows so little that one must grope for words, pass over misunderstandings, and be misunderstood.

'Do you model yourself on any other writers?' asked Ba, relentlessly.

'Not to my knowledge,' he said in a light tone. Originality means concealing origins, Oscar Wilde said. He recalled this grimly for his own amusement.

'I know I ask too many questions, but I am fascinated,' Ba said. Really, she was trying to cover up for Flora with a lot of prattle – Flora, who sat staring at the fire, miles away from them both. 'How do you find the names of your characters, for instance? I've often wondered that. Dickens used to get his off shop-fronts, didn't he? But his always seem so far-fetched to me.'

'It's difficult to say. I thought of Armitage Ware for one of my characters,' Patrick said, trying hard to oblige. 'But somehow it seemed vaguely familiar to me. Then I found that it was the name of my lavatory basin. I stare at it every day, but had only remembered it in my subconscious.'

'It's a good name,' Ba said seriously.

'What is?' asked Flora, returning to them.

'Armitage Ware,' said Ba.

Flora shook her head in a puzzled way.

*　　*　　*

Mrs Lodge could have bitten her tongue out. What a day! she kept thinking, as she prepared dinner. A sharp and buttery smell of gooseberry-pie came from the oven, when she opened it. She took out the pie and dusted its crust with sugar. It was rather a fine pie – in its middle it had a pastry rose with little leaves arranged round it.

Whatever possessed me? she asked herself.

But the atmosphere in this house had always been so open, so sunny, that she had never thought of there being secrets.

On Sunday evenings, on her way back from visiting her son, she had turned the corner of the Crescent and seen Elinor leaving and Richard at the gate seeing her off.

By the time Mrs Lodge had reached the house, the front door was shut. She let herself in, and met Richard coming from the drawing-room with two glasses in his hand. He had enquired about her day, and she had told him some of it, but not as much as she would have told Flora – for men, she knew, are very little interested in detailed descriptions of ordinary things. Then she took the glasses from him, and went downstairs to the basement. She reconstructed the events in her mind now, as if she were being questioned by the police.

Flora's manner – upstairs, a little while ago – had made it quite obvious that she had not been told of Elinor's visit. Perhaps he just forgot to mention it, Mrs Lodge thought. She probably only dropped in for a minute or two.

Then she heard voices in the hall above, and the front door slamming – after that, no more voices. So they had both gone. She put the potatoes on, and soon a smell of mint drifted upstairs, and greeted Richard on his return.

*   *   *

'Richard,' Flora began, when they were in bed that night.

She had waited until they were in the dark, lest he should see her blushing.

'Yes, darling,' he said peaceably, afraid lest she should go on some more about Mrs Lodge's departure.

'Did Elinor Pringle come here on Sunday – when I was at Mother's?'

'Yes. She did.'

There was no hesitation in his reply, and she felt some small relief at that.

'She was going down the road when I was putting the car away, and she came in for a drink. Why do you ask?'

'Why didn't you tell me?'

'I don't know. I didn't think any more about it.'

'But, darling, I only said to you yesterday that we hadn't seen them for ages. Why didn't you tell me then that you saw her on Sunday evening?'

He hesitated now, and instead of answering her question – as he could not – he coldly asked, 'What are you getting at, Flora?' He wasted precious time wondering how on earth she knew about it – when he should have been finding a reply to her question, which, after a second or two, she asked him again.

'I honestly don't know,' he said. 'I couldn't have been attending to what you were saying.'

This hardly passed, and he knew it.

'Do you see much of her?' she asked in a quiet voice.

'I haven't lately. I told you I dined there a lot, when you were in the nursing-home.'

'But Geoffrey was there then.'

'And what difference does that make? Darling, I don't know what you're driving at – but there's nothing secret or surreptitious between me and Elinor Pringle. I can assure you of that.'

'I hope I can manage to *be* assured.'

She sounded unhappy. He knew it had been an altogether unhappy day for her, apart from this silly little situation he had created – why, he could not fathom.

'You can't possibly believe there's anything I wouldn't like you to know,' he insisted.

'No. I'm sorry,' she said meekly, in an unconvinced little voice.

He drew her up close to him. 'My dear girl,' he said, his voice gathering confidence as she relaxed against him, 'Poor old Elinor's quite a nice person, but hardly the sort anyone could fall for, if that's the idea you've got in your head.'

Although he wasn't in love with Elinor, although that much was true, he felt greatly ashamed that he should do this dreadful thing – pity one woman before another. Self-preservation, and Flora's peace of mind, he thought; trying to excuse himself. He knew how easily wounded Flora could be. That must have been the reason for his secretiveness. He could really think of no other.

*　　*　　*

On the next afternoon, Patrick and Meg went to the Zoo. It was a summer holiday and, although she could not afford to go away, not to have to go to work, to lie later in bed, to avoid the rush-hour, to have time to cook other things than stews for Kit, was holiday enough for her.

It was a hot day. A shimmer of heat rose from the paths. The trees, water, iron railings had a gilded look. Lions yawned languorously.

To be out on an afternoon, strolling in daylight with Patrick was a wonderful surprise bonus added to her week. She did not particularly like zoos, but would face the pacing caged animals to be with him, and even, with her handkerchief over her nose, accompany him into the Lesser Cat House. She had to turn her eyes from the tormented ones of a beautiful black serval, which was lashing about furiously behind its bars, never giving up, going endlessly, rapidly from side to side.

'Come, I shall dream of it,' she said, and took his arm to urge him towards the door.

She was happier when they sat down on a seat and watched the seals slipping placidly in and out of the water, making a cool sound in the blazing afternoon.

His very bringing her to such a place made her feel like an indulged child, and, instinctively, she reacted with the proper enthusiasm, although her fatherless childhood had been short of the traditional treats and she had very little practice of how to behave.

'You look happy,' Patrick said.

Her dark-skinned, rather Oriental face was too often puckered into lines of anxiety; but today she seemed to have no care. Kit's job was a help with money and he himself was happier: there was even a nice young woman in his firm's reception office, whom he had brought out to Towersey for lunch on Sundays once or twice.

'If he suddenly gets married, you'll be lonely,' Patrick said, when she told him this.

He had used the word 'suddenly' to suggest that any distant marriage of Kit's might see Meg already married herself.

'I never thought of us being together all our lives,' she said.

'No, of course not. And you'll get married yourself.'

He did not want to cloud her afternoon, but the chance had come of saying something he had long felt bound to, and he could not let it slip by.

'Perhaps,' she said. He was trying to convey something else, she knew; and she wanted to say something in return, such as –'I'll settle for friendship, a dear companion; and in the end it may be all I'll want.'

'Yes, perhaps one day I might,' she said instead.

It was over, said and heard, and he felt an almost physical relief, like coughing up phlegm.

'What sort of person is Elinor Pringle?' he asked, as they strolled on.

'I don't know her very well.'

'Does Richard, do you think?'

'I don't know. Why?'

'Rather awkward, the other evening when I was there, Mrs Lodge told Flora that she – Elinor, I mean – had been there with Richard while Flora was away. She all too plainly let the cat out of the bag; for Richard, it appeared, hadn't mentioned the visit.'

'I dare say he forgot to.'

'Flora didn't think that.'

'I don't know why you think it has any significance.'

'Because Flora thought it had. There was a sticky quarter of an hour with her for Ba and me. At first, she chattered a lot of nervous nonsense, then she sat staring into the fire, as if we weren't there – which we weren't, as soon as we could get away.'

'But they're so happily married. It's the happiest marriage I know.'

'Well, I thought so, and I'm sure Flora always thought it, too – It's Richard we don't know about.'

One thing Meg had *not* envisaged guarding her freind

from – a wandering husband, a mesh of mysteries and evasions.

'But I'm sure it was nothing,' she said.

'When I went to see Flora in the nursing-home, she told me Richard was having dinner with the Pringles. The next morning, I read in a newspaper that Geoffrey was somewhere abroad on a delegation or a conference. Why tell silly lies?'

'You are something of a gossip, Patrick,' she said.

'Yes, I am,' he agreed, in a detached voice.

They stopped to watch a small mournful monkey. He was balancing himself on a tree branch, and staring at the crowd. Its laughter, when he fidgeted, shifted himself – like a rheumaticky old man – into a more comfortable position, made his sad glance back more dignified, more reproachful. He tilted his head, looked down his flat nose, then slowly turned dark golden, unblinking eyes to Meg, held her own unfaltering gaze and came towards her along the branch. He put his small hand through the wire. He had rough, broken finger-nails, like a neglected child's. For a long time, they were quite still, looking at one another. Meg felt that there was some attempt made of communication; of guilt, apology on her part; on his, she could not tell. She did not know if his steady eyes were expressionless, or just that they always held the *same* expression – was there emptiness, or bewildered woe? He seemed as if he might be troubled by the glimmerings of intelligence, perhaps by the intimation that there was a meaning in the sea of pale faces shifting before him, and all the loud and puzzling laughter. At last, he turned away and sat picking at his chest, and without a backward glance, Meg turned away.

'It must be like that, visiting people in prison,' she said to Patrick. 'No use.'

'What a very nice person you are,' he said. 'Even monkeys love you, and choose you for their friend.'

It was the best she could ever be, she thought – the very nice person in his life. She would try hard not to be less.

'Next time we have an afternoon off, we'll go to some place not quite so saddening,' he said.

Their shadows were no longer now on the sunny paths, and when they reached the gates he said, 'Have you time for a drink at that pub in Baker Street?' It was his way of letting her know that her outing with him was nearly at an end.

They went out into the glittering swirl of the rush-hour traffic.

She had all the time in the world. It was he who had not. This wasn't a Friday evening.

Fifteen

THE hot weather went on, but changed its quality. Open, sunny skies were lowered, contracted, as before thunder – which was predicted.

Patrick's little flat was stifling. On evenings when Frankie did not come, he took to walking in the quiet streets as it grew dark, waiting for it to get cooler so that he could go to bed.

The city was an oven – curtains hung without movement at wide-open, lighted windows. In a district of coloured people near by, West Indians sat out on porches or leaned against railings in quiet groups, fanning themselves with their wide-brimmed hats, relaxed, for once, in this alien city.

There was an air of informality, almost like wartime, Patrick thought. Slackly, idly, people strolled the streets, sauntering, laughing, looking in shop-windows; but, unlike wartime, all the pub doors stood open, showing the empty brightness within. No one wanted to be inside for long, 'Sultry,' barmaids said, agreeing with any customers who came. 'Well, it's too sudden, isn't it? Feels like there's thunder about.'

In Towersey, people were drawn towards the river. Liz Corbett, having come out of *The City of London*, leaned over a parapet, looking down at the dark, scummy water. She had spent most of the day not painting, but clearing out rubbish, Her dustbin was overflowing.

It had been a decisive day. All this clobber! she had suddenly thought that morning, looking with revulsion at disintegrating still lives, the chipped jug and the rest of the dusty débris. It had served its purpose. There were

enough shapes, patterns, colours in her head to last a lifetime, she believed. All day she had felt a sense of change –
a sense of being not in full control, of having been
mastered.

She could not stay in the bar. It was too hot and, after
her second glass of beer, she felt weakly drunk. With a
floating sensation, she had walked across the road to lean
over the parapet, and was there when she saw Kit come
sauntering along the embankment.

Since the turning-point of their quarrel, he had seen
her once or twice and, having been with Meg, was obliged
to speak to her. He had done so, as if from a great distance
and when, later, his aloofness was commented on by his
sister, he said, 'We had an argument.' (To put it mildly,
he thought.) 'Nothing important.'

This evening, seeing her leaning against the wall in the
lamplight, he would have liked to avoid her, but there was
no way of doing it. She turned and looked at him and, as
he hesitated, said, 'Have you still got that job? I hope.'

'Yes, I'm still there.'

'It was because of what I said, wasn't it? That you got
it, I mean. You were irked.'

Jeering triumph was in her voice – the triumph of the
successful reformer who, all the same, could not resist
mocking the reformed.

'Nothing to do with you,' he said evenly. 'Nothing you
said could ever make any difference to me.'

But it wasn't true. Her words had certainly lashed him
into action, caused an enormous upheaval in him – for the
better, it had turned out.

'So you're still angry?'

She wanted to detain him. Usually self-sufficient, this
evening she wanted company – a breathing-space before
whatever sort of work she was going to begin tomorrow.

'I was very angry at the time. Now I've forgotten it.'

'Then will you help me down with my dustbin?'

'Your dustbin?'

'I have to lug it down to the street, and it's too heavy.'

How could he refuse?

She turned and crossed the road, and he followed her up the familiar, creaking staircase. On the little landing at the top was the dustbin, crammed with the properties of her past life.

'What has happened?' he asked, seeing the dead cow-parsley, and the lustre jug in two halves.

She couldn't tell anyone, hardly knew herself. Without replying, she grasped one handle of the bin, as if she had no time to waste explaining. Slowly they carried it down the narrow stairs and across the pavement to the kerb. Even this small exertion had made his hands and face sweat, the evening was so heavy. He looked at her, not able now to say goodbye abruptly and be on his way.

'Would you like a drink?' he asked her.

She nodded.

Having more money had given him confidence, she thought. She was impressed when he even went so far as to ask her what she would like. This was quite unlike the old days.

'Just beer,' she said.

They sat down at the usual table in the corner. The landlord and one of his regular customers exchanged glances. It was all much as it had been before – except that he would never go to bed with her again, and she knew it.

* * *

Meg could not sleep. The window was such a small square, and very little air came through. She heard the church clock strike eleven. Kit was later than usual, but she did not wonder where he was. It was an odd relationship they had nowadays; they left the house and returned to it at different times; there were brief words on the wing, notes left on the table, no confidences. She loved him dearly and always had, but knew nothing of him, or he of her. It seemed almost by chance that they shared their existence in this little house.

But when he goes, as he will go, it will seem very strange, she thought. She put the idea out of her mind. No point in going halfway towards it. So she turned her pillow over to the cooler side and tried again to go to sleep.

* * *

The next day, the weather broke. Richard, having business to do in High Wycombe, drove afterwards to call on Flora's mother.

The thundery atmosphere had affected Mrs Secretan very much, and all day long she had suffered from headaches and forebodings. Miss Folley seemed especially irritating. As time went on, she had found herself able to think of other things than her wounded pride; but the scars remained: she still had thoughts her mind shied from, and if she said something unpremeditated which, on reflection, she could imagine Mrs Secretan smiling at, writing in a letter to Flora, she could be cross and defensive for the rest of the day.

Mrs Secretan, wretchedly oppressed, worked in the garden, snipping off dead roses, trying to forget the pain in her chest, and when she could not, trying instead to persuade herself that she was a hypochondriac. 'You are a morbid old woman,' she told herself sternly. But this was no use. The thoughts of death loomed larger and larger as the day wore on – her mind seemed so empty nowadays that these sick fancies could occupy it wholly.

Before tea-time, a sudden breeze ruffled the garden and all the bushes and branches began to jog. She emptied her gardening basket onto the rubbish heap and went indoors.

Death! said her pain, as she walked up and down the drawing-room. Sometimes, she felt she was growing accustomed to the idea of it. When it came, she had resolved to be as peaceful as she could. It would be the last thing she could do for Flora – to take perhaps the ugly fear of death out of her life. At other times, she was filled with panic, trapped, terrified, as this afternoon she was. She could not seem to settle to anything.

Suddenly the rain began to hiss down. She stood at the window watching. The delphiniums were such a sad blue against all the dripping green of grass and leaves. The rain drove like bayonets into the flower-beds. There was a rattle of thunder and at first she thought it was Miss Folley upstairs impatiently trying to shut a drawer that had stuck.

Whom to turn to? Mrs Secretan wondered. She often wondered. Lately, she had thought a great deal of her lost husband. She could have asked for his help in illness; but she could not ask her daughter.

Richard's car turned in at the gate and came slowly up the drive, rain bouncing off its roof. Incredulously, she watched it sweep round on the gravel and stop; then she hurried into the hall and opened the door.

She could tell at once, by his cheerful face, that it was all right; he had not come because anything was wrong with Flora.

'No, I just came to see you,' he said, in answer to her questions. 'I hoped you would be glad to see me.'

'Oh, I *am*, I *am*,' she said. When he had followed her into the drawing-room, she shut the door, leaned against it in an exhausted way, and said, 'I doubt if I have ever been so glad to see anyone in my life.'

He looked at her in surprise. She was very pale, thinner, her face as anxious as a frightened child's.

'You find me at the end of my tether,' she said, sinking down on the sofa. 'If I had known you were coming, I'd have put myself into a better frame of mind. What a day! I longed for some relief, and here you are! Like a miracle, an answer to a prayer.'

He sat down beside her on the sofa and looked at her with concern. 'My dear, are you ill?' he asked.

It could not be just a thunder-storm to have upset her so much.

'Yes, I'm afraid I am ill, Richard. And I've been afraid about it for such a very long time. But I don't want anybody worried. I don't want Flora worried.'

'What is it?'

'Aches and pains. Such a pain in my chest, you know.' It was a great relief to say it: it almost made it not be there.

'What does your doctor say?'

'I haven't seen him. I really haven't dared.'

'My dear Alice,' he began. He had never called her this before. Somehow, he had managed not to call her anything. He took one of her trembling hands and held it firmly. 'Before I leave this evening, I'm taking you to see your doctor. We'll find out the truth, and put your mind at rest.'

'It wouldn't be any use. He'd never *tell* me the truth – not if it were bad. We've been such good friends and neighbours.'

'Well, that's what we're going to do, none the less. We'll go down to his surgery the moment it's opened.'

'I've *never* been to his surgery,' she protested.

'We're going this evening. We'll sit there together and read *Punch*. And then I'll bring you home and you can have a good night's rest. You don't look as if you have for ages.'

'No, I haven't,' she murmured.

But suppose it's serious; suppose sleep's out of the question, both thought. I'd have to stay, he decided. Telephone Flora. Make up some rigmarole so that she won't be anxious.

Miss Folley brought in tea and looked at them both with curiosity. When she had gone, Mrs Secretan suddenly said flatly, 'I can't go, Richard I find I haven't the courage.'

She looked helplessly at the tea-tray, and then lifted the teapot. 'Not a very exciting tea, I'm afraid,' she said.

'Do you know what I think?' Richard said 'I think you need a complete change. Something really exciting. It can't be much fun, shut up endlessly with . . .' He waved a scone at the closed door.

'I have my friends in the village.' But not so many as I had, and no new ones, she thought.

'Something quite *different*,' he insisted, thinking hard. This conversation was to take her mind off the evening ahead.

'Now I look back,' she admitted. 'Everything seems to have been centred on Flora. I don't suppose any mother really gets over the loss of her daughter. Oh, what a thing to say – to you of all people Perhaps I made her too much my whole life. It's possible, you know And since she went, I've been adrift. I don't feel I've been wasting my life; but I haven't been making the most of it lately, and that gives one such a nasty feeling of guilt. Well, it's no use now to fret about it.'

'It *is* use now. It's not too late to live until you die. Think what you could do,' he added hastily. 'Really, you're awfully fortunate. For instance, you have plenty of money to travel.'

'My dear, I haven't travelled since Edward died.'

'Then now; *now*, for heaven's sake.'

'Oh, my goodness, I couldn't on my own. And, in any case, what capital I have I wanted to leave to little Alice.'

'No. It's not a thing to do. Money's to be used up, not left behind one. Alice will make her own way. And I'm not hard up for half a crown.'

'Of course . . . you know I didn't mean . . .I simply . . .'

'Children have their own world ahead of them. And I've no use for wills. When I read them in the newspapers,

I think, "Poor old so-and-so. Just couldn't manage to get through the last twenty thousand." '

He was speaking a little against his real views, in order to persuade her. 'Think of the places you could go to,' he went on. 'Florence, Rome, Greece, Turkey, Bangkok ...'

'Bangkok?' she echoed faintly.

'Yes.'

She looked at him in amazement; but by the time she had to fetch her hat and gloves to go with him, she was so filled with daring ideas that her pain seemed better already.

'I shan't be long,' she told Miss Folley.

'It's just on opening time,' said Richard, looking at his watch then winking at his mother-in-law.

'You won't tell Flora where we've been,' Mrs Secretan begged him, as she got into the car.

'No, I won't tell Flora,' he promised. But he hoped they would not have to wait too long.

*   *   *

No one came to see Flora that evening. The rain spinning down the streets, the complete disappearance of cabs, must have kept them away. Marooned by the weather, she felt rather dull and sad as she waited for Richard to come home.

All the day had been overshadowed by a dream of the night before, one in which she had come to her own house as a stranger. She had walked along Beatrice Crescent in a curious half-light, wondering who she was, wondering why the laburnum tree in the garden had been cut down. Inside the house, everything had been changed – the rose prints in the drawing-room were gone, the flowered curtains were plain; there were no photographs about the rooms, and the glass over the fireplace was blank when she looked in it. Terror mounted in her, as she went about the house. Some one else's clothes hung in her cupboard – drab coats, horrible woollen dresses, like those in jumble sales she had helped at as a girl. Mrs Lodge was still in the kitchen, but she did not glance up and, though Flora struggled to speak, she remained unaware, as she sat at the table stringing red-currants through the prongs of a fork – the fruit dropped like little drips of blood into a basin: Mrs Lodge's lips were set in a thin line. The voice-struggle put Flora into a panic and she fled from the kitchen, up, up, without touching the stairs, to Alice's nursery: and there was the child, tucked up and sleeping peacefully. Whoever it was who had taken over her home and made so many alterations, had kept Mrs Lodge, and Alice. But what of Richard? There was not a trace of him to be seen. Had he been thrown out with the pictures of roses, and all the other pretty things? She did not know whether she wanted him to have been kept or discarded, and woke up wondering, glad to find him in bed beside her, snoring softly. She had once heard that snoring is a sign of suppressed anger, so she pushed his shoulder gently, to stop him *He* had nothing to be angry about.

As it was Mrs Lodge's day off, Flora had made a special dish for Richard's dinner – his favourite steak pie. She had a feeling today that she must propitiate him, draw him close to her with every gyve she could find. This particular gyve, the steak pie, she kept taking out of the oven, then putting it back. The pastry seemed to be hardening.

She wandered about the house – went up to Alice several times: but as in the dream Alice slept peacefully, her legs on top of the light coverlet, her hair stuck to her head like damp feathers.

Richard was dreadfully late, and Flora began to feel wretched. Wherever he was – goodness knew where, somewhere, anywhere, in the growing darkness and the rain – she could not reach him and plead with him, let him know how upset she was, how the sacramental pie was spoiling, how the vision of Elinor Pringle kept coming into her mind. He had said that Elinor was unlovable; but his words had proved only a temporary comfort. She kept offering them to herself and rejecting them: yet she wanted so much to accept them.

'Is it jealousy,' she whispered through the lattice of her fingers, laced nervously together. The word – the name for what she was suffering – frightened her. It was one that had had no meaning before.

When Richard at last came home, he found her in the dark drawing-room, crying In the kitchen, for the fourth time, the pie had been taken from .the oven. She ran downstairs, out of his embrace, and put it back. Richard followed her.

'Is Alice all right?' he asked, for he could get no sense out of Flora, no explanation of her tears, only more tears. What a day! he thought. The earlier, trickier business interview was now the least of his stresses, was almost forgotten. Virtue had gone out of him, and he was hungry, soon would be past eating, though – the sick, sore feeling in his stomach coming on.

'I went to see your mother,' he said.

'But not all that time. She would never have let you stay so long and worry me so much.'

Well, he had made his promise that he would say nothing about the visit to the doctor, and he would keep it, he decided glumly. The risk of worrying Flora about her mother's health – and the doctor's reassuring words, his dismissal of anxieties had surely cancelled the risk – seemed to him less important than having Flora worried about his whereabouts. On the other hand, no doubt her mother now felt a little ashamed of herself, would feel sensitive about all the sick fancies she had had. She would not want Flora to know of those.

'I'll have some pie now,' he said. 'Will you?'

'I couldn't eat.'

'Well, I'll just have it here.' He sat down at the kitchen table.

'But I've laid it in the dining-room. And Mrs Lodge might come in. I'm sure the pie's not even warm yet. Oh, Richard, *where* have you been? If you knew what an evening I've had.'

'I take the trouble to go and see your own mother, and when I get back I'm accused of all sorts of unnamed things.' He had begun to shout; his stomach was curdling, going sour. 'What the hell do you think I've been doing? Where do you think I've been?'

She was silent, stopped crying and just looked at him. Then, very slowly, she went to the dresser drawer and took out a knife and fork.

'Don't bother!' he said. 'I've *had* it. I don't want anything now. You think I've been with Elinor Pringle, don't you ? '

She laid the knife and fork on the table, but said nothing. He pushed them aside.

'Oh, I see it now. That woman's on your mind, isn't she? Well, I can put it at rest. I can tell you that she's away – she's gone away to the seaside with her husband. Southend, or Margate, or some such place. To a conference.'

'I know she doesn't take any interest in politics, Richard.'

'You're calling me a liar. She's gone, I say.'

'Oh, don't shout at me. Please don't shout at me. I'm so sorry. I'm so ashamed. I was just so anxious, and time dragged, and my head filled up with horrible ideas, and I had such a nasty dream – a nightmare, really – it's been with me all day,' She babbled on. He couldn't understand what she was talking about, but as she became peaceably contrite, his anger receded and when she put the pie in front of him, he rearranged his knife and fork and watched her cutting into the crust. She put some sad-looking vegetables on the table and he began to eat.

After a while, she went over and kissed his brow and its furrows smoothed out. 'Forgive me,' she pleaded.

'Only if you never have such thoughts again,' he said, sensing his mastery. 'You must promise to trust me.'

'Yes, of course.'

She sat and watched him eating. When he had finished, he said, 'Now I'll tell you. I am sending your mother half round the world. That was why I was so long – trying to persuade her to go.' Surprised, and humble, Flora listened to him. 'She badly needs a holiday, a change. She hasn't been away for years.'

'She went to my uncle's for a fortnight last autumn,' Flora pointed out. 'And, anyway, she's so contented at home. She has all her old friends about her, and Miss Folley so devoted. Won't she be awfully lonely if she goes away?'

'It will do her good, take her out of herself.'

They were still discussing it, when Mrs Lodge returned.

'I'm sorry,' Richard said to her. 'I was so late home, it didn't seem worth while taking it all upstairs.'

'That's all right, sir,' she said, her face stern with disapproval.

*　　*　　*

After they had been lying in bed for a while, Flora asked softly, 'Richard! Richard, how did you *know* that Elinor is away?'

But Richard pretended to be asleep.

*　　*　　*

The next morning, Mrs Secretan woke up, ready as usual to review her situation with courage; then, gently, the realisation washed over her that no courage was needed.

Dear, dear Richard! she thought, staring up at the ceiling, her eyes swimming with tears of relief and gratitude. He had done more for her than any person in her life; Flora, even.

She got up and went to the window – the morning was hazy, the sun breaking gently through. The sky was like rice-paper.

She could at last enjoy what she loved, instead of being pained by it – her garden; the river; the world beyond, as much of it as she desired. 'I shall be keeping an eye on you,' Doctor Wilson had said. This had given her confidence, a feeling of security and of having been taken over; but there wouldn't be any more pains: they had dissolved there, in his surgery, the previous evening. The dreaded names of diseases had suddenly lost their potency – cancer, angina pectoris, coronary thrombosis.

She dressed and went downstairs, out into the garden, which was washed bright from last night's rain, full of floating strands and webs. Yet all that heavy rain had not washed the roses clean. Close to the walls, the blight was thick on the stems of buds, like thick, embroidered stitches of bright green. She would have to be busy again: not desultory, and half-hearted, as she had been of late.

Flora's doves were walking on the roof; other birds came down on to the lawn, stabbing their beaks between the blades of grass, into the rain-softened earth. The landscape was cleansed, made radiant; renewed, as her heart was.

She went out of the garden and walked along the towing-path. She had walked here with Edward, and with Flora, and now was quite content, walking alone. The river this morning was almost milk-white, misty, speared with brilliant, emerald reeds. The little almond-scented, yellow lilies were still clenched tight, would open later when the sun grew strong. She saw a heron, then a kingfisher, though both were so much rarer than when she had come to this place as a young woman.

After a while, she turned, and began to walk back. I'm hungry, she thought exultantly.

Miss Folley, from her bedroom window, had seen the

track of footprints across the wet lawn. She got up and went downstairs to cook the breakfast. When Mrs Secretan entered the house by the back door, she smelt bacon and tomatoes frying, coffee percolating.

'I'm so hungry,' she said, going into the kitchen.

'You ought to change your shoes. They're wet,' Miss Folley said.

'It doesn't matter. Do you know, what we'll do today is give ourselves a little treat. We'll have a car and go out to lunch. *The Compleat Angler*, or somewhere like that. Would you like to?'

Miss Folley's face brightened. 'I ordered the chops,' she said.

'They will do for tomorrow.'

Mrs Secretan turned a piece of toast on the grill. 'We're getting too set in our ways,' she said. 'We mustn't waste the summer doing nothing.' She hummed a little tune, watching the toast.

'Well, it would be very nice,' Miss Folley said. 'It really would be very nice indeed.'

Sixteen

LIZ CORBETT, creature of rules, of disciplined habits, had spent the summer days indoors. Her studio was hot and stuffy; but she was only vaguely aware of discomfort, standing before the easel, her swollen-veined feet bare on the dusty floor-boards.

'Where's the enchantment gone?' Patrick rather affectedly asked one evening, as she turned her latest finished painting from the wall to show him.

'I don't want to enchant people. I want to shake them up,' she said. 'People under spells are half dead.'

All the feathers, and the flowers and shells were broken and torn. The pale faces of the girls were disorganised, the features reassembled into stronger, but unfamiliar forms. None of the past was wasted, but seemed to have been subject to fission: the new paintings were a form of schizo-genesis, Patrick thought, propping the canvas on the arms of a chair and stepping back.

'As far as I'm concerned,' he said, 'you're on your own now. I'm not there any longer.'

He felt sadly deprived of an old magic her painting had had for him, and resented the limit to his appreciation.

'I've a lifetime's work in my head,' Liz said, not having listened to him. 'Some explorations to be made.' She had never before wanted to talk about work; had seen no useful point in doing so; but now a yeasty excitement, almost like drunkenness, impelled her to it.

'I shan't be able to keep up from this point,' he said, 'but if you put your shoes on, I'll take you down to the pub for supper.'

She searched vaguely for them, found a pair of sandals

under the bed, one with a buckle missing; then began to look for a comb, but soon gave up.

She carried the broken sandal down the stairs. In the street, she put it on and limped along beside him into the pub.

The sight of the bottle of bright red sauce on the table, congealed and sticky round the stopper, almost made Patrick heave. But he really did not think Liz clean enough to be taken to the hotel instead.

She was happy where she was, a good day's work off her shoulders. When some fish wrapped in a yellow, shrinking batter was put in front of them, she stretched across the table for the sauce bottle, shook it energetically, and poured a dollop on to her plate. Patrick looked aside. Then, hesitantly, he extracted a piece of fish from the middle of the batter, and ate it doubtfully.

She had the effect on him of making him seem over-dainty to himself, old-maidish. He sipped his wine. It had been a mistake to order it, and doing so had caused a little commotion; the landlord had to take keys and leave the bar to see what he could find. What he had found was fairly horrible. Patrick put the glass down again and re-sumed his search for morsels of fish inside the batter. He was not really at ease in pubs.

'Aren't you eating that?' Liz asked. 'Because if you won't, I will,' She kept spearing bits off his plate with her fork and popping them into her mouth. She waved away a fly – of which there were a good many circling about them – and knocked over her glass. She looked at the wet tablecloth with indifference, and reached for the bottle of wine and refilled her glass, before Patrick could do so for her.

I wish I were with Meg, he thought. Dear, peaceful, gentle Meg. He had come all this way to see her – and it was not a Friday – as soon as he had heard that she was ill. He had found her lying in bed, a little feverish from influenza, and it had seemed quite clear to him that she wished he had not come, that she wanted to be alone, not having to talk or listen, just drifting in and out of sleep, waiting patiently for the fever to pass. He had gently sponged her face and wrists, smoothed her hair, arranged some grapes on a plate beside her and brought her the two thinnest slices of bread-and-butter he had ever cut in his life, and watched her turning them drily, dutifully in her mouth. But she was so full of apologies, gratitude, anxiety lest he should have germs from her, that he decided he was unsettling her, and said goodbye.

'I left some smoked salmon between two plates in the kitchen cupboard,' he told Liz. 'If you could give her that for lunch, Kit can see to her supper. The key is hanging from a string inside the letter-box.'

'Don't fuss,' said Liz. 'I'll fix it.'

'She might like her sheets changed. . . .'

'Don't fuss.'

He could not imagine Liz being much of a nurse, but he had made her promise to do what she could. It was a pity that Flora had gone to stay with her mother for a day or two. She would have been lavish with sympathy and delicacies in such a situation.

When Liz had finished her fish – and Patrick's – she leaned back in her chair and, for the first time during the meal, looked at him. Replete, he thought, glancing away from her, afraid for a moment that she might belch. She pressed her finger-tips into some crumbs on her plate, and licked them. Plates were now quite clean. Nothing was left.

'How's that awful Flora woman?' she suddenly asked, as if thoughts of the world, of other people, could enter her head now that she had finished eating.

'Flora's not awful. What on earth do you mean? You don't know her.'

'Don't I just!'

'I dote on Flora. I won't have a word . . .'

'I know what I know,' Liz said cryptically. He finished his glass of wine, took his wallet from his pocket, bored with her mysteries.

'I shall have to go,' he said. 'And you won't forget about tomorrow.'

But she wasn't going to waste words on any more of those assurances. She slid her foot back into her broken sandal and clopped awkwardly across the bar. Outside, they said goodbye, and he walked off towards the station. He glanced back once and saw her standing in her doorway. She waved her sandal at him, and called goodnight again.

*　　*　　*

Patrick's visit had only made Meg more miserable. It was so kind of him to have come, she thought – and not on a Friday, either; but the room, and particularly herself lying in it, seemed so sordid to her that his presence had mortified her.

She had not had the strength to tidy her bedroom, and all the time he was sitting there, she had been irked by the sight of the disorder – the dressing-gown dropped to the floor, a dirty glass with a spoon in it, her clothes draping a chair, with dangling suspenders, and a slip, with a shoulder strap she had torn in her feverish haste to crawl into bed the night before.

If only she could have washed, or brushed her hair, she thought, lying tousled and sweating in the crumpled sheets, shrinking with horrified embarrassment as he came close to her and dabbed timidly at her face with a wet flannel and smoothed her tangled hair back from her forehead.

When he had gone, she tried not to cry, tried to reason away her shame. I couldn't take anything from him with grace, she thought mournfully.

It was different when Kit came home. She was glad and relieved to see him, and very grateful that he had given up an outing with the girl he knew at work. He had hurried back to Meg and came bounding upstairs with a bag of grapes.

'Oh, I see you've got some,' he said. 'Mine aren't such nice ones. Who came?' He sat down by the window, eating grapes from the bag, and spitting pips out into the garden.

'Patrick.'

Kit made a sarcastic noise. 'There go the Adalats for their evening walk,' he said, looking out of the window, at the family from next door setting out. 'Mrs has a pink sari and stiletto heels, Pa a double-breasted blazer and winkle-pickers, little girl a big blue bow on top of her head, carries a plastic Donald Duck.'

He watched them going sedately down the road. Through the open window, they could hear boats hooting on the river and, very faintly, a band playing Gilbert and Sullivan in the Public Gardens. Soon it would play no more; for the summer season was nearly over.

When the Adalats had disappeared, Kit turned back to Meg, glanced round the room and decided to tidy it as best he could. 'Shall I bung all this lot into a drawer?' he asked, gathering up her clothes.

She nodded. To have it put out of sight would be something. He pottered about, straightening things, and Meg closed her eyes tightly, not able to watch his clumsy movement, ashamed of her impatience.

'Poor old Meg,' he suddenly said, and it was not just because she had influenza that he did so. 'And how was Patrick?' he went on, trying to be kind.

'Oh, I hope he hasn't caught anything from me,' Meg said fretfully. 'I hope *you* don't, either.'

'You know I don't catch things. And if *he* does, it won't be the end of the world: it's only 'flu.'

'Who would look after him?'

There was a silence. They both felt that they knew who probably would not. Then Kit, in a different voice, said, 'No woman would ever play the devil with him as that boy does.'

He had never referred to Frankie before, and the moment he had done so, he was alarmed that he should have chosen such a moment, such a situation.

Meg only turned her head wearily on the pillow and said, 'You know that *anyone* can play the devil with *anyone*.'

'I didn't. . . . I wish I hadn't said that.'

'No, no, it doesn't matter. We both know. Everybody knows. What are you going to have for your supper?'

'I'll soon find something.'

He went downstairs, and she heard him clattering about, dropping saucepans, filling the kettle. She slipped into a doze, and it seemed a long time later that she woke again. Kit was standing over her. He helped to hoist her up against her pillows and put a tray in front of her. There was a cup of tea and a boiled egg as hard as a stone. He watched her – with a look of pride and affection – as she began to eat.

'And when you've finished that, I'll make your bed for you,' he said.

'That would be nice.'

'Egg's a bit over-done, isn't it?'

'Not really. Have you had yours?'

'Just going to. Is there anything else you'd like? I found some chocolate cake in a tin.'

'No more, thank you.' With relief, she gave up the tray and slid down in the bed. 'Thank you, Kit. It was so good of you. I'll be better tomorrow,' she promised.

Seventeen

ELINOR escaped from the bright-red hotel on the esplanade to mingle with the holiday-makeıs. It was drizzling,
and all the town's inhabitants seemed to be on the move,
aimlessly shuffling and drifting about the streets, rain-
coated, plastic-hooded, ugly, staring into shop-windows,
thronging steamy Woolworths, licking ice-creams, trying
to make the best of their belated holidays.

The tide was in and rasped the shingle. From the distant fun fair, came the thudding, rolling noises of the giant
coaster, and screams – wave after wave of high-pitched
screams.

Elinor's escape was from what was called a 'get-together'
in the bar after the usual meeting. Geoffrey and his col-
leagues would all come in together, jovial and anticipatory,
relieved – most of them – to have put the morning's business behind them. 'And now what have *you* been up to?'
Some of the older men would ask Elinor. 'Spending all
your hubby's money?' She found it an unenlightened
approach to the economics of marriage, but was mag-
nanimous enough to believe it insincere. Those chaffing
gallantries had happened yesterday, and the day before,
and the day before that. There were one or two serious
young women, who did not want to put the meeting behind
them, and who would sit and continue to talk about it to
Geoffrey across Elinor, who did not seem to be there, as
far as they were concerned.

There had been no point in her coming to this place.
When she was alone, then that was what she was: and
when all the business was done and Geoffrey free to be
with her, he had to be with the otheıs, too. He even danced

– very badly – with a stout mayoress or a thin lecturer in economics – or what he called one of the Party battle-axes – trundling them sedately round the room. He would never have danced for any but a political reason. Conferences were held to keep up the morale of the party workers, and on these occasions, he was indefatigably jolly. Elinor had seen quite a new side to him; but she could not develop a new side to herself: she had dismally failed in gaiety, and had had the added misery of offending people, had met too many strangers and could not remember their faces, let alone their names, and so defaulted her husband, growing more and more nervous and incoherent.

This was her first escape, the first time she had not felt able to sit out the get-together. It was not much of an escape. The town seemed to her to be England at its worst, full of people trying to enjoy themselves and not managing it for various reasons – perhaps chiefly those of the weather and the deeply-rooted dullness it had caused. Girls in cowboy hats affected high spirits, walking arm-in-arm along the promenade, singing: they were strident, but not gay. Elderly people sat in the porches of private hotels, above the spreading pink hydrangeas and clumps of golden privet. Passively, they were waiting for lunch, to file into those dining-rooms Elinor could see behind net curtains, and to sit down at the tables with the vases of plastic flowers. The Albemarle, The Waldorf, The Clarence, were the grand names the little hotels had.

Towards the pier, this gentility was lost in a confusion of fun fairs, Bingo parlours, fish and chip shops, and old-fashioned pubs with Ladies Only bars. Part of a child's holiday pleasure, apparently, was to be pushed through the turnstiles on to the pier to see the Chamber of Horrors, with its Spanish Inquisition Set Piece and Mediaeval Torture Chamber; or to have a photograph taken, sitting astride a mangy-looking stuffed donkey.

In its gilded pagoda, the band was playing. The con-

ductor – a small bent man with a waxed moustache –
looked as if he were whipping up a pudding with his baton.
One or two people, hunched up in mackintoshes, with
damp newspapers on their heads, sat listening amongst
the rows of empty seats; but when the rain began to
quicken from a drizzle to a steady fall, even they gave up
and moved on, leaving the band to finish to themselves
something very pom-pom of Messager.

Rain hissed hard into the bright, clean shingle and the
crowds scurried for shelter. Elinor was pleased that she
would be able to explain how she had been caught in the
deluge and delayed. By the time she arrived back at the
hotel, the gathering in the bar would have dispersed; they
would have gone into the restaurant for lunch.

To get out of the rain, she turned into a dim, echoing
arcade, which smelled of damp, trodden sand, and candy
floss, and spent some time choosing a picture postcard to
send to Richard and Flora.

*　　*　　*

So here was the card confirming that Elinor was out of
town – just as Richard had said she was. Flora looked at it
again. There were some crudely-coloured gardens, and the
sea, with the pier like a thin arm and clenched fist reaching out into it. 'Simply ghastly!' Elinor had written on the
other side. Then why go? why stay? Flora wondered.

She had just come home from her mother's, where she
had found Mrs Secretan surrounded by travel brochures,
and full of schemes about them. To Flora's astonishment
she was quite seriously weighing the pros and cons – of
Hellenic tours ('might be too scholarly'), India ('But I
dare say it is spoiled, now that it doesn't belong to us'), the
Holy Land for Christmas.

'Yes, I might plump for the Holy Land for Christmas,'
she had told Flora, who had been deeply shocked. At
Christmas! she had thought in dismay. So what shall *we*

do? Christmas had always been a sacred time, with cherished customs, not one for taking oneself off to the Holy Land.

'I believe it's been terribly commercialised,' was all she could reply.

'I think you've rather unsettled Mother,' she said to Richard when he came home from work.

'Good! Jolly good.'

He bounced Alice on his knee and a thread of milk ran down her chin. Her eyes goggled and she belched; then she smiled at him, showing her two front teeth. Well, she can be sure of *me*, he thought. Until the day I die. And I'll see that everything she has is a damn sight better than anybody else's.

Being a parent sets mirrors round one, so that one can catch an oblique, surprising glimpse of other people, even of their previous lives. Richard suddenly saw his father as a young man, full of ambitious plans for his son, and he wondered if he, Percy, had ever danced *his* child on his knee, hurried home from work to do so; if he had felt this fierce protectiveness. It was one of the strangest ideas Richard had ever had, and it made him uneasy.

'A woman came for an interview,' Flora said.

'Any good?'

'She didn't like the stairs.'

'Pity.'

'No one's any good. Even if they were, I couldn't take to them.'

'Go on trying. Something will turn up.'

'And poor Meg telephoned. She sounded awfully low. Now Kit's got the 'flu and Meg has had to go back to work, because Miss Whatshername's away.'

Richard kept poking Alice in the stomach to make her laugh, and Flora wondered if he ought to.

'I'll go over tomorrow to see him,' she said. 'Mrs Lodge cooked some extra fish, and I can warm it up for him.'

'Is it wise, Flora? You'll catch the 'flu yourself, and give it to Alice.'

'All the same, I must go. I don't catch things, as you know. I'll have to put her to bed now. It's getting late.'

Richard handed the baby over and she grabbed at his hair, trying to stay with him. Really, a baby's flattery is devastating, he thought, straightening his tie, smoothing his hair. He poured himself out a drink and strolled about the room, feeling content. When Flora came back, he was looking at Elinor's postcard.

'Oh, that came by the afternoon post,' she said, off-handedly.

She had always collected picture postcards and kept them in a gilt rack in the downstairs lavatory, but when he had put this one aside, she tore it across and dropped it into the waste-paper basket.

Eighteen

Kit lay and groaned and talked to himself aloud. 'Who will come? Who will come?' he moaned pettishly. It seemed hours since Meg had gone off to work, and since then his case had altered. Now he had a pain at the base of his spine and at the back of his eyes. What's wrong with me? What's going wrong? he wondered, in the panicky way of a person who is seldom ill.

He wondered if it were meningitis which prevented one from looking upwards – or else made it impossible to do anything but. He had heard or read something of the kind, and wished now that he had paid more heed to it. Trying to roll his eyes back to look at the wall behind him, he very painfully succeeded. Or was it polio-myelitis? he wondered. Ought not someone to have seen that he was inoculated against it? In a flash, he had a clear picture of himself lying in an iron lung.

But I couldn't stand it, he thought in a panic. I haven't the patience. I wouldn't have that wonderful spirit some people have. I'd weep and shout and get into a state.

He had read in a newspaper of a woman who had spent years in an iron lung. She had to be fed, letters had to be read to her. Yet she was the life and soul of the hospital. 'My most cheerful patient,' the Matron had said.

But I shan't be like that, Kit decided. I shall curse all day long at the top of my voice. 'Your vocabulary!' they would reprimand him, in terrible nurses' voices.

Despair swept through him. Well, I can't take responsibility now; for myself, or anything else, he thought. I'll just be ill for ever. There won't be the fag of going to work, or the boredom of being there. I won't blame myself any more for being a failure, and no one else will dare to. Someone will have to look after me.

He slept for a while and when he woke, and before he opened his eyes, he could hear someone moving stealthily about, the floor-boards gently creaking, as someone came and went. A cup was put gently on to a saucer. The closing door brushed over the carpet.

Everything had subtly changed since he had fallen asleep. The patch of sunlight had moved across the bed, and when he opened his eyes he saw a jar of dahlias that had not been there before. Soon, he heard someone coming upstairs; the door opened again, and there was Flora, carrying a tray.

'You will try to eat it, won't you?' she said.

His delighted relief at seeing her made it out of the question that he should not try.

'Dearest, lovely Flora,' he murmured. His weakness gave him the idea of speaking to her as he would not have done in health.

She put her strong arms round him and hoisted him up against the pillows. He wanted to stay there in her arms, but she moved away and fetched the tray. It was very prettily arranged: he looked down at the smallest piece of fish he had ever seen in his life, palely golden, flecked with parsley and decorated by butterflies of lemon. He had not seen anything like it since his mother died.

'You are so good,' he said, staring without appetite at the tray. 'So awfully good.'

'I'll leave you while you eat it. There are some things I want to do downstairs,' she said briskly.

When she had gone, he began to eat, staring before him, his hair worked up into a cockscomb from the pillows, his mind as nearly vacant as it could be. It was just after midday, he thought; for he heard the Adalat child come home from school, rattling the letter-box and calling through it to her mother. Then the street, the room, were quiet again: there was just the peaceful sound of his knife and fork on the plate. The fish, though so small, had taken him a long time to eat, and he was grateful to Flora for knowing that that was all he could take. He was grateful to her for everything; for she seemed to know all that there was to be known about people. He pined for her to come back upstairs to him.

When he had finished, he pushed the tray aside, put on his dressing-gown and went, on feeble legs, along the passage to the lavatory. She was making his bed when he returned – pillows were arranged like an armchair and there was a splendid tension on the bottom sheet. He slid into it, feeling worn out after his walk along the passage, and she drew the bedclothes gently over him and handed him a cup of tea.

'Do try to drink it,' she urged him, and sat down by the window with a cup for herself.

'Did you have something to eat?' he asked her.

She nodded.

'You are so good to come,' he said presently.

'Don't be silly.' She took the empty cup from him, and he lay back and closed his eyes.

'Suppose I have some dreadful, catching thing wrong with me,' he suggested, in a pathetic voice. 'I couldn't bear anything to happen to you.'

'What dreadful thing could be wrong with you?' she asked. 'It's only 'flu, and you'll be better in a day or two, and be able to work again, like Meg.'

'Don't mention it,' he implored her. 'And this can't be just what Meg had. I feel so bloody ill.'

'So did she, while it lasted. Even now she feels weak and depressed. I think one always does. You must be prepared for it.'

He longed for her to come nearer to him and hold his hand. It seemed to him that then he could die happy – a better thing than to have her sitting hour after hour, day after day, beside his iron lung. Even she would in the end tire of that. Other alternatives, like taking up the old life again, or of trying to begin a new one, without faith or inspiration, he had not the strength to consider.

'I can't hear you from over there,' he said. A lorry went rattling down the street and drowned whatever she was saying. When she had moved her chair closer to the bed, she repeated it. 'Would you like me to read to you?'

'Talk to me.' He groped for her hand and held it. 'You're so beautiful, Flora. I've always adored you.'

'What a sweet, kind thing to say!' Her words were as cool as the hand she put on his forehead.

'I wish I could do something terrific to please you, make you admire me a little,' he went on, 'but I'm quite useless. It was pointless, having those plans for me.'

'The 'flu is making you sorry for yourself,' she said.

'That stupid job I've got, for instance. I can't see where it can lead.'

'There's no need for it to lead anywhere. Just look upon it as a temporary thing.'

'But I can't do anything *else*.' He closed his eyes, turned aside his head.

'"You know perfectly well that I don't believe that.' Almost as if she were attempting to hypnotise him, she clasped his hand firmly in both of hers, and leaned forward, imparting strength, willing it. She *could* do it: she felt that she could. 'Kit, dear, I truly believe in you.'

'Yes, I think you do. It's that that worries me when I fail.'

'Between us we'll arrange something; but you don't have to worry now.'

'It's now that I've got the time to worry. I can't help it.'

'Well, for one thing, I hear that Geoffrey Pringle's writing another play. *This* time perhaps we can do something about it. Yes, I think I know of a way. Richard might have a word with Elinor,' she said, in a resolute voice.

He sighed.

'I know you have this gift,' she said.

Her words made him even more light-headed. He seemed to float, and her clear voice echoed about him. Even this unlikely chance of being alone with her, of their actually being hand-in-hand, could not keep him awake. His mind became blurred and muddled as he drifted into sleep.

When he awoke, the room was darker. All of the sunlight had gone from it, and Flora stood by the window, wearing her coat.

'I'm sorry if I woke you, but I have to go,' she said.

'I'm furious that I fell asleep.'

'It's the best thing.'

'Not while you're here.'

'I've left some supper ready for when Meg gets home. I'm afraid I can't come tomorrow, because Richard has asked someone to lunch. I hope you'll be better and, darling, promise not to worry about anything.'

He promised. She kissed him or, rather, laid her cheek briefly against his, and went downstairs.

As she was getting into her car, a short, ungainly young woman with straggly hair came along the street. She stared blankly at Flora, then opened the gate and went up the path. Flora hesitated for a moment before starting the engine, then she saw the girl pull the key through the letter-box, open the door, and go inside.

* * *

As Flora drove home, she felt invigorated, sure that she had accomplished something for Kit, had left him uplifted and inspired. It was the gift *she* had – to be able to do this for him, to give him something to lie and think about and hope for.

When she reached home, Patrick was there waiting for her. 'How was Kit?' he asked.

'I think I managed to put new heart and hope into him.'
Her words were like the warning sound of a maroon.
'I must try to go to see him tomorrow,' he said.

* * *

'That was your goddess, wasn't it?' Liz asked Kit,
standing by the window eating an apple.

He didn't answer, wished she had not come, for he
wanted to cling fast to the mood of Flora's visit, to go over
all the words of hope again and again.

'I looked in to see if there was anything I could do,' Liz
said, looking round the room. 'But I see there's not. The
healing hand has passed over everything. That's fine. I can
get back to work.'

'It was kind of you to come,' he said quickly.

'So *I* thought.'

He closed his eyes, as if he could not keep awake. When
she had finished crunching her apple, she threw the core
out of the window, and went downstairs, slamming first
the front door, so that the house shook, and then the gate.
He gritted his teeth. Even noise could make sweat spring
from him.

'I know you've got this gift,' Flora had said. He repeated
it in his mind, over and over again, shifting the emphasis
from one word to another, as he tried to recall her firm
and certain tone.

As the time went by, and he lay there alone, the feeling
of euphoria slipped away from him and when it had gone,
he was worse off than ever, lowered as if by a worn-off
drug; there was no way out, and nothing for him. He
wanted to die.

* * *

Patrick did not go to see Kit the next day, for Frankie
arrived unexpectedly, having an afternoon off, and was

full of a new idea he had had for them to take an autumn holiday together.

Patrick knew that he could not spare the time to go away; and knew, too, that he deceived himself by being flattered by the suggestion. Half of him saw and understood what Frankie was, so that he was twice the victim – of his own perceptiveness, and of Frankie's capriciousness and greed.

Of course they would go, wherever Frankie chose – to Cannes, or Monte Carlo: it did not matter where, for it was sure to be the kind of resort where Patrick would sink into despondency. Before they went, he would have to work much harder than he cared to. And there would be other claims on his time. There always were. For instance, the next afternoon, instead of settling down at his desk, he felt obliged to go out to Towersey.

He could guess what mood he would find Kit in – depressed and upset after Flora's visit, and he blamed himself for not having gone the day before.

In the next-door garden to Meg's the Pakistani neighbour was clipping a privet bush. It was a very neat little garden, with decorative pebble work and white-washed stones and bright dahlias.

Patrick went up the path to the front door. The key was not hanging inside the letter box as usual, and this made him feel quite irritable and indignant. It was bad enough having to give up his afternoon. He put his hand through and groped, but could find nothing; he tried to peer through into the dark passage. Then nausea and panic overcame him. He could smell gas.

There was silence everywhere, except for Mr Adalat's rhythmically clipping shears. Patrick turned and called out to him. 'There's something wrong going on, and I can't get in.' Senselessly, he lunged his shoulder against the door. Better break a window, he thought. He had never been a man of quick action, and could not think which way to turn.

But Mr Adalat had dropped his shears, and was through his own front door in a flash. Patrick, less nimbly, began to follow. I didn't want to be the first one there, he thought. And I shan't be. He had always been sure that in a crisis he would fail.

He entered the house, and a little girl pressed back against the passage wall as he passed. He went through the kitchen into the yard, where Mrs Adalat, wearing a cardigan over her sari, was looking over the low wall into the next back-yard, wringing her hands, her bracelets tinkling.

Fearfully, Patrick looked over the wall, Kit was lying sprawled face-down on the bricks, and Mr Adalat was kneeling over him. He pushed at Kit's shoulder-blades, pressed his knee into the small of his back and suddenly a thin stream of vomit flew out of Kit's mouth.

Mrs Adalat put an orange-box by the wall and Patrick climbed up and jumped down on the other side. The smell of gas and vomit was horrible.

Now Mr Adalat was pumping Kit's arms backwards and forwards. 'He is not dead,' he said to Patrick. 'His head had fallen away from the oven. He must have hit it on the door.'

Blood was trickling from the side of Kit's forehead. His face was ghastly.

'I'll get a doctor,' Patrick said. That was something he could do. But Mr Adalat gave him a shrewd look and shook his head. 'It is better not,' he said.

'It is better not,' his wife echoed with certainty over the wall. It was as if they were familiar with the circumstances, perfectly experienced; and Patrick was like a child to them.

'I can't take the responsibility,' he said. 'His sister . . .'

'He will be quite all right.' Mr Adalat now gathered Kit up against himself, felt his forehead, and then the pulse in his wrist. 'Open the front door,' he told Patrick. 'When the house is clear, we'll put him to bed, and he will sleep for a little.'

Patrick went quickly through the kitchen, without taking a breath. He flung open the front door and all the windows upstairs and down. On a table in the passage were two letters – one addressed to Meg, one to Flora. He put them in his pocket. Then he went back to the yard and stood by Kit, who began to moan and move his lips. Mr Adalat nodded with satisfaction.

'Look, I don't think we're doing the right thing,' Patrick said.

Mr Adalat could not be bothered to answer. He was wiping vomit from Kit's face and neck.

'At any rate, I must telephone his sister and say there's been an accident.'

'Sure,' said Mr Adalat. 'Now you and I will carry him upstairs, and I will sit by him while you go to the phone-box.'

The wind was streaming through the house. Curtains flapped, were blown back into the rooms.

Poor boy! thought Patrick, when they had put Kit into bed. He had created appalling problems, trying to solve others.

Mr Adalat sat down primly at the side of the bed, his hands folded patiently in his lap.

'Are you sure?' Patrick began.

'You go to the phone-box; but be sure to tell her not to worry.'

Mrs Adalat was in the front garden when Patrick went out. The little girl stood close to her.

'I am going to telephone his sister,' Patrick said, feeling he had to make the explanation.

She nodded gravely. 'At the corner, by the shop,' she directed him.

Going down the street, he prayed. 'Please God, give me the words to tell her.' But were there any words? None that he could think of.

Nineteen

'He might try to do it again,' Meg said to Patrick.

'People don't, you know; once they've tried,' he said, as casually as he could.

'I don't think that's true.'

Patrick didn't think so, either.

He was with her as much as he could be, during what seemed to them like Kit's convalescence from death. They were days of shame and embarrassment. Kit got up, he loitered glumly about the house, secretly wincing whenever he went into the kitchen, or glimpsed Mr Adalat returning from night shift. He had no reference as to how to behave. To keep being apologetic to the remorseful only deepened the consternation. Nothing true was really said between himself and Meg. Patrick had made an attempt, had asked a question or two and been painfully endured. When they were alone, he had handed over the two letters addressed to Meg and Flora. Colour had sprung smartly across Kit's face, as if it had been struck with a whip.

'We don't know how to behave to one another,' Meg said to Patrick. 'There's an awful ravine between us, and my voice simply doesn't carry across it. But the worst thing is that, even if I could make him hear, I really haven't anything to say. I can't get over the truth. That he wanted to be done with us. It's so difficult to forgive – that one has been of so little account.'

There was also Flora for her to try to forgive.

'He was quite happy,' she insisted. 'Before all this, he was quite happy.'

Trying to convince herself made her vehement.

It was Sunday. He had persuaded her to come out and

walk by the river – for her own good, and because he knew
that her constant presence was unnerving Kit, who obviously felt as if he were on probation.

Autumn was in the air, and in this fine weather, trees
had an edge of light to them.

'He had given up all thoughts of that acting nonsense,'
Meg went on. 'I thought he was quite in love with that
girl in the office – Caroline. He was well away from Flora
and those little tea-parties when she used to put those
impossible ideas into his head.'

Patrick listened gravely. He had heard it all several
times during this weekend.

'She upset him ' Meg said. 'Dragged him back to her,
made him feel a failure again.'

'He'll go back to work. It will be just as it was before.
All this will be forgotten,' Patrick said.

They sat down on a seat and watched a string of barges
going up the river.

'I'm so tired,' she said. 'Fagged out. Oh, excuse me.'
She yawned, patted her mouth with her fist.

She was pale and thin. It was *she* who needed the holiday, Patrick thought. He would have liked to take her
away, to the sort of place they would both like. But he
wouldn't: he would go to the South of France with Frankie.

'I feel I don't want to see Flora ever again,' said Meg.
'She has so much, and always wants more.'

'To harm anyone is the last thing she'd ever have in
mind. She would be astonished to hear you talking like this.'

'Someone ought to tell her then; if she can't see it for
herself.'

'There's no point in adding to the general misery,' he
said gently.

'No.' Her voice flagged suddenly.

'Let's go back. It's not warm enough for sitting about.'

'Liz Corbett agrees with me about Flora,' Meg said as
they walked on.

'What on earth has it got to do with Liz Corbett?'

'She seems fond of Kit.'

'Then he *had* better look out.'

'She was there that afternoon, after Flora left; and then again the next day when she went to see him, she said he was in a bad way. He wouldn't eat anything.'

'If *she* cooked it, I can't blame him.'

'He turned his face to the wall, she said. He was still like it when I got home. He wouldn't talk.'

Patrick knew. That day had been gone over and over. He supposed it was natural, and it was not so tiring to lend an ear now, because his replies came automatically.

As they turned into Alpha Terrace, they met the Adalat family going for their Sunday walk. The Adalats had lapsed into their former reserve, and bowed stiffly.

At home, Kit had begun to get the tea. The kettle was singing, and he was clumsily cutting bread and butter.

*　　*　　*

The next day was Flora's birthday. For a treat, she had breakfast in bed, and sat up with the tray beside her, her presents and wrapping-paper all over the eiderdown. Richard brought up the post and she opened her cards. There was one from Patrick, but nothing from Meg. That must surely come later, for Meg never forgot.

Richard, watching her, thought how like a child she looked, really pleased, really excited by her birthday.

'I must get off to work,' he said, standing up and glancing at his watch. He was all ready, wearing his dark suit. Monday morning. There was always a strangeness about it – people hurrying through the streets, out of the Underground stations, off buses, hastening to take up the threads again, but somehow subtly changed by Sunday.

'Richard!'

He turned quickly to see Flora's altered face, her startled eyes, her trembling hands holding out a letter. He took it and read, frowning. He picked up the envelope and looked at the postmark. S.E. 12.

Flora had her fingers pressed to her lips, was staring at him.

'What does it mean?' she cried.

'I don't know,' he said slowly, reading again.

'What does it mean,' she said again – 'that Kit tried to kill himself? Who can have sent it? Why don't they say; why don't they sign it? Are they mad?'

'"No point in putting my name. You don't know me,"' Richard read out. 'What a bloody horrible thing for any-one to do.'

'Let me read it again!' She took the letter and stared at it with revulsion. It was scribbled in pencil on a piece of paper torn roughly from a sketching-pad. '*My* interfer-ence!' she said, in horrified amazement. 'Why do they blame *me*? I've tried and tried and tried to do all I could for Kit. There's no one I've tried *more* over. I'm so fond of him. I love him as if he were *my* brother, not just Meg's. And I know he wouldn't do anything like that. Why should he? Why, I only saw him the other day. And who in the world hates me so much as to send me this dread-ful . . .' She dropped the letter, put her face in her hands and began to weep – with long, shocked gasping sobs. Richard sat on the edge of the bed and put his arms round her. 'On my birthday, too,' she wept.

'Darling, I'm so sorry. It's probably someone who is quite mad.'

'But how do they know about *me*?'

'I don't know, but I'll find out. I'll take the filthy letter to the police.' He paused, then said, 'No, on second thoughts, of course I can't.'

'Those awful names! To be accused of such dreadful things. To be blamed . . . I know it isn't true. I've never done anything to harm anyone in all my life.'

'No; of course not, darling. No one is kinder.'

'Will you ring up Meg and make sure it isn't true?'

'I can't ring her up at her office about a thing like this.'

Flora stopped crying and looked up at him. 'She didn't send me a birthday card,' she said.

'Oh, that will come later,' he said. 'That's nothing to worry about.'

'All this about Kit being in love with me. You know that's all lies, don't you?'

'Yes, of course.'

'A boy of *that* age! Oh, I feel so sick, so terribly sick.'

She struggled from bed, and cards and wrapping-paper rustled to the floor. She went to the bathroom and Richard could hear her retching. He looked at his watch anxiously. He had an appointment in half an hour.

At the sight of her, when she returned, shivering violently, holding her wrap round her with blue hands, his heart ached with pity. It was Flora disintegrated, her poor face shattered with grief. He had never imagined that she could look like this. It was as if she had woken from a happy dream into a nightmarish reality. If he could, he would have done – would do – great violence to whoever had caused this change in her.

'Don't leave me, Richard.'

He took her in his arms and looked at his watch again over her shoulder. 'My love, I must. I'll come back to lunch. I promise I won't be gone long.'

'How can I find out what's happened?'

'I'll find out somehow. I'll think of a way.'

She let him go, turned away. 'Will you ask Mrs Lodge to come up?'

'Yes, of course. What will you tell her?'

'The truth,' Flora said. 'The truth.'

She collapsed on the bed and sobbed again.

He had to leave her. He went downstairs and called to Mrs Lodge, who went hurrying anxiously upstairs.

As he opened the front door, an errand boy came up the

path, with some red and pink carnations done up in cellophane.

*　　*　　*

Patrick was just getting into the stride of the day's work when the telephone rang. It was Richard ringing up from his office.

'Yes, it is true,' Patrick said cautiously. 'I'm afraid he did. . . . Well, perhaps not on the telephone, d'you think?' Tiredly, he rubbed his face, staring at the papers on the desk in front of him, and listened. 'Poor Flora,' he said after a while. 'So unpleasant. I'm most dreadfully sorry. No, of course I don't know who it could be.' (He had known straight away.) 'I'm most dreadfully sorry,' he said again. 'Yes, I'll go round at once.' He put down the telephone, tidied the papers on his desk, and went to get ready.

'Madam's not herself,' Mrs Lodge said when she opened the door to him. 'You see what you can do.' Then I can get on, she thought.

Flora was in the drawing-room surrounded by carnations. Her face was swollen, her lips puffy, her eyes bloodshot. Patrick put his arm round her, but she was so much taller than he that she might have been drawing him to her shoulder to comfort *him*.

'Richard rang me up,' he said, and added, when the tears began to run down her cheeks, 'It's only an anonymous letter. You're not the only one in the world to get one of those.'

'Well, have *you* ever had one?'

'Yes.'

She looked up through her tears, astonished. 'Whatever about?'

'I couldn't tell you.'

She looked quickly away, feeling she had had enough shocks for one morning. Her head ached, her lips were dry and salty.

211

'So it's all untrue – about Kit?' she asked.

'No.'

'You mean, he really tried to kill himself? Kit, of all people? Why did no one tell me?'

'I've come to tell you now.'

She sat, with her hand on her forehead, listening to him, and could find nothing to say until he'd finished. Then she got up and fetched the letter and its envelope from her desk, and handed it to him.

'There!' she said. 'Who on earth can have written it? Do you know? Please tell me.'

'Yes, I think I do; but the name would mean nothing to you, because it's no one you know. I'm so sorry, Flora dear.'

'Well, it isn't your fault, is it?'

'No. No, of course it isn't.' I blame myself far too much, he decided. Then he said, 'It's the most despicable thing for anyone to have done.'

'And *why* should anyone?'

'Perhaps in love with Kit.'

'A woman then?'

He said nothing.

'A rather horrible-looking young woman called there, just as I was leaving the other day.'

'Flora, do listen! Don't go on and on. It's useless. I should like to help if I can. . . .'

'But I don't understand anything any longer. If it means one can't be good to one's friends, and do the best for them, inspire and encourage them. . . .'

'People just aren't up to it, you know.'

'So you are turning against me, too?'

'I never shall. I never could.'

'But Meg must have done. She didn't come to see me this weekend. She hasn't remembered my birthday. Oh, it was so kind of *you* to remember, Patrick. Thank you very much,' she added childishly. 'I shall go to see her this evening – and Kit.' It would be dreadful, she thought. She did not know what to say to people who had been so near to death – and by their own hands, too.

'Don't go,' Patrick said. 'Let her come to you.'

'But she might *not* come.'

'She will, if you give her time. She doesn't much like to leave Kit alone at present.'

'I can't see how she can ever leave him alone for the rest of her life.'

'They're getting over it. Kit's better. I told you. I'm afraid I haven't done much good,' he said, getting up to go.

'Won't you have a drink?' she asked, trying to detain him.

'No, I must get back to work. Don't cry any more, Flora, for your lovely face's sake.'

But the moment he'd gone, she began again.

*   *   *

Meg did not come the next day, or the next. On the second day, Ba called on Flora, and found her very altered. Someone she knew had been very ill, she explained to Ba. The story must not go round, Patrick had warned her.

While Ba was out, Percy played the gramophone, very loud, beginning with the *Cockaigne Overture*. On the top of the bookcase he kept a special stick, which he used as a baton for conducting orchestras when he was alone. Sometimes there were complaints from the adjoining flat; but he had never in his life taken much notice of complaints.

His conducting was a hobby he had to keep for when Ba was out. He would not have revealed to anyone the great pleasure it gave him to take the orchestra safely through the Ride of the Valkyries or the last movement of Brahms's First Symphony – two of his favourites.

He took off his jacket – for it was exhausting work – then, just as he had brought in the woodwind and strings, the outer door slammed. He was building the music to a climax, and to have to discard it was like being interrupted when making love.

By the time Ba came into the room, he was sitting back in his arm-chair, twiddling his thumbs, but she noticed that he had beads of sweat on his forehead.

'Are you all right, honey?'

He opened his eyes, as if he had not heard her come in. 'Yes, of course I'm all right.'

'Why on earth are you sitting there in your shirt sleeves?'

'It's very close in here.'

I, wouldn't have thought so.' She went and laid a hand on one of the old-fashioned radiators, which scarcely gave out any heat. 'I went to Flora's. There's been some trouble there.'

'She'll get over it,' said Percy, not wanting to hear. He was put out, and cross with her for coming back so soon. She was always hanging about the house during the day, or abandoning him completely and going off to France.

The old order had been much better – to be alone in the daytime with his piano and his gramophone, to look forward to visiting his mistress in the evenings. He had no mistress now, and nothing to look forward to, either.

'Flora looked awful,' Ba said, untying a bunch of chrysanthemums she had brought in. 'Oh, dear, aren't they wintry? There just wasn't anything else. I wonder what's happened to upset her so? She was very evasive.'

'Perhaps Richards' put his foot down about that Barlow chap always being there.'

'I don't think it would be that.'

'Young people must sort things out for themselves.'

'But she looked very ill – as if she'd been crying for hours, or days. Tears kept plopping on to Alice while she was spooning slops into her.'

'I'm glad I wasn't there,' Percy said, thinking of the tears and slops.

'Do put your jacket on, my love.'

He had just been going to do so. Perhaps she could read his thoughts.

'I'm too hot, It's far too stuffy in here,' he complained.

* * *

'No,' Meg said. 'I have no taste for it.' She turned coldly away from Patrick, feeling that he had failed her. 'You are all running true to course, but I shall not. I shall *not*,' she repeated, drumming her fingers on the back of a chair, because she was trembling.

'You will in the end,' he said listlessly. He had come all the way to Towersey to plead with her to do something he hardly believed in. 'That letter gave her a glimpse of herself as someone she could never bear to live with.'

'Other people have to live with the truth about themselves.'

'But this dreadful weeping . . .'

'Temper,' Meg said shortly, like a cross Nannie.

'She's destroying herself before our very eyes. I can't bear destruction.'

'It's our punishment for having had that horrid glimpse of her she had herself. She'll go on and on until we rally round and build up the image again.'

'I've already rallied round.'

'At the first crack in the façade. . . .'

'Such an alarming crack. It frightens me to see beauty ravaged. She does seem, literally, to be crying her eyes out. I'm too squeamish for it.'

'I'm not.'

'It's hell for Richard.'

'Yes, I'm sorry about that,' Meg said reasonably. This cool tone of voice made her seem to him more adamant than ever. He sighed.

'But it's you she wants. More than anyone,' he said.

'It's not a scrap of use being artful. And if she does, it's only because I'm the last one to capitulate.'

That 'last' sounded more hopeful to him; but at once she said, 'The only one *not* to,' correcting herself.

'It's very uncomfortable in that house.'

His one, untroubled relaxation at the end of a working day was gone – and that knowledge of the kind welcome he would get from pretty Flora in the pretty room. Now he must steel himself to enter the house. And he knew that she would go on and on until she had her way.

'It's not very comfortable in *this* house, either,' Meg said. 'I could never tell anyone how terrible it is. The dreadful awkwardness and embarrassment.'

'They are under-rated forms of suffering,' he agreed.

Emotionally tired, he had a fit of yawning. Catching as it always is, it spread to Meg.

'I'm tired, so tired,' she said into her hands.

Patrick wiped his eyes. 'They say that Goya lived ten lives,' he said. 'I've lived half a one, and found it too much.'

*　　*　　*

Elinor had lately bought a dog to keep her company. It was obviously inadequate, for she had taken to exercising it along Beatrice Crescent. Once, she met Flora there, slowly pushing the pram, looking not herself, wearing sunglasses, though autumn mists softened the light

'Hallo, Flora.'

'Hallo, Elinor.'

They smiled at one another and passed on. Not a word was spoken about child or dog or husband or anything else.

On another evening, she met Richard coming home from work. As he approached, she wondered if he might invite her in for a drink as he had done before.

'Hallo, Elinor,' he said, lifting his bowler hat, opening

his gate. The very name 'Elinor' upset Flora and there was enough bother in his world, he thought, unlocking the front door and wondering what lay on the other side of it this evening.

Elinor walked slowly down the hill. To be spurned by a friend seemed to her as bad as to be spurned by a lover. Her pace slackened as she drew nearer to her empty house.

* * *

On Saturday afternoon, Meg got off the bus and walked along Beatrice Crescent. Richard would be out, he had promised when he telephoned. A stiff little note had come from Mrs Lodge. *Dear Miss Driscoll, Madam would be ever so pleased to see you anytime you see clear to drop in but kindly do not mention this letter. Yours faithfully, Mrs Lodge.*

'Oh, Meg dear!' said Flora opening the door, 'I saw you coming up the path, and there couldn't have been a more welcome sight.'

She was carrying Alice, and Meg touched the child's cheek self-consciously.

The drawing-room was full of flowers; there were invitation cards on the chimney-piece and toys on the floor.

'I see that life jogs on,' Meg said in a dull voice. She had come to comfort Flora, put her mind at rest. Those were her instructions.

'How is Kit?' Flora asked tremulously. Meg had come at last, as she had longed for her to do; but now that she was here – it was hard to find anything to say.

'Kit's all right. As far as you're concerned, he just had 'flu.'

'Yes, I understand.' After a pause, she suddenly asked, 'Would you like to hold Alice?' – like a placatory child offering a sweet, a toy.

'I'm not much good with babies,' Meg said. 'They usually cry.'

In a rush, Flora said, 'I suppose Patrick told you . . .'

'Yes, I think Patrick's told me the lot. But, Flora, I can't discuss it.'

'I know. I only wanted to be sure that you don't blame me for anything. If I have ever interfered. . . . Oh, I've worried so. I haven't been able to sleep.'

That's why I'm here, Meg thought. It was unthinkable to them all that Flora could not sleep.

'I *don't* blame you,' she said meekly.

'I couldn't understand it. You stayed away so long.'

'I had other things to do.'

'Where is Kit this afternoon?'

'He has gone out with a girl called Caroline.'

'And he seems quite happy again?'

'Yes, quite happy.' Telling people what they wanted to hear was really Flora's prerogative, thought Meg – with her, an impulse; with Meg herself, a grudged concession. The goosefeather bed that Flora must lie on, to make her sleep.

'Shall we have toast for tea? I'll go and fetch the tray.'

Flora sprang up – a different person now – and went downstairs to Mrs Lodge. When she had gone, Meg went over to Alice, who was lying on the sofa. She knelt beside her and shyly took her hand. At once, Alice's face darkened, her mouth stiffened with displeasure, and before she could cry, Meg hastily went over to the other side of the room. They *know*, she thought. People always say they know – like horses that bite, and dogs that snarl. Know *what*, though, she wondered.

When Flora came back with the tray, she looked cheerful and her old self again, and Meg knew that the nightmare of the last week would never be referred to again.

'You and Kit must come for Christmas,' Flora said. 'I've been thinking it all out while I was waiting for the kettle to boil. We'll have a lovely Christmas all together here.'

'Won't you be going to your mother's?'

'I'm afraid Mother will be in the Holy Land,' Flora said disapprovingly. 'But, never mind that. *We'll* have a nice time, in spite of it. Alice's first Christmas.'

When Richard returned, they were both sitting before the fire, making toast. Even Meg's usually pale cheeks were bright red. Alice lay on her back cooing, turning her wrists and watching them, pedalling her plump legs in the air. It was a scene of domestic contentment.

'We're making plans about Christmas,' Flora told him – though Meg, so far, hadn't said one word.

*   *   *

Mrs Lodge, having cut the bread for the toast, swept the crumbs off the board into her hand and threw them out of the window for her tame robin; but it was too late: he had turned in for the night, was in some secret place, waiting for darkness. She stood for a while at the area window, sniffing the air – the sharp, smoky smell of a London dusk. Leaves were beginning to clutter the garden. They floated on the air, and someone near by was burning them. As Mrs Lodge turned away from the window, she sighed. It seemed to have been quite forgotten that she was ever leaving.

ELIZABETH TAYLOR

was born Elizabeth Coles in Reading, Berkshire, in 1912. The daughter of an insurance inspector, she was educated at the Abbey School, Reading, and after leaving school worked as a governess and, later, in a library. At the age of twenty-four she married John William Kendall Taylor, a businessman, with whom she had two children.

Elizabeth Taylor wrote her first novel, *At Mrs. Lippincote's* (1945), during the war while her husband was in the Royal Air Force. This was followed by *Palladian* (1946), *A View of the Harbour* (1947), *A Wreath of Roses* (1949), *A Game of Hide-and-Seek* (1951), *The Sleeping Beauty* (1953), *Angel* (1957), *In a Summer Season* (1961), *The Soul of Kindness* (1964), *The Wedding Group* (1968), *Mrs. Palfrey at the Claremont* (1971) and *Blaming*, published posthumously in 1976. She has also published four volumes of short stories: *Hester Lilly and Other Stories* (1954), *The Blush and Other Stories* (1958), *A Dedicated Man and Other Stories* (1965) and *The Devastating Boys* (1972). Elizabeth Taylor has written a book for children, *Mossy Trotter* (1967); her short stories have been published in *The New Yorker*, *Harper's Bazaar*, *Harper's* magazine, *Vogue* and the *Saturday Evening Post*, and she is included in *Penguin Modern Stories 6*.

Elizabeth Taylor lived much of her married life in the village of Penn in Buckinghamshire. She died in 1975.

Critically Elizabeth Taylor is one of the most acclaimed British novelists of this century; of her works, Dial is also publishing *The Sleeping Beauty*, *Mrs. Palfrey at the Claremont*, and *In a Summer Season*; others are to follow.